WHEN YOU ARE NEAR

Books by Tracie Peterson

BROOKSTONE BRIDES
When You Are Near

GOLDEN GATE SECRETS
In Places Hidden • In Dreams Forgotten
In Times Gone By

HEART OF THE FRONTIER
Treasured Grace • Beloved Hope
Cherished Mercy

THE HEART OF ALASKA★★
In the Shadow of Denali • Out of the Ashes
Under the Midnight Sun

SAPPHIRE BRIDES
A Treasure Concealed
A Beauty Refined • A Love Transformed

BRIDES OF SEATTLE
Steadfast Heart
Refining Fire • Love Everlasting

LONE STAR BRIDES
A Sensible Arrangement
A Moment in Time • A Matter of Heart
Lone Star Brides (3 in 1)

LAND OF SHINING WATER
The Icecutter's Daughter
The Quarryman's Bride • The Miner's Lady

LAND OF THE LONE STAR
Chasing the Sun
Touching the Sky • Taming the Wind

BRIDAL VEIL ISLAND★
To Have and To Hold
To Love and Cherish • To Honor and Trust

STRIKING A MATCH
Embers of Love
Hearts Aglow • Hope Rekindled

SONG OF ALASKA
Dawn's Prelude
Morning's Refrain • Twilight's Serenade

ALASKAN QUEST
Summer of the Midnight Sun
Under the Northern Lights
Whispers of Winter
Alaskan Quest (3 in 1)

BRIDES OF GALLATIN COUNTY
A Promise to Believe In
A Love to Last Forever
A Dream to Call My Own

THE BROADMOOR LEGACY★
A Daughter's Inheritance
An Unexpected Love
A Surrendered Heart

BELLS OF LOWELL★
Daughter of the Loom
A Fragile Design
These Tangled Threads

LIGHTS OF LOWELL★
A Tapestry of Hope
A Love Woven True
The Pattern of Her Heart

All Things Hidden★★
Beyond the Silence★★
House of Secrets
A Slender Thread
What She Left for Me
Where My Heart Belongs

★with Judith Miller ★★with Kimberley Woodhouse

For a complete list of titles, please visit www.traciepeterson.com

WHEN YOU ARE NEAR

TRACIE PETERSON

WITHDRAWN

BETHANYHOUSE
a division of Baker Publishing Group
Minneapolis, Minnesota

© 2019 by Peterson Ink, Inc.

Published by Bethany House Publishers
11400 Hampshire Avenue South
Bloomington, Minnesota 55438
www.bethanyhouse.com

Bethany House Publishers is a division of
Baker Publishing Group, Grand Rapids, Michigan

Printed in the United States of America

Library of Congress Cataloging-in-Publication Data

Names: Peterson, Tracie, author.
Title: When you are near / Tracie Peterson.
Description: Minneapolis, Minnesota : Bethany House Publishers, a division of Baker Publishing Group, [2019] | Series: Brookstone brides ; 1
Identifiers: LCCN 2018034300| ISBN 9780764219023 (trade paper) | ISBN 9780764232879 (cloth) | ISBN 9780764232886 (large print) | ISBN 9781493417223 (e-book)
Subjects: | GSAFD: Christian fiction. | Mystery fiction.
Classification: LCC PS3566.E7717 W48 2019 | DDC 813/.54—dc23
LC record available at https://lccn.loc.gov/2018034300

Scripture quotations are from the King James Version of the Bible.

This is a work of fiction. Names, characters, incidents, and dialogues are products of the author's imagination and are not to be construed as real. Any resemblance to actual events or persons, living or dead, is entirely coincidental.

Cover design by Jennifer Parker
Cover photography by Mike Habermann Photography, LLC

19 20 21 22 23 24 25   7 6 5 4 3 2 1

With thanks to Karen Vold and Linda Scholtz for your amazing insight and help with trick riding. It was so much fun to see the history you both have in trick riding and rodeo. Attending your clinic was so much fun and gave me a much better understanding and love for what you do.

Thanks too, to Amber Miller—another amazing trick rider who has answered my questions faithfully. I appreciate your patience and help.

"Come one, come all to the Brookstone Wild West Extravaganza—the only wild west show to give you all-female performers of extraordinary bravery and beauty! Women whose talent and proficiency will amaze and delight people of every age!"

═ ONE ═

SEPTEMBER 1900
WASHINGTON, D.C.

Lizzy Brookstone sat atop her perfectly groomed horse, Longfellow, and waited for her cue. The sleek Morgan-Quarter horse crossbreed was a dazzling buckskin with sooty dappling. Named for one of Lizzy's favorite poets, Longfellow was one of two buckskins she used for the wild west show her father and uncle had started back in 1893.

The horse did a nervous side step, and Lizzy gave him a pat. "Easy, boy. I'm just as anxious as you are, but you know the routine."

She glanced down at her prim English riding costume. The outfit had been created to break away easily, and under it was her basic performing costume—a comfortable split skirt tucked into knee-high boots to allow her a full range of motion. Under the restrictive lady's jacket, she wore a specially designed blouse that easily accommodated her acrobatics. But at first glance she looked like nothing less than a refined lady of society out for an afternoon ride. She even wore riding gloves and a proper top hat with a netted veil.

The crowds cheered as her uncle Oliver continued to build up their anticipation for the show. He was the perfect master of ceremonies, and the audience always loved him. He announced every event and explained each of the three main acts.

"And so without further ado, I proudly present my darling niece, Elizabeth Brookstone—the most accomplished horsewoman in the world today!"

The crowds roared with approval.

Lizzy straightened in the saddle. "That's our cue, Longfellow." She drew a deep breath and urged him forward.

The cheers were thunderous as she entered the arena. Lizzy put Longfellow into a trot and gave a ladylike wave with her gloved hand as they circled. This was her chance to assess the audience. The stands were packed to full capacity, just as all Brookstone events were. Souvenir banners were waved by those who had purchased them, while others waved handkerchiefs or simply clapped. Lizzy had ridden with the show since her father and uncle created it, and had never known anything but sold-out shows and crowds such as these. The Brookstone show was known far and wide to be of the utmost quality and satisfaction.

"Isn't she lovely, ladies and gentlemen?" Oliver Brookstone asked through his megaphone. The audience roared even louder.

Lizzy set Longfellow into his paces. She signaled him to rear, causing the crowd to gasp. Longfellow began to prance and rear as if agitated and out of control. Lizzy let her top hat fall to the ground. Her chestnut brown hair tumbled down her back. She gave every pretense of being in peril as she signaled Longfellow to gallop.

As the gelding picked up speed, Lizzy pretended to be in trouble. She threw herself across the saddle first one way and then the other in order to rip away the special skirt and jacket. The audience that only moments earlier had been cheering now fell silent except for an occasional woman's startled cry. This was how the audience always reacted. Lizzy saw one of the other trick riders racing out to pick up her discarded articles of clothing. Freed of impediments, Lizzy slipped her foot into one of the special straps on her custom-made saddle and went into a layover, looking as if she would fall headfirst off the saddle.

From this point on, she didn't hear the crowd or pay them any attention. Her act required her full attention.

Since she was a little girl, Lizzy had performed tricks on horseback. Her father and uncle had been part of Buffalo Bill Cody's Wild West show. They'd joined up in 1883, when their friend William Cody had decided to put together his famous show. Lizzy's mother had been needed to help with cooking for the crew, and naturally that meant bringing Lizzy along. Lizzy had grown to adulthood under the show's influence, performing her first tricks with the help of her father when she was just twelve. Every winter they'd gone home to Grandfather Brookstone's ranch in Montana to rest and plan new tricks. It was an unusual life to be certain, but one Lizzy enjoyed—probably because her father loved it so.

"You are the very heart of me, Lizzy," her father had often told her. *"You and your mother. Without either one of you, I'm not sure I could go on."*

But he had never considered how they might go on without him. Earlier that year, Mark Brookstone had suffered a heart attack. He had lingered for several hours after the initial onset, and during that time, he had made his wishes known before dying in the arms of his beloved wife.

Lizzy's body shifted in the wrong direction. *Focus on what you're doing or you'll get yourself killed.*

She pushed the memory aside. Focus was key to not getting hurt. She went into a trick that put her upside down along the horse's neck. The gelding didn't even seem to notice and continued to gallop around the arena. The audience applauded, now understanding that Lizzy's situation was quite under control.

Lizzy swung back into the saddle and gave a wave. The crowds went wild with cheers and the fluttering of the colorful Brookstone Wild West Extravaganza pennants they'd purchased.

She performed various moves for nearly twenty minutes, wowing the crowds with layovers, saddle spins, and shoulder stands, then ending with a death-defying drag that put her upside down, her hair and hand sweeping the floor of the arena. The people loved it. They were on their feet, cheering and whistling. The applause was thunderous as she reclaimed her seat and rode out of the arena.

The other nine performers for the show were waiting on horseback. Lizzy's was the final performance, but now the entire troupe would go out to take their bows. Lizzy positioned Longfellow while the others made their way out to the cheers of the audience. They lined up the horses, and each rider raised her hand high as the horses bowed.

An old man rushed to Lizzy's side, holding up a flag. With quick action, she secured straps over her feet and took the unfurled cloth. She returned to the arena, standing in the saddle and hoisting an American flag as she circled the ring. It was hard to imagine possible, but the cheers grew even louder.

Lizzy smiled and waved the symbol of America back and forth just as her father had taught her.

"People love a good finish, Lizzy. Give them a surprise and something to cheer, and they'll never forget you."

Longfellow headed out of the arena once again with the other riders following close behind. The audience continued to cheer and clap. As usual, no matter how much the performers gave, the audience wanted more.

Lizzy pulled off to the side, and the same older man who had given her the flag now retrieved it.

"Thanks, Zeb. I'm sure glad that's over." Lizzy had pushed herself nearly beyond endurance, having given a private performance for the president and his friends earlier in the day. She was tired and sore and relieved that her obligations were concluded. She could feel in Longfellow's gait that he was too.

"Wonderful performance, Lizzy," August Reichert declared, taking hold of Longfellow's bridle. "You were amazing."

"Thanks." She smiled at the sandy-haired head wrangler, who was the brother of her dear friend Mary. He had once tried to pay her court, but Lizzy kept everything professional. She had no interest in losing her heart to anyone in the show or anywhere else. Falling in love was even more dangerous than the act she'd just performed.

She slid from the saddle. Longfellow gave a soft nicker, knowing they'd both done well. "That's my boy." Lizzy kissed the horse's velvety nose. "You were wonderful. You always are." The horse was puffing and sweating but bobbed his head as if agreeing with her. "I'll bring you some treats later tonight." She gave him one last stroke as August loosened the cinch. "Take good care of him, August. He needs to walk awhile." She knew she didn't need to tell August his job, but it was a force of habit.

"I'll see to it, Lizzy." August led the horse away.

She made her way to the small room where her mother was waiting. Rebecca Brookstone was a fine-looking woman with a slender figure. Just shy of fifty years old, she and Lizzy shared many features. Both had chestnut brown hair, although Rebecca's bore gray as well. They had dark brown eyes—a trait passed down from Rebecca's mother's side of the family—and a brilliant smile. Although Mother smiled less these days. Losing her husband had clearly left Rebecca Brookstone with a broken heart.

"I'm so glad you're safe," Mother said. "Were there any problems?"

"No. None." Lizzy gave her mother a kiss on the cheek. "Are you ready to go?"

The black-clad widow nodded. "I am. I'll be glad to be back on the train."

"Me too." Lizzy picked up the one remaining bag her mother motioned toward and offered Mother her arm. "Let's get out of here before anyone spies us."

Her mother happily complied, and they made their way to their home on wheels. Usually there would be a carriage or wagon to drive them, but the train station was only six blocks away, and Lizzy and her mother had walked it more than once that day. The walk helped Lizzy clear her head, and on this particularly warm night, it was pleasant just to stroll and let the evening breeze cool them.

"The capital is a fascinating city, isn't it?" Mother stated more than asked.

Lizzy nodded. "It is, but given the upcoming election, it seems to almost be running amok."

"I suppose that's to be expected. Still, it was a lovely visit at the White House. I thought Mrs. McKinley such an amiable hostess."

"I remember the first time we met her." Lizzy paused at a busy street corner to wait until the traffic cleared. The other pedestrians around them seemed less inclined and dodged in and out of the traffic, much to the annoyance of the drivers. When they were once again on their way, Lizzy continued. "Do you suppose the president will be reelected?"

"I think so," Mother said, nodding. "The country has returned to prosperity, and industry is progressing. I believe most people will see the president as having a part in that."

They reached the train depot and made their way to the area where the Brookstone railcars awaited. There were eight bright red cars in total, artistically painted with performance scenes. Each bore the lettering, *THE BROOKSTONE WILD WEST EXTRAVAGANZA*, and all were customized to their personal needs. Half were dedicated to the animals' welfare and equipment, while the other four were set up for sleeping and living on the rails.

Lizzy made her way to the family car and helped her mother up onto the temporary wooden platform. Once they were inside, both women heaved a sigh in unison.

Mother smiled, but it didn't quite reach her eyes. "We're a sorry pair."

"We're tired. It's always hard when we get to the end of the season. I'm just thankful that you don't have to furnish the evening refreshments. Mrs. McKinley was so kind to send over all that food from the White House."

"She was indeed. I don't think I would have had the energy to lay out a table this evening. I'm glad there won't be too many more meals to arrange for this tour."

"Maybe we should hire someone to assist you next year."

Mother shook her head. "No, this is my last tour."

Lizzy wasn't all that surprised to hear this declaration. Since Father had died, neither of them had much passion for the show. They would have quit immediately had he not begged them to continue.

"The show must go on," he had said in barely audible words. *"Promise me you'll finish out the tour."*

They had promised, although neither had the heart to continue.

"I think it shall be my last as well," Lizzy said, plopping down on the comfortable sofa. "After all, I'm twenty-eight. I'm getting a little long in the tooth to be doing this." She rubbed her abdomen. "I get sorer with each performance, it seems."

"Besides, you should consider settling down, getting married and having a family. I would find it a great comfort to have grandchildren." Her mother took off her black veiled hat and set it aside.

Lizzy shook her head. "I'm sorry that I've disappointed in that area, but I'm not sure it's ever going to happen." She couldn't say that seeing her mother's pain from Father's death had made her look at romance and marriage in a completely different way.

"There's always Wes," Mother said. "He's free now. We both know he married Clarissa out of pity, but he's always cared about you."

This was not the conversation Lizzy wanted to be having. She had watched her mother go through the overwhelming grief of losing the man she loved. It had made Lizzy rethink her dreamy notions of marriage. She had loved Wes since she was a child, but he had never cared about her in the same way, and maybe that was for the best.

"There are other things in life besides marrying and having a family. Wes has his own life, and I have mine. Besides, he thinks of me as his sister," Lizzy said, shaking her head. "Nothing more than a pesky sibling."

"But that could change," Mother countered.

Thinking about Wesley DeShazer, their ranch foreman, always made Lizzy's heart ache. She had first met him when Wes was just eighteen and she was eleven. Her adoration of the young ranch worker had been overwhelming. She followed Wes around like a puppy for days, asking him questions and showing off her tricks. Wes had been kind and fun. He had treated her with tenderness. He was never condescending toward her, which only served to endear him to her all the more. It had been hard to leave him behind each spring when they returned to the wild west show. Lizzy would count the days until they returned, and when they did, she had rejoiced to find him still working at the ranch and more handsome than she'd remembered. As he grew into a man and took on more and more ranch responsibilities, Lizzy had determined he was the man she intended to marry.

"Lizzy?"

She glanced up to find her mother watching her. Lizzy smiled. "Sorry, I'm tired. What were you saying?"

Mother sat down beside her. "I was speaking of Wes."

"Ah, yes."

"Clarissa's been gone two years now."

"True, but during those two years, Wes has avoided me whenever we've been home. I don't think there's any future with him. If we were meant to be together, he wouldn't have married Clarissa."

"You were just a child when he married."

Lizzy frowned. "I was eighteen. Hardly a child." She yawned. "I'm sorry. I'm too tired to talk about this. I think I'll get ready for bed."

Mother took her hand. "Darling girl, you mustn't give up on true love. If Wesley is the man God has for you, then it will come about."

"And if he's not?" Lizzy already knew the answer but voiced the question anyway.

"Then you wouldn't want him for a husband. We need to rest in God's will for our lives, Lizzy. You know that. To seek our own would only result in a world of hurt and problems."

"Seems we have that anyway."

Her mother's eyes filled with tears. "I know. It's been so hard without your father." Tears trailed down her cheeks. "I don't know why God took him from us. He was so loved."

Lizzy hated seeing her mother cry. She put her arm around her mother's shoulders and hugged her close. "I don't know either. I do my best to trust God for the future, but losing Father makes the future seem grim."

Her mother sobbed into her hands. Lizzy couldn't count the number of times her mother had broken down like this, which was exactly the reason she couldn't be honest with her mother about her own feelings. "Come on, Mother. We're both done in and will soon be lost in our tears. Let me help you get to bed." She helped her mother to her feet and led her to one of the four private sleeping rooms in the family car.

The space wasn't all that large, but there was a small built-in dresser and a rod to hang clothes on beside a double bed, which was also built in with a nice ledge at the side of the headboard. One of the cleaning girls had opened the window and lit the kerosene lamp, which was affixed to the wall above the bed. Lizzy wished they could spare the extra money to electrify the car. It would be much safer, less smelly, and far easier to manage an electric switch.

Still pondering that matter, Lizzy helped her mother undress. She hung up the discarded clothes while her mother donned her nightgown.

"Would you like me to help with your hair?"

"No, I'm fine. You go ahead and get to bed yourself. I know you're tired."

Lizzy smiled. "I'll fetch you a glass of milk. I know you enjoy that before bed."

"No. Don't bother." Her mother sat down on the edge of the bed. "I just want to read my Bible for a while." Her tears returned, and Lizzy knew it was better to just go.

She slipped from the room and pulled the door shut behind her. Her own sleeping quarters were next to her mother's. Close enough to hear her sobs well into the night. Lizzy prayed God would give her mother comfort.

Maybe it was best not to marry. She couldn't imagine the pain her mother was bearing. Losing a father was misery enough, but losing a lifelong companion had to be like losing part of yourself. An amputation of the very worst kind.

Lizzy went into her small room, sat on the bed, and began unlacing her boots. She spied the pitcher of water, steam rising from the open top. The cleaning girl was no doubt responsible. Once she was rid of her boots, Lizzy poured some of the water into the bowl and washed her face, then began discarding her clothes.

Just as she'd anticipated, her mother's sobs could be heard through the thin wall. How Lizzy wished she could comfort her mother, but as Uncle Oliver had told her, this was a burden a wife or husband must bear alone. No one else understood the pain of a marriage severed. Especially when it involved a couple who had loved each other as deeply as Mark and Rebecca Brookstone had loved.

Lizzy looked at her reflection in the mirror on the wall. *Why would I ever want to experience that sorrow and pain? Loving Wes and being rejected was painful enough. I can't imagine how hard it would be to share his love and then have him die.* No, the best way to avoid widowhood was to avoid love.

She quickly finished washing up, then readied herself for bed. With her hair braided and nightgown in place, she extinguished the lamp before crawling beneath the covers. Her window was still open, and she heard Uncle Oliver conversing with someone as they drew near the car. No doubt he was settling last-minute problems before their railcars were hooked up to the next westbound locomotive. It was a strange life, living on the rails. Sometime in the next hour they'd feel the gentle—or not-so-gentle—bump of the cars being coupled, and then they'd begin to move as they were transported to their next stop. At each city where they performed, their eight cars were moved onto a siding, and there they would live until the performances were complete. It was an exciting life—seeing America, meeting new people. Lizzy had even met three presidents: Grover Cleveland, Benjamin Harrison, and William McKinley.

When Lizzy was younger, her mother had always seen to it that they visited places of historic importance at each stop. Lizzy had learned so much along the way. The trips had always been something she looked forward to. Now, however, there was no joy. She was ready to be done with it all.

"But then what?" Her voice was a barely audible whisper.

The ranch in Montana was home, but without Father, it wouldn't seem that way. Then there was Wesley. If she quit the show and stayed on the ranch with her mother, could they find a way to just be friends?

"Can *I* find a way?" Lizzy gazed at the top of her berth, then closed her eyes.

Her mind whirred with questions, but by the time the train car began to move, she was starting to fade off to sleep. Sadly, without any hope of answers.

TWO

Lizzy and her mother sat at the table, reading the local paper and eating a hot breakfast brought to them from their current stop. While the railroad men handled their routine business, Uncle Oliver had left the car to make certain the rest of Brookstone's workforce had what they needed before the train started up again.

"It says here that the Galveston hurricane last month may have killed as many as twelve thousand people," Mother said, lowering the paper. "Can you imagine? Oliver told me there are only about two hundred thousand people in all of Montana."

"I can't imagine it," Lizzy admitted. "To think of that many people suddenly killed is beyond me. Those hurricanes must be terrible storms to endure. I hope we never encounter one."

"It says the loss of livestock and crops was unimaginable." Mother shook her head. "Seems the newspaper is full of such sad things these days."

A knock sounded on the car door, but before Lizzy could get to her feet, it opened and her uncle peered inside.

"Oh good, you're both awake and ready to receive," Uncle Oliver declared. "I want you to meet someone."

Lizzy stood and smiled as her uncle stepped into the car. The young man who followed him was expensively clothed and nearly a head taller than Uncle Oliver. He carried himself like a man who had been brought up in privilege. He glanced around their accommodations, seeming to assess the situation. Lizzy wondered if he thought their little home on wheels quaint or appalling. Finally, his gaze settled on Lizzy and then Mother. He offered them a wide smile that seemed sincere enough and took off his hat.

Uncle Oliver did likewise and offered an introduction. "This is Jason Adler. He joined us last night, but you ladies had already gone to bed."

Mother and Lizzy exchanged a look. Lizzy knew that Henry Adler was responsible for her father and uncle having the money to start their own wild west show back in the day, but she had no idea who Jason was. Better still, what was his purpose here?

As if reading her thoughts, Uncle Oliver added clarity. "He's the son of Henry Adler. Jason, this is my brother's widow, Mrs. Rebecca Brookstone, and her daughter, Elizabeth."

Mother spoke first. "I'm pleased to meet you, Mr. Adler. My husband spoke so highly of your father."

"And my father spoke highly of your husband. He sends his deepest regrets, Mrs. Brookstone." Jason Adler gave a slight bow. He looked at Lizzy. "We are sorry for your loss as well, Miss Brookstone."

"Call her Lizzy," Uncle Oliver declared. "Everyone does."

Lizzy wasn't sure what Jason Adler was doing here, but she couldn't deny that he was quite the dashing gentleman. He looked about her age, maybe a little older, and his accent clearly revealed his English heritage.

"Jason has come on board to help me," Uncle Oliver continued. "He has all sorts of ideas for benefiting the show."

"Won't you join us?" Mother said. "There's hot coffee and extra pastries, though I'm afraid if you want something hot to eat, we'll have to send someone out."

"We've had our breakfast, Rebecca, but a cup of coffee would suit me right down to my boots. How about it, Jason? Coffee?"

Jason Adler smiled. "I'd be happy to share coffee with two such lovely ladies."

The men put their hats aside and took the empty chairs at the small table for four. Lizzy retrieved extra cups and brought them to the table. She didn't understand Jason's purpose. Uncle Oliver said the Englishman had all sorts of ideas, but Lizzy couldn't see any reason they needed his or his father's thoughts on the show.

Once Mother had poured the coffee and Uncle Oliver had made small talk about the weather, Lizzy decided to press the matter.

"I'm afraid I don't understand the reason for having Mr. Adler join the show. You mentioned he has ideas for us, but I wasn't aware that we needed . . . ideas."

She glanced at Mr. Adler to judge whether or not he'd taken offense. He seemed completely at ease, however, and merely sipped his black coffee. He met her gaze over the rim of his cup, and it looked to Lizzy as if there was a twinkle in his blue eyes. He seemed amused.

Uncle Oliver, on the other hand, looked a bit sheepish. "Well . . . you see . . . a while back, I sold part of the show to Henry Adler."

"What?" the women questioned in unison.

Jason Adler slowly lowered his cup while Uncle Oliver held up his hands. "It's a long story, but the show has been struggling to make a profit. I thought some fresh ideas might benefit us. Mr. Adler has proven very helpful in the past."

"Still, you should have discussed it with Mother, at least. She speaks in place of my father now," Lizzy replied. She knew her tone revealed her outrage.

To his credit, Jason Adler said nothing.

"I think in time you'll see how good this will be for us. Jason's ideas are good ones—things I know your father would have approved."

What could she say to that? If Lizzy even thought to argue, it would no doubt bring on another round of tears from her mother. No opinion was worth causing her mother pain.

For several minutes and another cup of coffee, her uncle explained that the Adlers were devoted to the best interests of the Brookstone family.

Finally, Jason spoke up. "My father—in fact, my entire family—is eternally grateful for what your father and uncle did for us. He often speaks of the hunting trip in the Rockies that your father and uncle guided him on. The fact that they saved his life will never be forgotten. Now, if there is a way for us to help you save the show, then we want to do whatever we can."

"Save the show?" Lizzy asked, looking to her uncle. "What is he talking about?"

Again, her uncle looked uncomfortable. "The fact is, we can't go on like this. There isn't enough money to go around. We're barely able to make our payroll."

"But we're always sold out." Lizzy knew there was a great deal of pride in her voice, but she couldn't help herself. "We have more towns asking for performances than we can say yes to."

"Indeed," Jason said. "It's more a matter of management. There are ways to save money and economize. Your father and uncle were not . . . well . . ."

"We weren't schooled for such things, Lizzy," Uncle Oliver said. "We've managed as best we could, but Jason here is educated. He and his father both attended college, and they've run all sorts of businesses and know how to manage money better than I do."

A knock at the door interrupted their conversation. Lizzy got up to answer it, and Jason stood quickly to help her from her chair. She didn't feel very hospitable toward him but forced herself to be polite. "Thank you."

She opened the door to find Agnes, the show's head seamstress. "Mrs. Brookstone," she called from the platform, "I wonder if you could come to the costume room when you have time."

Mother started to rise, and again Jason was there to lend a hand. She gave him a warm smile, much more sincere than the one Lizzy had offered him. "I'll come right now." She looked to the men. "If you'll excuse me. Oliver, I trust you to manage the matter. You've always had our best interests at heart."

"August asked me to tell Mr. Brookstone that he needed to consult him on a matter related to the horses," Agnes added. "He said he needed to speak to you before we pulled out of the station."

Uncle Oliver got to his feet. "Jason, perhaps you could stay and explain some of your ideas to Lizzy. I want you two to become good friends."

Lizzy didn't want to contradict her uncle even though sitting and talking with Jason was the last thing she wanted to do. She walked back to the table and found Jason waiting to help her with her chair. She certainly couldn't fault his manners.

Once she was seated and the others had departed, Lizzy looked at Jason. Previously he had been seated beside her, but now he took the seat opposite her, where Mother had been sitting. His expression was concerned. "I suppose this is a rather uncomfortable situation for you."

"*Uncomfortable* isn't the word I would choose." She shrugged. "I'm confused and concerned, but not uncomfortable."

"I'm glad to hear it." His blue eyes sparkled, and his expression relaxed. "I wouldn't like you to feel uncomfortable in my presence. Like your uncle, I very much want us to be friends."

Lizzy tried to put aside her suspicion. "Why don't you explain your money-saving ideas? Then perhaps I'll be less concerned and confused."

"I'd be happy to." He tugged absentmindedly at the cuffs of his shirt. "As you know, a show such as yours is hardly guaranteed an income. There are all sorts of overhead costs and unexpected problems."

"Isn't that true of all industries?"

"Quite right. However, a performance-based industry such as yours has many variables that other businesses might never have to concern themselves with. Your business is in constant motion. You take it on the road, and for most of the year you go from place to place. The wear and tear takes its toll. The business is also dependent on living, breathing beings, both human and animal, for its success. That only serves to increase the risk and expense."

"But all industry and business requires living, breathing beings." Lizzy didn't know why she felt so at odds with Jason. He was only trying to help, she supposed, but he wasn't family, and the fact that he would be allowed to help make decisions in their business irritated her sense of balance.

He shifted in his seat and gave a hint of a shrug. "It's true that any business is only as good as the individuals running and working it. However, Brookstone's adds an additional element to that. In other industries, when a worker is injured or falls ill, there are many others who can step in to manage their position. The same is true for industries reliant upon horses. However, in your situation, that isn't the case."

Lizzy had to concede he was right. "I

understand what you're saying. It wouldn't be possible to suddenly procure animals as well-trained as my horses, should something happen to them."

"Exactly so." He smiled. "Even harder to replace the rider." His right brow rose, as if daring her to contradict him.

Lizzy remained silent but gave a nod.

"The most important thing is to assure quality housing and care for yourselves as well as your stock. I'd like to see the railcars inspected and repairs made. There are new, safer ways to transport horses, for instance. I can show you some of the designs I have with me. Perhaps later, when we're actually on our way."

"Yes, I'd like to see what you have in mind."

"The key is to keep both performers and livestock at their optimum health and ability. After all, venues will hardly pay if there is no performance."

"I imagine our contracts allow for some sort of compensation."

Jason shook his head. "The contracts created by your father and uncle were hardly more than handshakes and letters. In the twentieth century, attention to detail is required. My father had our solicitor put together some sample contracts that we might use. We can discuss this when the time is right."

She felt her anger building. "I see. So our problem is that my uncle and father mismanaged the show?"

"Not entirely. They did what had been done in the past. What they learned from the show in which they had once performed. I'm not here to point out fault, but to help. I hope you won't always be hostile toward me."

"If someone came into your home, started suggesting changes, and told you that your father hadn't sense enough to know how to manage his affairs, wouldn't you feel a tad hostile?" She fixed him with a stern gaze.

"If my father had asked someone to help him figure out how he might better his home and family," Jason replied calmly, "I would hope that the remaining members of the household wouldn't treat that person as the enemy."

Lizzy forced herself to calm down. He was right. He wasn't here to be her enemy. "So what do you suggest, besides improving the railcars and new contracts?"

"It will be necessary to look at the operation and see where money can be saved. Perhaps we can start by eliminating some of the men who work with the stock and equipment. I've noticed quite a few are well into their years and able to do very little. It seems the younger men could handle their responsibilities along with their own, thus saving money in wages."

"Those older men are friends of my family. They were given jobs with the show because they aren't able to work full-time on our ranch. They've been with us for a long time, and although broken and aged, they still provide good help."

"I know it's hard to imagine letting them go, but no one will earn a wage if there is no longer a show."

Lizzy hadn't realized things were so dire. She wanted to ask Jason about the details, but at the same time, she didn't want anything to do with him. Apparently he noted this dilemma as well.

"Over time, we can go over the ledgers and review where costs might be saved. For now, however, just let me say that I think the show is amazing. I know the crowds love it and will continue to do so. I want your help to figure out how we can keep it alive."

His change of direction made Lizzy remember her own thoughts from the night before. "My mother doesn't plan to continue with the show. It's been so hard on her since my father's death."

"I can't begin to imagine. Why didn't she return to the ranch with . . . your father?"

"She wanted to." Lizzy felt her anger fade.

"She would have, had she not promised him to stay with the show. Father was a firm believer in honoring his commitments, and he didn't want to disappoint the people who were looking forward to our performances. He made Mother and I promise we'd stay on until the end of the tour this year." She shook her head. "I think he also knew that Mother would be lost in her grief if she didn't have something to do."

"And now she'll return to the ranch?"

"Yes." Lizzy met his sympathetic expression. "I may remain with her."

He frowned. "But why? You're the main attraction."

"I am only one of several, if you'll recall. I'm also twenty-eight. It's getting harder to perform those tricks. Besides, without my father, I've lost the heart of it all."

"But your fans can surely help reinstate that passion. They're devoted to you. You may not realize this, but some people actually follow you from show to show—at least within a certain radius of their homes. If you leave the show, I believe it will fail. Like it or not, you are the main attraction and the reason the show continues to garner large audiences."

"I wouldn't go without training a replacement. The other girls who trick ride are quite good. With some practice, they could take over my tricks—even mimic my costumes and styles. No one will ever know the difference. They come for the Brookstone all-female wild west show. Not for Elizabeth Brookstone."

"I don't think you realize your importance." Jason shook his head. "People know exactly who you are. You receive fan letters, don't you?"

"Yes, but so do the others."

He leaned forward. "Miss Brookstone, would you please at least delay making your final decision until the end of the tour? I'd like to convince you to stay on for at least one more year. The changes I'm going to suggest will upset things enough, but if you leave, then I can guarantee the show will fall apart."

Lizzy sighed. She didn't want to be the reason the show failed. In some ways it would be like losing her father all over again, and it would break her uncle's heart. Uncle Oliver would never give up the show. He loved it too much. The show was his entire life, although since her father had died, Oliver had taken to drinking a bit too much, and she wasn't sure how much life he had left in him.

Jason leaned forward. "Just give me some time, Miss Brookstone. Think about staying on for one more year. Please."

His pleading tone stirred something deep within her. Lizzy knew what it felt like to desperately want something to work out. She also knew how it felt when the one key person refused to do their part.

"I'll pray on it, Mr. Adler." She met his gaze. "That's the best I can give you."

He smiled. "It's enough. For now."

❖⸱═ THREE ═⸱❖

Their next show was in four days and would take place in St. Louis, Missouri. It was the second to last show for the season, and Lizzy found herself counting down the days. She longed to return to the family ranch in Montana, where the show would spend the winter. She had memorized every inch of their large house, and there was nowhere she could go in the ten-bedroom, two-story house without remembering something pleasant or humorous. It was a haven—a sanctuary of love. It was there she had grown up, and hopefully it was there she might one day raise a family.

Lizzy gazed out the train window at the Kentucky countryside gently rolling past. Before the show in St. Louis, they had a stop to make.

Jason Adler loomed in the open doorway of the railcar. "I hope you don't mind the interruption."

Uncle Oliver had told them Jason was to be treated like family, so Lizzy welcomed him into their car and pushed aside thoughts of her father. "Not at all. We'll arrive at the station soon, and then the railroad will move us to a siding and we'll head to Fleming Farm." She shrugged. "But I'm sure you know all of that."

"Yes." He took a seat on a ladder-backed wooden chair near her spot on the sofa. "You look quite lovely."

Lizzy glanced down at her simple mauve promenade suit. It wasn't the most current style, but was one of her better outfits. "Thank you. It may not be fashionable, but it is very comfortable."

"You make it look quite fashionable. I especially like the way you've done up your hair."

She flushed and looked at her folded hands. "That would be Mother. I'm used to braids and tight little buns. However, since we're visiting the Flemings, it's important to look our best. They're very splendid and proper."

"Ah, yes. The Flemings. Your uncle explained the arrangement. I understand their horses are important for the show."

"Yes, after a fashion." Lizzy was glad the focus had moved away from her appearance. "We've always used Morgan-Quarter horse mixes. We have a very fine older quarter horse stallion at the ranch, but we lost one of our mares, and the others are getting up in years. We need a couple of new breeders. Mother and Father were both of a mind to expand the ranch to breed horses."

"I see. And this mix of bloodlines is what they hoped to promote?"

She could hear the doubt in his voice. "I suppose it's difficult for you to understand, not having grown up around a ranch and wild west show."

"I did, however, grow up—at least part of the time—on our country estate, and we had a fine stable of animals. I know the value of a good brood mare."

"I'm glad to hear it. I'm sure it's difficult enough to comprehend why we do what we do." She tried not to sound sarcastic.

His expression grew serious. "Then tell me. Start with the ranch in Montana. Did you always live there?"

Lizzy knew they still had time before reaching the station. "The ranch belonged to my granddad, father, and uncle jointly. Granddad inherited some money and had always wanted to move west. My uncle and father were both like-minded. They sold everything, and we relocated to some land several miles outside of Miles City, Montana. I was ten years old when we moved. I saw the move as a grand adventure, but my aunts—Granddad's daughters with his second wife—cried and whined all the way."

"Perhaps they were leaving suitors?"

"Yes, I'm sure that didn't help. There were five of them, but the elder two were already married. The other three were certainly of marriageable age, although I don't recall if they were serious about anyone at the time of the move. I do recall that my mother and grandmother were the only women in our party who were in favor of the move."

Jason chuckled and crossed his legs. "Please go on."

"When we arrived, we found there wasn't much to this ranch Granddad had purchased, but thanks to his inheritance, that wasn't an issue. He knew the tiny house already in place would never work for us and had logs and finished lumber brought in to make a colossal two-story house. Granddad had visions of his sons having large families to fill it and stay on with him and Grandmother. There are ten bedrooms in the house, which I suppose sounds terribly overdone, but Granddad was always a big dreamer."

"It sounds charming," Jason said.

Lizzy remembered then that he came from a wealthy family—a father who was an English lord and well-propertied. "I suppose I sound silly. I'm sure you must have a much larger estate and a great deal of finery."

"Our country estate is quite large, but our London house is smaller. I'll tell you all about it sometime, but right now I'd like to know more about your upbringing. Did you enjoy living out there in the wilds? As I understood it from my father, there aren't many cities or people."

She nodded. "That much is true. There still isn't all that much, but yes, I love it. I wouldn't live anywhere else."

"Perhaps you only say that because you haven't yet seen a better place." His smooth voice was compelling.

"Perhaps." Lizzy shrugged. "But I've toured all over this country."

"Maybe," he said, his voice lowering, "it isn't in this country."

Lizzy felt her cheeks grow warm. "Well, anyway, by 1885 my aunts had married, and of course my father and uncle had decided to take up the offer from their friend Bill Cody to join the wild west show he was putting together."

"And you and your mother went along?"

"Yes. Mr. Cody wanted Mother to cook for him, and they figured I might as well come along. Mother and Father both agreed it would be a grand education. And it was. I learned a great deal and saw so many places of historical relevance."

"So why did your father and uncle quit the show?"

Lizzy remembered it as if it were yesterday. "We were home for our winter break when Grandmother fell ill. She never recovered and died in the spring of 1886. We were all devastated. Even though she wasn't my father and uncle's natural mother, she was the only mother they could remember, and she had been so good to them. She was dear to all of us." The words seemed to back up in her throat, choking her. Lizzy coughed.

"How old were you?" Jason asked. His gaze was sympathetic.

"I was fourteen." She thought of her sadness and how much she had cried. "Grandmother was an incredible woman. To know her was to love her. My father was home from the wild west show, recovering from an injury. He and Uncle knew that Granddad could never bear it if we left, so they resigned from the show, and we stayed on the ranch." Lizzy drew a deep breath and let it go. "The summer that followed was hot and dry, and then winter came early and hard. By January, things went from bad to worse. Are you familiar with the winter of 1886 and 1887?"

He shook his head. "I don't believe I am."

"Most of the ranchers hadn't put up feed for the winter. When the snow came early and deep, the cattle were already underweight because of the drought that summer. In January, there came a warming that melted some of the snow. We thought maybe the worst was over, but of course it wasn't. The temperatures dropped, and the melted snow formed a thick ice crust that the cattle couldn't break through. Then more snow came. By spring, the loss was nearly total for all ranchers. We were no exception. I think Granddad lost the will to live after Grandmother died, but if not then, he certainly did when he found his entire herd dead. He and my father and uncle worked day and night to dispose of the carcasses, and Granddad caught pneumonia. He was dead within a week." She felt her chest tighten. She didn't want to remember those days.

"That must have been truly difficult for someone with such a tender heart."

The train slowed and brought Lizzy back to the present. She glanced out the window to see they were still some distance from town. The Fleming horse farm was not far from Louisville, and they planned to stop there for two days. The year before, Lizzy's father had made arrangements to buy twin four-year-old mares. He'd watched the fillies almost since birth—checking on them each year. After the second year, he told Fleming he wanted the pair, but Fleming had thought to keep them for himself. Finally, after some bartering back and forth, Fleming gave in and sold them. Father had been proud of that accomplishment. The mares were buckskin, a favorite of the Brookstone family. Just before he'd died, Father had talked with such excitement about bringing the horses home.

Jason seemed to read her mind. "If I might change the subject, tell me why you prefer the Morgan-Quarter horse mix. Your uncle said that most of the performing horses are of this cross."

Lizzy appreciated the chance to focus on something else. "They're marvelous. Spirited and easily trained."

"But so too are Thoroughbreds."

Lizzy nodded. "But they're too tall and their backs are much too long. In order to do tricks, you must have just the right-sized animal. Of course, that is totally dependent on the rider's size. We do have one horse that's a Thoroughbred-Morgan, but I still find the back too long, which makes it difficult to perform some tricks. One of the other girls, however, loves him."

"And what of other breeds?" He leaned back and crossed his legs in a casual manner.

"Well, with the American Saddlebred the neck isn't quite right. It's too difficult to do stands and vaults. Morgans by themselves are too stocky, and Arabians can't manage the shifting of weight that's required." She considered other breeds for a moment. "The Standardbred is better suited to harness racing."

"I quite agree," Jason said. "And I presume that while Barbs would be small enough, their gait is too unpredictable for trick riding. They're more suited to racing."

Lizzy could see he was knowledgeable on the topic of horses. It gave her a bit of respect for him. "Yes. Over the years we've just found the quarter horse and Morgan make the best horse for trick riding. I'm sure you've seen my horses, Longfellow and Thoreau."

"Beautiful buckskins. I particularly like the dappling on Longfellow. I also appreciate the names. Are you a fan of Longfellow's and Thoreau's writings?"

"I am. I enjoy a great many writers, but particularly poets. We also have horses at the ranch named Blake, Burns, and Byron."

Jason grew thoughtful and closed his eyes. "'She walks in beauty, like the night of cloudless climes and starry skies; and all that's best of dark and bright meet in her aspect and her eyes: thus mellowed to that tender light which heaven to gaudy day denies.'" He opened his eyes and gazed at her with such intensity that Lizzy found herself unable to look away.

"Umm, yes. Exactly," she said when he finished.

"I'm a fan of Byron's work. He always captured a depth of emotion that appealed to my spirit."

Lizzy had no desire to discuss Jason Adler's spirit. "I recall Mother saying something about you having American relatives." The train was now nearing the station and barely crept along. The braking made for a jerky ride.

"Yes. There are a great many Americans on my mother's side. She is, you see, American herself."

"Oh." Lizzy gave a closed-mouth smile.

He laughed. "I thought perhaps you already knew. Her family is quite wealthy, which was no doubt one of the many reasons my father married her."

"I hope he also married for love."

Jason shrugged. "If not, love is surely the reason they remain together. Father adores her and her family. Her people are industrialists from New York."

The door opened at the end of the car, and Uncle Oliver strolled in as if he were making his way through the park. "Lovely day. Just perfectly lovely, Lizzy. Is your mother awake?"

Lizzy shrugged as the train continued to jerk as it slowed down. The whine of metal wheels on metal rails was enough to wake the dead. "I'm sure she is now. I'll go see if she needs help dressing." She glanced at Jason and gave a little nod. "If you'll excuse me."

He jumped to his feet and helped her up. "I enjoyed our conversation. I hope it will be the first of many."

His thumb rubbed the back of her knuckles. When he didn't let go, Lizzy pulled her hand away. "I must go." Her tone was curt, perhaps edging on harsh. But it was necessary.

The last thing she wanted or needed was for Jason Adler to try to woo her.

FOUR

Your home is just as lovely as I remember it," Mrs. Brookstone said, patting Beatrix Fleming's hand.

Ella Fleming watched her mother graciously welcome the Brookstones to their estate. She smiled when her gaze met Elizabeth Brookstone's. She liked Lizzy very much. Ella had in fact found a kindred spirit in her, even though Lizzy was eight years her senior.

"It's so good to see you again, Ella," Lizzy said, coming forward.

"Did you have a good journey?"

Lizzy glanced around the room as if familiarizing herself with the house again. It had been over a year since she'd been here, after all. "It was the same as always." She looked at Ella. "I just love how bright this foyer is. You've done something different, haven't you?"

"We did. Mother thought it much too dull, and we repapered it in this lovely gold stripe. We also added a few mirrors to reflect the light."

"I like it very much. Perhaps we can do something like this at home to brighten the interior."

"I'm so glad you've come. I so enjoy our visits." Ella lowered her voice. "Father rarely allows me to entertain."

"What are you girls whispering about?" Ella's mother asked.

Ella put her arm around Lizzy's waist. "We're hoping to have a chance to ride together."

"There's no reason you shouldn't," Mother replied. "The weather has been lovely." She returned her attention to Lizzy's mother.

"Forgive me," Ella whispered. "I'll explain everything later."

Lizzy looked concerned, but she said nothing.

Ella saw her father and Mr. Brookstone speaking with a tall, handsome stranger. She lowered voice and leaned closer to Lizzy. "Who is that?"

Lizzy glanced over her shoulder. "That's Mr. Jason Adler. He's from England and apparently will be with our show for a time."

Ella returned her attention to Lizzy. "Doing what? I thought it was all female performers."

"He'll be helping Uncle Oliver. You did hear that my father passed away earlier this year, didn't you?"

Ella felt the blood drain from her face. How unfeeling she'd been not to mention it first thing. "I apologize. How thoughtless of me. I'm so sorry for your loss. We received your uncle's telegram and were devastated for you."

Lizzy was all graciousness. "Don't feel bad. My father was an amazing man, and he will be missed, but he was also very practical. In fact, he insisted that the show had to continue—that it was his legacy and the only memorial he wanted. He begged Mother and me to continue with the performances. I suppose he knew that by keeping us busy, we would have less time to be swallowed up in sadness."

"I liked your father. He was always so pleasant—even humorous. So unlike my father." Ella fell silent, knowing she'd said too much. "I'm sure you must be tired. There's time to rest before supper. Why don't I show you upstairs, where you can take a nap or at least freshen up? I'm sure the servants have already taken up the bags."

"Well, I wouldn't want to desert my mother," Lizzy replied, "but I would like to be able to talk to you without everyone else listening in."

Ella took her hand. "Mama will see to your mother's needs. Come along."

"Thank you."

Taking the grand staircase in the deliberately slow manner she'd been taught, Ella glanced back down at the guests still speaking in the foyer. "Mr. Adler is quite handsome."

"I suppose he is." Lizzy sounded distant.

"Is something wrong?" Ella hoped she hadn't offended.

"No, not really. I suppose I'm still wondering what role he'll play in our show. Apparently there has been some concern about

how we're managing the business and, well
. . . everything related to it."

They reached the top of the stairs, and
Ella stopped. "I know we're not all that close,
although I consider you my dearest friend."

"I feel the same and must contradict you.
We're very close," Lizzy said, smiling. "I don't
confide in many people as I do with you."

Ella glanced down the hall where a black
woman stood dusting one of the tables. She
lowered her voice even more. "We need each
other, then."

She hurried to pull Lizzy down the hall
and past the uniformed woman. When they
reached the final door on the right, Ella opened
it and all but dragged Lizzy inside.

"I'm sorry to seem so rude, but there is
always someone listening in on conversations around here." Ella let go of Lizzy and
glanced around the room. There was no sign
of Lizzy's suitcase. "They'll bring your things
up soon, but in the meantime, let me open a
window. It's rather stuffy."

Ella could feel Lizzy's gaze on her. She
had been hoping they might have a chance
to talk about Ella's situation. It was unseemly
to involve an outsider in family matters, but
Ella was starting to feel nervous. Still, it would
be best to wait until they could be away from
the house. Perhaps on their ride tomorrow.

"You seem upset." Lizzy's voice was soothing and kind.

Ella grew a deep breath and turned back to face her. It was silly to pretend nothing was wrong. "There is . . . a problem. But I can't speak of it just now."

As if to stress the point, a knock sounded on the bedroom door.

"Come in," Ella called.

"I has Miz Brookstone's things," the young man declared. He brought in the bags and set them at the foot of the bed. "Mara say she be in by and by to put 'em away."

"Thank you, Elijah. You may go."

He gave a bit of a bow, then hurried from the room.

Lizzy looked at Ella. "We could go for a walk. I'm really not all that tired."

Ella shook her head. "No. It will keep. I probably shouldn't bother you with it at all." She bit her lower lip. Had she already said too much? "Get some rest. Dinner will be served promptly at seven. Tell Mara what you intend to wear. She'll have it pressed and ready for you."

Lizzy nodded. The look of worry on her face left Ella feeling guiltier than before.

"Everything is just fine," Ella said, forcing a smile. But it wasn't fine. Nothing in her life was fine.

When they came down to supper that evening, things went from bad to worse. Jefferson was there. Jefferson Spiby was the basest form of man. He was also Ella's fiancé, thanks to her father's business arrangements. They had been engaged since she was fifteen, and the only reason they hadn't married yet was that Mother insisted Ella was too young. But now that she was twenty, that excuse no longer applied. The wedding was planned for Christmas.

Jefferson spotted Ella and smiled in that suggestive way of his. It was embarrassing and terrifying at the same time and always left her feeling like she wanted a bath, even if she'd just come from one.

She had very nearly convinced herself that she should say nothing to Lizzy Brookstone, but seeing Jefferson here and knowing what he planned for her, Ella couldn't remain silent. She had been making plans for weeks, ever since learning that Lizzy was coming to the farm. If she didn't see them through, her fate with Jefferson would be sealed.

"Ella darling, your intended could not stay away," her father declared as she and Lizzy joined the family in the large parlor.

Jefferson watched her like a cat eyeing its prey. He made his way to her, sleek and calculating in his moves. When he finally stood before her and Lizzy, he smiled and took Ella's hand.

"My dear, you are deliciously beautiful." His words were barely whispered, and no wonder. Ella knew her father would never allow such talk. He kissed her hand, rather than hover over it respectfully, and touched his tongue to her knuckles, leaving Ella nauseated.

"Lizzy, this is Jefferson Spiby," she said. "Jefferson, this is Miss Brookstone. Her father and uncle are the owners of the Brookstone Wild West Extravaganza."

He straightened and let go of Ella. Turning to Lizzy, he smiled and extended his hand to take hers. He lowered his head until his lips nearly touched her knuckles, but then quickly straightened. "Miss Brookstone, I am charmed."

Lizzy's expression was guarded. She looked at Jefferson as if she were assessing the truth of his statement. Ella should have warned her that he couldn't be trusted, but that would have required further explanation.

"I understand you are a trick rider, Miss Brookstone," Jefferson said.

"I am," Lizzy replied.

His smile turned to something more like a leer. "You must get into some very . . . interesting positions."

Ella was mortified at his suggestive tone and glanced around quickly to make certain no one else had overheard. Everyone seemed otherwise occupied in conversation, however. She looked back just as Lizzy replied.

"You have me at a disadvantage, Mr. Spiby. You know my relationship to Ella and the Flemings, but I know nothing of why you're here."

Ella wanted to laugh out loud at the look on Jefferson's face. He wasn't used to women standing up to him. He regained his control quickly, however, and looked at Ella. "Why, I'm our dear Ella's fiancé. We're to be married very soon. Christmas, in fact."

A servant appeared at the entryway. "Dinner is served."

"Ah, thank goodness," Mr. Fleming declared. "I'm positively famished. He extended his arm to Lizzy's mother. "Might I escort you to dinner, my dear? I'll trust your brother-in-law and Mr. Adler to bring my wife."

"And I'll bring along Ella and Miss Brookstone," Jefferson announced. "That will leave Robert to bring up the rear."

Ella glanced at her brother Robert, who stood gazing into the eyes of his wife, Virginia. They had been married for five years and had two little boys, but they were still very much in love. Robert put his arm around his wife's waist and smiled. "I'd be delighted," he said.

They made their way into the dining room and, once everyone was seated, began to enjoy the delectable dishes Cook had created. Ella tried to keep her mind on the meal and polite conversation, but Jefferson made it nearly impossible. Not only had he broken with protocol to position himself at her side, but he insisted Lizzy sit at his side as well. Ella had hoped she might have Lizzy to herself.

The table was set with Mother's finest Royal Worcester china in the Pompadour pattern. The cream-colored china was artistically exquisite, with gold-painted leaves, flowers, laurels, and other delicate designs. Created prior to her mother's family coming to America, the set was their very best. Everything on the table was of the finest quality, from the crystal to the silver. This dinner was staged to impress. Something her father loved to do.

The evening passed surprisingly enough in easy conversation. Oliver Brookstone was full of stories and entertained them all. Ella had very nearly forgotten about Jefferson and her own troubles when one of the serving girls tripped and spilled orange sauce on the sleeve of Lizzy's gown.

"Oh, I'm sorry. I'm so sorry," the poor woman said, looking frantically for a napkin.

"You stupid girl," Jefferson declared, jumping to his feet. "You should be whipped."

Lizzy only smiled and shook her head. "It's not a problem, I assure you." She had her own napkin in hand and waved the girl away. "It wouldn't be the first time I spilled something or had something spilled on me. Please, don't worry about it."

Ella tried to hide her horror. She glanced toward her father. He looked livid. She knew he wouldn't make a scene here, but later he would punish the girl for her clumsiness, maybe even fire her. He could be so cruel at times.

Jefferson muttered something and reclaimed his seat. The lighthearted atmosphere faded quickly, and from that point on, everything seemed to be on edge. Gone were the entertaining stories of the wild west show and soft laughter.

When supper was finally concluded, Ella's father rose. "Rather than take our brandy and cigars in the library, I suggest we make our way to the stables. I know you're anxious, Mr. Brookstone, to have a look at your horses, and we can enjoy our cigars while considering their merits. Then we can have a brandy before retiring."

Ella hoped the men might spend a good long time there and give her a chance to speak to Lizzy about her trouble, but it wasn't to be.

"If we're going to look at the horses," Oliver Brookstone declared, "then I want Lizzy to accompany us. She knows more about horseflesh than anyone in our family save my brother, and in his absence, I'll trust her to know that the animals are fit for our needs."

It felt as if a hand had tightened around Ella's throat. No one challenged her father, and no one ever suggested that a woman was qualified to pass judgment on Fleming horses. She couldn't even bear to look at him for fear of what she might see in his expression. The entire room went silent, and even the servants went rigid, awaiting the coming storm.

"Well then," her father finally said after a lengthy silence, "I suppose we can forgo the cigars. After all, I wouldn't want to offend a lady's delicate constitution."

Lizzy had the audacity to smile. "I assure you, Mr. Fleming, my constitution can bear up under most anything."

Ella would have groaned aloud had she not feared the repercussions. Here was yet another challenge to her father's authority.

He motioned for one of the footmen. "Have the groom bring the Brookstone mares to the sale room. I wouldn't want Miss Brookstone getting her lovely gown dirty by traipsing all over the grounds."

Thankfully Lizzy didn't comment further.

Ella knew that would have been more than her father's temper could have tolerated.

"If the rest of you ladies would excuse us—" He paused, then without warning called Ella's name. "Why don't you join us? Ella also knows horses, and it might be nice for Lizzy to have her friend along. Certainly more appropriate." He didn't give anyone a chance to speak but turned and led the way.

There would be a price to pay for all of this later, but for now, Ella took up her shawl and kept very close to Lizzy Brookstone.

Lizzy could see that Mr. Fleming was unhappy with the turn of events. She had learned long ago that men of his breeding were often reluctant to believe a woman held any value outside of keeping a house and bearing children. She hadn't meant to comment on his remark, but the words were out of her mouth before she could hold them in check.

"You can see for yourself they are a handsome pair," Mr. Fleming announced as a uniformed groom lead the mares into the showroom. "I'm still disappointed in myself for agreeing to part with them."

The four-year-old Morgans were finer than any Lizzy had seen. Their large brown eyes seemed to watch her with concentrated care. They were nervous at the new attention, but Lizzy could see their quality and the remarkable strength of character, even in this brief encounter. Her father had told her about the horses long before she'd ever seen them, and his instincts about them had been right.

"They are very fine." She moved slightly to the right to better see them.

"Samson," Mr. Fleming called, "walk them around the room."

The man quickly followed the command. He led the mares together, one on either side of him. He walked them the full length of the showroom and back.

They were superb. Their buckskin coats glistened in the lamplight. They bore all the Morgan qualities Lizzy loved. Delicate, fine-chiseled features marked their heads. Their elegant necks were draped with black manes, and their tails bore the same ebony hue. Lizzy could only imagine the beautiful foals they would bear.

"They are handsome," Uncle Oliver declared. "My brother never failed to find the best. That's why he preferred your farm to any other."

Mr. Fleming smiled for the first time since the trouble at dinner. "I'm glad to be appreciated."

Lizzy looked at Ella, who stood between her father and fiancé. Spiby held on to her in a possessive manner, and Ella looked miserable. They were completely mismatched. Ella was petite and childlike, while Spiby was at least twice her age and stood a head and a half taller. It was appalling to imagine her having to marry the much older man.

A cat skittered through the room and spooked the mares. The one on the right started to rear, which upset her twin. Neither horse would easily calm. Lizzy watched as Jefferson Spiby stepped forward and yanked down on the rope that held the mare on the left.

"You must show them who has control," he said even as the horse backed away from him and shook its head. He reached up and twisted hard on the mare's ear. The horse on the right became even more agitated.

Lizzy started to say something, but Uncle Oliver put his hand on her arm. The look he gave her urged restraint.

"For pity's sake, Samson, control those animals," Mr. Fleming demanded. He turned back to Lizzy and her uncle. "As you can see, they're high-spirited, but with the right trainer, they will perform in whatever manner you choose."

Spiby finally had his horse under control

and looked back at them with a broad smile. "Rather like a good woman."

Lizzy stiffened and considered throwing back a sarcastic comment, but one glance at Ella changed her mind. Spiby wasn't worth it, especially if it only served to cause her friend more pain.

Thankfully, August Reichert, the Brookstones' head wrangler, took that moment to appear and try to get the attention of Lizzy's uncle. Lizzy could see the other men were already deep in conversation about something, so she went to August, curious at the look of perplexity upon his face.

"Good evening, August. Do you need something from Uncle Oliver?"

"Since he's busy, maybe we could have a word in private, you and me?"

She smiled. "Of course." She glanced back at Ella. "If you'll excuse me."

Lizzy followed August from the showroom, and once they were well away, he stopped to look back at the building. "They're a touchy lot around here. I'll be glad when we leave."

"Why do you say that?"

They were far enough from the lanterns that lit the path from the house that Lizzy could barely make out the frown on August's face. "I turned our horses out in the field as

I was instructed, but when I came back to the stables, lookin' for some liniment to rub on Betty's black, I was all but strong-armed out by Fleming's men and accused of snooping. I tried to explain what I needed and that I wasn't trying to cause a ruckus, but they wouldn't hear me out."

Lizzy considered this. Mr. Fleming had allowed them to graze the Brookstones' horses in his pastureland, but apparently his generosity only went so far. "I admit that Mr. Fleming and Mr. Spiby are hardly the sort I like doing business with. Father never spoke much about them except to say they produced excellent stock."

"Well, I just want to let you know that I'll be riding back to the train to get some of our own liniment and salve. I didn't want anyone wonderin' where I'd gotten off to, and the other boys are in town for a night of fun."

"That's fine, August. Since the horses are in the pasture, I don't foresee any problems. I'll let my uncle know when he's finished with Mr. Fleming." She gave a slight shrug. "Perhaps I'll even mention what happened in front of Mr. Fleming so that it doesn't happen again. There's nothing quite like embarrassing a man in front of his guests to bring about better behavior."

August shook his head. "Or worse."

⤝ FIVE ⤜

Wesley DeShazer sorted through the stack of bills. He had taken a chance and bought extra feed and hay. The old-timers felt certain it was going to be a bad winter. Maybe not as bad at '86–'87, but sure to be rough. Eastern Montana wasn't known to be kind when the months turned bitter.

He leaned back in the well-worn leather chair and stretched his arms over his head. The show folks would soon return to the ranch, and that would mean extra work and animals. Extra men to help with the herd as well.

It also meant Elizabeth Brookstone would be in residence. He tried not to think about her, but once in a while her memory snuck in like a fox to the henhouse.

He'd first met Lizzy when she was no more than a scrawny tomboy yet already an accomplished equestrian. He had marveled at how she could crawl all over the body of her mount at a full gallop. He could still see her standing on the back of her horse, her dark brown hair flying out behind her and her arms raised heavenward, as if she might be able to touch the sky.

As a child, Lizzy had been carefree and inquisitive. She'd taken to Wes immediately and hung around him like a faithful puppy. He pretended to be annoyed, but they both knew he didn't mind. He was barely a man doing his first real job and so homesick that having a little sister around, chattering about whatever popped into her head, made life away from home bearable.

It wasn't long before he met Clarissa Strong in Miles City—or Milestown, as some of the old-timers called it. She was the only daughter to a sickly mother and an abusive father. Her father was a good-for-nothing drunk who seemed to take special delight in tormenting his wife and child. Mrs. Strong worked at taking in laundry and mending, and Mr. Strong worked occasionally helping the blacksmith. His real job, however, seemed to be drinking up whatever earnings they made. It got to be so bad that Clarissa had to leave school and get a job at the local bakery in order to keep a roof over their heads.

They barely scraped by, and Wes had always felt sorry for them. Clarissa in particular. Her father thought nothing of hitting her for the most minor offense. It wasn't at all unusual to see her with a black eye, or hobbling because her father had kicked her repeatedly. Wes had wanted to confront the old man, but Clarissa told him it would only make matters worse.

When her mother died, things took a truly grim turn. Her father's anger surged, and it wasn't long before he wasn't even allowed in the local drinking halls. No one wanted to deal with his violent temper. Clarissa had barely turned eighteen when her father got himself killed in a fight. After that, Clarissa had few choices. She could marry one of the local cowboys or find a job that paid enough to support her in the tiny shack her father had leased. Bakery work certainly couldn't pay enough, and Clarissa hadn't the skills to earn more. Wesley had felt obligated to help her and proposed marriage.

They'd both known it wasn't a love match. Wes was fond of Clarissa, but more than anything, he wanted to save her from a plight worse than death. Clarissa had known her prospects were limited and eagerly accepted his offer. Plenty of men wanted her, but most were like her father, and the decent ones were just as bad off financially as she was. Wesley was the better choice. He had a good job—a foreman at a ranch—with his own little cabin to live in.

When Wes returned to the ranch with a wife in tow, the Brookstone family had been congratulatory and generous. Mrs. Brookstone went to work immediately to dress up his bachelor cabin. Not only that, but she'd taken Clarissa under her wing and helped her learn all she needed to know about ranch life.

Lizzy, however, hadn't taken the news well at all. He hadn't registered it then, but she and Clarissa were the same age, or nearly so. Lizzy had declared herself in love with him, but he'd figured it was just the silly notion of a little girl that would pass soon enough. Instead, Lizzy had been truly hurt by his marriage.

For weeks he hadn't understood her attitude toward him. It took her father's comment one day to open Wesley's eyes to the truth.

"It'll take time for her to get used to you having another woman in your life," Mark Brookstone had told him after Lizzy snubbed Wes during branding. *"But her heart will mend in time."*

Wes banged his fist on the desk. Thinking about the past wasn't going to get his work done. The Brookstones would soon be home, and he needed to be able to account for the year to Oliver rather than to his brother Mark. Wes was sad that Lizzy's father was gone. He had been good to work for, and he'd always known how to coax Wes to talk about what troubled him and then given great advice. But now he was dead. The ranch wouldn't be the same without him.

Without warning, Wes's office door opened.

Matt, one of the hands, gave a nod toward something behind him. "Fella here says he needs to see you. Says he's your brother."

Wesley's eyes narrowed. Phillip? Here? "Send him in."

Wes gathered his papers and ledger and stuffed them into the top drawer. He got to his feet just as his brother strolled into the room, acting as if they had seen each other only the day before.

Phillip grinned. "I guess you're surprised to see me."

The reply stuck in Wes's throat. He hadn't seen his kid brother since their father's funeral. Wes had been a bridegroom only a few months when word came that their father had been killed. He'd seen Phillip at the funeral, but not again—until now, over ten years later.

But it *was* Phillip, as sure as they lived and breathed. He was taller, but not by much, and still scrawny, although as Phillip pulled off his coat, Wes could see he'd muscled up over the years.

"I know I've given you a shock, but you could at least say something," Phillip declared.

"I guess I'm not sure what to say." Wes sat back down and just stared.

"Well, maybe you could say you're glad to see me. Or maybe, 'How are you doin'?'"

"Or how about 'Where have you been?'

Or 'Why didn't you bother to show up when our mother died?'" Wes asked in a snide tone. Anger was beginning to replace his surprise.

Phillip held out his hands. "That wasn't my fault. I didn't hear about it until the day of the funeral, and I wasn't able to leave." He grinned. "I was a guest of the city jail in Cheyenne." He pulled up a chair and turned it around backwards before plopping down. He leaned his arms across the back. "I would have come if I could. Ma knew how I felt. I'm sure she forgave me."

Wes clenched his teeth. He didn't want to fight with his brother—not when it was the first time they'd seen each other in a decade. "Where have you been?"

"Everywhere. Mostly Wyoming." Phillip gave a shrug. "Been workin' wherever I could get hired on. I'm good with horses, like you. There ain't a mount I can't break."

"Is that a fact?" Wes crossed his arms. He really was glad to see Phillip. He'd feared his brother was running with outlaws or dead.

Phillip laughed. "You know I always liked to do whatever my big brother could do . . . only better."

"I reckon I do."

"Well, I heard you were still up this way and figured it was about time I checked up on you. Thought you might be glad to see me."

Wesley nodded. "I am. I would have been glad to see you nine years ago or even five at Ma's funeral. I would have been glad just to get a letter. Do you have any idea how worried we were about you?"

"Ma always said worry was a sin." Phillip straightened and gave another of his good-natured smiles. "Besides, I wrote Ma twice."

Wes shook his head. "Twice in how many years?"

Phillip smacked the back of the chair. "That's all in the past. I can't make up for it now. I thought maybe we could just put it behind us."

"Funny how people who've done wrong are always the first to want everyone to forget about it."

"Well, we were always told that good Christians were supposed to forgive and forget. Ma would have wanted that."

For all that Phillip was twenty-six years old, Wesley couldn't help seeing him as a little boy. There had been times when their father had taken Phillip to task for one offense or another, and Phillip had sat before him with the same look on his face. He was so willing to receive correction, but just as willing to turn around and repeat the wrongdoing. Their folks were hard-pressed to get mad, however. Phillip was just too sweet, and his joyful countenance made it impossible to stay mad at him.

But Wesley wasn't sure he felt that way anymore. His brother had broken their mother's heart by disappearing after Pa's funeral. With each week that passed without word, she'd grown more concerned that Phillip might have fallen on hard times, gotten sick, or maybe even died. She refused to move to the ranch where Wes could take care of her for fear that Phillip would come home and not know where to find her. Then a letter would finally come, and all of Ma's worries were forgotten.

Until another stretch of time passed without word.

Yes, there had been two letters. She'd read both until the writing was faded and barely legible. She'd held on to the hope that there would be more letters and that Phillip would one day return to her, but that day never came. How was Wesley supposed to forgive and forget that?

"You mustn't hold it against him," Ma had said just before succumbing to her sickness. *"He doesn't know what he's done—how he's hurt us. He never meant to hurt anyone. That was never his way. Forgive him, Wes."*

The memory of his mother's words haunted him. She would have welcomed Phillip with open arms and never questioned the missing years. But Wes wasn't his mother, and he didn't know if he could forgive.

"What do you want, Phillip?" Wes finally asked, unable to find any peace in his heart.

Phillip's grin reappeared. "Why, that's simple. A job."

"Now can you tell me what's wrong?" Lizzy asked as she and Ella began their ride across the large open pasture the next day.

"I'll try, but you must swear to say nothing." Ella rode beside Lizzy on her favorite gelding. She called him Pepper because of his black coat. "If word ever got back to my father . . . well, it wouldn't be pleasant. You saw how angry he was last night when you mentioned what happened to your wrangler."

"I was surprised by how enraged he became. It was terrible when he promised to whip the grooms involved. I've never heard of such things in this day and age. So don't worry, I promise your father and the others will hear nothing of it from me," Lizzy assured.

"As you know, I'm supposed to marry in December."

"Yes, but I get the feeling it isn't what you want." Lizzy looked over at Ella with unwavering concern. "And frankly I can't fault you for that."

"I don't want to marry him. Jefferson is old enough to be my father. Well, nearly so. He is Father's dearest friend and confidant. They have many business dealings between them, and I happen to be one of them."

Lizzy looked away, as if contemplating the landscape. "It's 1900. Arranged marriages went out of fashion long ago."

"Not here. Proper young ladies only marry with their father's approval, and often that approval is only given in arranged marriages." Ella glanced over her shoulder, still not completely comfortable discussing the matter aloud. "But I am afraid I can't be a proper young lady. Not if it means marrying Jefferson. He's cruel and lewd. I've heard horrible rumors about him. They say he has not one, but three mistresses."

"Good grief!" Lizzy turned to her with a look of stunned disbelief. "Three?"

Ella nodded. "He has a reputation for being with women of all kinds, and he gambles and deceives. Whenever he's here and we're alone, he tries to take liberties."

"Have you mentioned it to your father? Surely he doesn't approve."

"I tried to talk to Father. He told me Jefferson is just overcome with love for me and anxious for us to wed. I mentioned the other women, but Father told me that men of power have needs that go beyond the home. He said that I need to concern myself only with being a wife and mother and that I'm not to listen to any of the rumors. But how can I not? And how can I bear a life with that man?"

"Why can't you just refuse to marry him?"

Ella's shoulders slumped. "Father said he would force me if I refused."

"But surely a minister would insist on your being willing."

"Father has powerful people on his side. He told me he would have one of his judge friends sign all the papers and declare us married, even without my permission. Almost every man in the county owes my father for something."

Lizzy considered that for a moment, then spoke. "But wouldn't that be an embarrassment to the family? I know reputations down here are important. If the community knew that he'd forced you to marry against your will, wouldn't that bring shame upon him?"

"He wouldn't allow me to say anything of the kind. I'm sure I'd be whisked away and locked in a room with Jefferson until I agreed to cooperate. I heard Father tell Jefferson that he'd be wise to get me with child as soon as possible." She shook her head. "Like I'm a brood mare and nothing more. Certainly not a cherished daughter." Tears formed in her eyes. "I don't know what I'm going to do."

"Why don't you leave? Didn't you tell me you have a sister in Chicago? Surely you could go live with her."

"They won't allow it. I'm virtually a prisoner. If I showed up in town to purchase a train ticket, my father would hear about it and drag me back home. Either him or Jefferson."

They rode on in silence for some time. It was clear there was no easy solution, but Ella couldn't help hoping that Lizzy might have an idea. God knew, Ella was out of ideas herself. She'd tried praying for direction, but God seemed strangely silent.

"What about your friends?" Lizzy asked after some time. "Isn't there someone nearby who could help you get away?

"My girlhood friends are all married with families of their own. I've lived a very secluded life the last two years. Once my betrothal was formally announced, Father and Jefferson sought to keep me away from my friends. They always make excuses for why I'm not at various parties. I attend church with Mother and Father, and of course Jefferson, but I'm not allowed to be alone or say much to anyone."

"And no one thinks this strange?" Lizzy

asked. Her tone was astonished. "What's wrong with the people around here?"

"They are in my father's debt, for one thing. His or Jefferson's. No one questions their actions or deeds. Those who benefit from them are more than happy to keep the truth from being known, and those who would protest or condemn are quickly silenced or ruined."

The sun was rapidly sliding toward the horizon, and Ella knew they'd soon have to return to the house and dress for supper. "I'm sorry for involving you in this, Lizzy. You don't deserve having to listen to all of this."

"I'm the one who's sorry. I had no idea anything like this was happening . . . or could happen." Lizzy looked around. "How were you allowed to come out alone with me?"

Ella tried to appear nonchalant. "I didn't tell them. Father was busy with your uncle and Mr. Adler, and Jefferson wasn't here. I'm sure once they figure it out, Father will send someone to find us."

"I'm so sorry, Ella. I don't know what to do. We'll be gone so soon."

Ella could hear the sincerity in Lizzy's voice. A thought came to her, sparked by her friend's words. "I don't know how we might pull it off, but perhaps I could . . . sneak away with the show."

"What?" Lizzy pulled back on the reins.

A smile broke across her face. "Why, that's a brilliant idea. No one would ever expect that."

Ella felt hope wash over her. "I know it would be a risk, but I think if I could just get out of town and far enough from here, I could catch a train to Chicago, where my sister lives."

She could see that Lizzy was pondering how to make it work. "We're heading back to town around noon tomorrow. Mother has some shopping to see to, and I promised I'd help. Then there are the other performers' needs to take care of. Our horses won't be rounded up until evening, however."

Ella nodded, remembering that the Brookstones' horses had been given one of the Flemings' pastures. "I could feign a headache and retire early, then sneak out and ride in."

"But how would you get to the train? That's several miles from here. And you'd be in town, so someone might see you."

"I'll get Mara to help me. She can get Elijah to take my horse out to the edge of the trees. When it's good and dark and Father is busy with seeing your horses returned, I can ride into town through the woods. None of our people will accompany the horses back to town, just yours."

"If you can manage to meet August down the road, I can get him to put your horse in with the others. He's our head wrangler and loyal to a fault. He'll keep our secret. Do you think Mara could help you to dress like one of the wranglers?"

Ella brightened. "You want me to look like a boy . . . a man."

"Yes. When you reach town, you'll appear to be one of the Brookstone workers. August can board your horse with the others and then show you which car is mine. You'll stay with me and Mother. Once the horses are loaded, we'll leave with the late train bound for St. Louis."

"It sounds like it could work." Ella could feel her burden lighten.

Lizzy nodded. "I'm positive it can work. You'll see. We'll get you out of here and then figure out how to get you to your sister's place."

"August, could I bother you for a moment?" Lizzy asked as she came upon him tending to Betty's horse. "Is he better?"

The wrangler released the gelding's leg and nodded. "He's doing just fine. This rest has done the trick. Couldn't have come at a better time."

"I'm glad to hear it. I've enjoyed the rest myself."

August gave the black a pat. "He's a good

animal." He pushed back his hat. "Just let me get him back in the field, and you can have my full attention."

"I'll walk with you. I'd rather no one overhear us."

August frowned. "Secrets?"

Lizzy nodded and tried her best to look perfectly at ease. "Yes. A rather delicate one."

They said nothing more as they walked Betty's horse back to the white-fenced field where the rest of the Brookstones' horses were grazing. Lizzy opened the gate for August and waited for him to release the horse. She didn't like involving him in the situation, but it couldn't be helped. She pitied Ella more than any woman she'd ever known, and Lizzy knew she couldn't stand by and do nothing.

August joined her, wrapping the lead around his arm and grinning. "What can I do for you?"

"I need your word that you'll say nothing about this to anyone. It's very important—very nearly a matter of life and death."

That wiped the smile from his face. "I promise."

Lizzy nodded. "Miss Fleming needs our help. She must get away from here, or she'll be forced to marry that awful Mr. Spiby. I've told her that if she can disguise herself enough to get away and join you when you bring our horses back to the train tomorrow night, we'll hide her and take her with the show."

"But won't her people think of that first thing?" He leaned back against the fence and shook his head. "I can't help but think they'll come to us looking for her."

"I've thought of that as well. That's why no one but you and me will know anything about it. Ella will get to the woods and then join you in the dark. After that, you'll come to the train. I'll be waiting, so just have her hide somewhere if it doesn't look possible to get her to my family's train car unseen. After that, I'll take care of her. She has a sister she can go to in time, but for now we're her only hope."

"All right. I'll do it, because I've got a bad feeling about this place and don't blame her one bit for wanting to leave. Did you know that Fleming whipped his men for what they did to me?"

"I heard. I don't like it any more than you do. It was never my intention that anyone come to harm."

"Nor mine. I'm sorry I ever said anything about it."

"Don't be. Whatever the reason for the way the men acted, whatever Fleming's issues, I won't have our people treated badly." She could see her uncle and Mr. Fleming making their way from the stables. Uncle Oliver waved to her. "I think I'm wanted. Please remember: Don't breathe a word of this to anyone. I'm counting on you."

August grinned. "Miss Lizzy, you know there's nothing I wouldn't do for you."

She smiled. "I do know that, August, which is exactly why I came to you in the first place."

<hr>

The next day Ella felt as though she were floating on air. She listened patiently as her father finalized plans with the Brookstones, then bid Lizzy good-bye without hesitation. She had arranged for Mara to bring boy's clothes to her room. Given Ella's tiny frame and short stature, there was no hope of being able to wear the clothes of a full-grown man. It was a pity Robert's boys were so young, or she might have snuck into the nursery to borrow some of their things.

The only problem came when Jefferson made an unannounced appearance in the late afternoon. Ella had been about to take an afternoon ride, and rather than deal with her fiancé, she hurried down the servants' stairs and slipped out to the stables unnoticed. She hurried one of the stableboys through saddling Pepper and was out and away from the house before anyone could stop her. Hopefully her exit that night would be just as easy.

Unfortunately, when she returned from her ride, she heard her father's unmistakable voice in the stable. He was angry, shouting and ranting about something. Her blood chilled as Jefferson replied.

"I'll take care of it. That man won't cause us any trouble, because he won't be allowed to speak about what he's seen."

"You'll have to act quickly," Father replied. "If he talks about what he's witnessed, we'll be ruined."

"Hardly that. Who would believe him?"

"I can't take the chance," Ella's father answered. "Neither can you."

Ella froze in place, afraid to advance farther into the stable. What were they talking about? What man? What had he seen?

"I said I would handle it, and I will," Jefferson said. "After today, it will no longer be a concern."

SIX

The day dragged by for Lizzy. She and Mother handled the shopping with the help of Zeb and Thomas, two of the oldest of their show's crew. The men had worked a great many years for the Brookstones, having been hired by Lizzy's grandfather. Now they were nearing the end of their days, and their options for earning a living were extremely limited. What were old cowboys supposed to do when they could no longer handle the physical strain of the job? They had no family to take care of them, no money saved with which to support themselves in their final years. She thought of Jason's desire to eliminate their positions in order to save money. Where would these old men go then? Who would take care of them? She couldn't bear the idea of them being turned out.

But on top of her worries over them and what Jason would suggest or even demand be done, Lizzy couldn't stop thinking about Ella's situation. She was glad to be able to help, but the problem would not disappear just because Ella managed to leave her father's farm. Men like Mr. Fleming and that Mr. Spiby would never give up. They would hunt Ella down, and they had the money to do whatever was necessary to find her.

Am I just putting my family in danger by helping her?

Several times Lizzy had thought about telling her mother about Ella, but the time was never right. She worried that someone might overhear and word would get back to the Flemings, and then all would be lost and whatever small effort Lizzy might have managed would be for naught. No. It would be better to wait until Ella was on the train and they were safely on their way to St. Louis.

"Look, there's Agnes. She must have finished sooner than she expected," Mother announced. "I still need to go to the market to pick up some things for our supper tonight. Time's getting away from us, and if I'm going to have it ready on time, I'll need to get right to work."

Lizzy glanced down the street to the bakery they'd passed earlier. "Why don't we keep supper simple? I could go to the bakery and buy bread and perhaps a cake. Then we could get some ham and cheese for sandwiches. I'm sure everyone would get their fill, and that way you wouldn't have to work so hard."

"I suppose we could," Mother said. "Mrs. Fleming sent a wagon full of homemade canned goods as well as jams and jellies. They were made from her own garden and orchards."

Lizzy was relieved. "See, we'll have plenty to eat."

Mother smiled. "I suppose that would make it easy on everyone."

They finished the shopping and made their way back to the train. Lizzy found a certain comfort in being on board. It wasn't that she hadn't enjoyed their time at Fleming Farm, but the train car reminded her of her father. His influence and choices were everywhere, as he had designed the car to be set up just as it was. He had made much of the furniture and found smart ways to secure things in place.

How she missed him.

"Would you help me change my clothes?" Mother asked as she pulled the pin from her hat. "I feel too overdressed for preparing a meal. Even wearing black."

Lizzy felt the same way. "I don't mind getting dressed up from time to time, but I much prefer my riding clothes and costumes." She smiled and gave a shrug. "If you were hoping for a frilly and fancy daughter, I'm afraid I must disappoint."

Mother reached out and touched Lizzy's cheek. "I am never disappointed in you, Lizzy. You've always been good about just being yourself. No one can fault you for that."

"Oh, some can and do." The words slipped out before she could hold them in check.

Mother looked at her. "Who would fault you?"

Lizzy shook her head. "It isn't important. Frankly, I had no one particular in mind." Although now that she was contemplating it, she easily recalled more than once when Wesley had chided her for her tomboyish ways.

Mother touched her cheek again. There were tears in her eyes. "You are a beautiful young woman. Just remember that your love for God would make you that way even if you weren't otherwise pleasing." She sniffed. "Your father always said he could see the love of Jesus shining through your eyes."

Lizzy's throat tightened, but she would not allow herself to cry. She patted her mother's hand. "He said the same of you. I'm so glad we have the Lord to guide us and help us through our sorrows. Now, come on. You undo my back buttons, and I'll undo yours." Lizzy forced a smile. "Then I'll help you with supper."

The troupe shared their evening meals in what was called the entertainment car. One train car was set up to be a gathering place for all the performers and crew who weren't needed in the livestock or tack cars. At one end was the show's office, and at the other Agnes's sewing room. When en route, it was here that the crew passed the hours reading, playing cards, writing letters, or even singing. More than once, the ladies had come together as a choir to entertain the others.

Lizzy usually spent her time on the rails in the family car, however. Especially now that her father was gone. She didn't feel much like socializing. She was still open and willing to discuss whatever was necessary with her fellow performers, but she preferred the quiet of her own space. She supposed that was another reason she didn't particularly want to have to treat Jason Adler as family. He seemed to always seek her out and want to talk. Tonight was no exception. Three times now he'd tried to corner her, and all she wanted was to be left alone to keep watch for Ella.

Finally, as the hour grew late, Uncle Oliver became her savior.

"Jason, why don't you come with me and the boys?" Uncle Oliver announced. "The horses will be arriving soon, and I'd like you to see how we handle the loading."

"I'd be glad to," Jason said, casting a glance at Lizzy. "Perhaps we could speak later?"

Lizzy shook her head. "No, I plan to go to bed early. Maybe tomorrow."

She hurried back to the family car before he could speak. She didn't want him trying to change her mind.

"I don't need you courting me, Jason Adler."

———◆◆◆◆———

Ella paced her room frantically, hoping and praying the time would pass quickly. Each time she stopped in front of the fireplace, she glanced at the beautiful ceramic clock. Was it even working? She was certain the hands hadn't moved in hours.

She still had to get through supper without giving herself away. That wouldn't be easy. Her father seemed to note her every mood. Still, she could easily excuse her silence and reflective manner by explaining that she was sorry to see Lizzy go. He'd believe her. He had no reason not to. He was the one, along with Jefferson, who had made her a virtual prisoner at the farm. He was the one who saw to it that she received very few guests. She would perhaps emphasize her sadness and remind him that she had no friends.

She shook her head. "It would serve no purpose. He doesn't care, and I'll soon be gone."

Mara appeared to help Ella dress for dinner. The maid knew about her plan to escape and had even offered to go with her. Poor Mara. She had been at the receiving end of Father's anger more than once.

"Elijah say he'll have Pepper waitin' for you just over the bridge and in the trees," Mara whispered as she did up the buttons on the back of Ella's silk dress. The gown was a new creation her mother had ordered from Paris. It was lush and beautiful, exactly the kind of dress any young woman would love. Ella had to admit she would miss the finery her father's money could buy. But her sister Margaret was by no means poor. She'd married well enough. Her husband, Isaac, was in business with his father and brother, and together they owned Knox Saddlery. Their saddles were sought out far and wide. Margaret and Isaac lived quite well on a beautiful estate outside of Chicago, but they weren't as rich as Father.

"I'll come back after supper—early, if need be," Ella said in a hushed voice. "Did you get the clothes?"

"Yes'm. I gots 'em, and I'll have 'em ready." The black woman led Ella to the vanity chair in order to arrange her hair. "I also packed you some other things you be needin'. Elijah gonna bring them with your horse."

Ella had figured she'd have to go with nothing but the clothes on her back. "Truly? That's wonderful. Would it include a change of clothes?"

"Yes'm. It's all in your small travel bag. He'll be havin' it for you, never you fear."

Ella sighed. "I'm going to miss you, Mara." She looked up at the dark-skinned woman. She and Mara had been raised together. Mara's mother, Lucille, had cared for Ella throughout her childhood. Lucille had taught Ella not only to embroider, but to actually sew. Mother would have had a fit had she seen her daughter on the floor with the servants, cutting apart clothes and making patterns from each piece. Of course, Mother and Father both would have had a fit if they'd known Ella had learned to Roman ride and do other stunts on horseback. Her brother and one of the servant boys had taught her when she'd been barely old enough to ride alone. It was just one more reason she felt a close bond with Lizzy Brookstone. She longed for the same freedom Lizzy enjoyed.

"I'll be missin' you too, Miss Ella." Mara's eyes were damp with tears, but she held on to her emotions and continued to arrange Ella's blond hair into an acceptable fashion. When she was done, Mara stepped back. "I be finished."

Ella stood and nodded. "I'll be back as soon as I can without arousing suspicion."

She made her way downstairs and found her brother and sister-in-law in the family parlor. Virginia smiled as Ella came into the room, but it was Robert who spoke.

"My, but don't you look pretty. Jefferson is sure to press for an earlier wedding day."

"That's hardly my goal." Ella looked around. "Is he here again?"

"Of course, little sister. He's not going to let you get far from sight. Frankly, I'm surprised he hasn't taken a room here." Her brother chuckled.

"Don't say as much to Father, or he'll no doubt extend the invitation." Ella went to the window and pulled back the sheers to look outside.

Robert joined her at the window. "You could do much worse than Jefferson Spiby. You'll always have a life of comfort and ease married to him."

"Especially if he spends more time in town visiting his mistresses than with me at home."

Her brother frowned. "He isn't the man I would have chosen for you, but you'll have a good life. Jefferson would never allow his wife to lift a finger. And not only that, but you'll always be close to home—no fear of him taking you off away from the family."

"But what if I want to lift a finger? What if I want to move far away?" Ella looked up at him. "You know as well as anyone that I'm kept here against my will. I'm never allowed to go to town unless Mother and Father are at my side, and usually Jefferson as well."

"They're only looking out for your well-being. You know there have been difficulties in town. Some of the women have complained about not feeling safe," Virginia said, joining them. "I, for one, am always glad to have Robert along."

He nodded and put his arm around his wife's shoulders. "It's far better to be over-protected than abused."

Ella sighed. "I have no desire to marry Jefferson. You both know his reputation."

"You're nearly twenty-one," Virginia protested. "People would already be talking about you if not for your engagement."

"Jefferson is more than double my age. I don't want to marry an old man."

Virginia took her hand. "If you feel so adamant about it, perhaps you should speak to your father again."

"He won't hear me on the matter. He's told me quite firmly that I am never to bring it up. He doesn't care that Jefferson is a bully, nor about his reputation as a womanizer. He only tells me to keep my thoughts to myself and be a good girl who allows the men in her life to speak for her."

Virginia frowned and looked up at Robert. "Well . . . I have heard that Mr. Spiby doesn't always conduct himself in a good Christian manner."

"As have I, but Father is right. Ella just needs to be silent and let him direct her. Father would never want anything bad for you, Ella." He smiled down at her. "Just trust him. He'll see that Jefferson does right by you."

Nothing more was said, because her mother

stepped into the room. "Goodness, why are you all gathered at the window? Is there something interesting to see?"

Robert laughed and led Virginia across the room. He bent to kiss Beatrix Fleming's cheek. "Good evening, Mother. How lovely you look."

Their mother smiled. "Thank you, Robert. You're quite dashing yourself." She smiled at Virginia. "And you are lovely, my dear. I told you that butternut color was perfect for your complexion."

"You did, and I'm very pleased with the results," Virginia said, running her hand down the side of her pigeon-breasted, lace-embellished gown.

Father chose that moment to enter. Jefferson was at his side, as usual, and the two had their heads close together in low conversation. They looked up and separated quickly, however, at the sight of the others. Both looked quite grim.

"What is it, George?" Mother asked.

"I'm afraid there's been an accident."

Mother put a hand to her mouth.

"What kind of accident?" Ella asked, coming to her mother's side.

"The Brookstones' wrangler has been killed."

Everyone gasped, and the color drained from Mother's face.

"What happened?" Robert asked as Ella led her mother to a chair.

"Horse trampled him," Jefferson answered before Ella's father could speak.

"That's awful," Virginia murmured. "Poor man."

"One of the risks of the job. We've sent word to the train. Our men will take the horses in and . . . the body."

Ella felt her stomach knot. This was terrible. Not only because of the loss of the poor man, but her plans were now in jeopardy. What could she do? She could hardly go along with the Fleming Farm workers. They'd know who she was, even in boy's clothes.

"We'll have them move out as soon as the sheriff arrives," Father said. "He'll have to ask his questions before the body can be moved."

"Oh, dear. I'm afraid I don't feel very well," Mother said. "I must go lie down."

Father nodded. "I think it would wise for all of you ladies to take supper in your rooms tonight. This is a terrible affair, and we will need to explain the situation to the sheriff."

Ella nodded. "I'll see that Mother gets to her room." She tried to think past the moment. How could she use this terrible situation to her advantage?

Once upstairs, Ella summoned her mother's maid. "Serena, Mother has had a shock.

Please see she gets to bed. I'll have some food sent up." The maid took Ella's mother in hand and led her away to the bedroom.

Ella quickly returned to her own room, and it wasn't long before Mara appeared. She had already heard the news and wondered if Ella's plans had changed.

"No, I still want to go. Only now I figure I'll have to leave when the sheriff arrives. Everyone will be too busy to notice. Please have Elijah take my horse now. They won't go into the family stables—at least I presume they won't. I figure the accident must have happened on the west end, where they'd gathered the Brookstones' horses. After you instruct Elijah, please hurry back here to help me with my clothes."

"Yes'm." Mara raced from the room while Ella began to do what she could to undress.

She heard the arrival of the sheriff, since her bedroom faced the front of the house. He'd come with several other men, including the doctor. She couldn't see well enough to tell who the other men were. Everyone raced toward the far west stables, just as Ella had figured.

She went to her jewelry box and opened the lid. She had several pieces that had been given to her by her parents. None of them were family heirlooms, so Ella stuffed them into a little drawstring bag. She would sell them in St. Louis to get money for her new start. She started to turn away but noticed the bracelet Jefferson had given her. She wanted nothing to remind her of him, but it was sterling and jade. Perhaps it would bring her a few extra dollars. She took it as well.

Mara returned and helped Ella change. They had never managed so quickly. Mara was perspiring profusely. No doubt she was just as scared as Ella. Until this moment, it hadn't dawned on Ella that Mara might be punished.

"Look, no matter what," Ella said, stopping to take Mara's hand, "I don't want you to get in trouble. When they ask you where I am, tell them I went to bed, sickened by all that's happened, and said I didn't want to be disturbed."

Ella went to her vanity and picked up her room key. "Lock the door, then hide the key. Throw it away, even. Whatever you do, don't take it back to your room, because they're sure to look there when they start to suspect you might know where I went. In the morning, make a fuss. Come down crying or upset and tell Mother that I won't open my door. That way it will be clear that you still think I'm in my room."

Mara nodded. "Yes'm. I'll do just that."

Ella gave her a hug. "I love you, Mara. You're like a sister to me." This would be the first time they'd ever been separated.

"I be prayin' for you, Miss Ella. Prayin' real hard," Mara said as Ella pulled away.

"I know you will. I'll be praying for you as well. If all goes well, Father won't find me until after I turn twenty-one. That's just until January, and then maybe I can send for you." She doubted her father would ever allow Mara to join Ella, but it comforted her to say as much.

Glancing once more out the window, Ella could see lanterns and all sorts of activity at the far end of the stables. "I must go. It's now or never." She pulled an old hat down over her blond hair. "Do I look passable?"

"In the dark, nobody'll know." Mara went to the door and opened it. She looked out, then nodded.

Ella slipped quietly down the back stairs. She stopped often to listen and make sure no one was nearby. She had to reach the trees, and it wouldn't be easy to cross the long, open lawns without someone seeing her. Hopefully anyone who did see her would presume she was just one of the boys searching for something.

She'd nearly reached the kitchen when she stopped cold at the sound of Jefferson and her father. They were speaking in hushed, quick statements.

"There was no other way."

"But now we've got this to deal with," her father said.

"He'd seen and heard too much."

"I know." It sounded like they were moving toward the back door. "I just don't like that you had to kill him."

Ella thought her heart might stop. She pressed hard against the wall of the stairs.

Jefferson actually laughed. "It wasn't my first killing, nor will it be my last. Now, you do your part and manage the explaining." His tone turned sarcastic. "I shouldn't have to do everything."

She heard them leave the room, and only after the screen door slammed shut did she feel she could continue. But Jefferson so casually admitting murder kept her frozen in place. He was the reason August Reichert was dead. The wrangler had seen too much.

But what in the world had he seen that merited death?

SEVEN

Wes looked around for his brother. It was nearly eight o'clock, and most of the men were headed to bed, if not already asleep. They were getting up at three in the morning to take calves to market, and every man there knew it would be a long day.

Wes left the bunkhouse and went to the barn. If Phillip's horse was gone, then he'd know the day of hard work hadn't agreed with his brother and he'd left. Probably for good. If that were the case, Wes figured it would be for the best. He was still uncertain about hiring his brother, but he'd promised their mother he would watch out for Phillip if he ever came around again.

The barn door was open, which gave him hope that Phillip might be there. Maybe he was just grooming his horse or taking care of his gear.

"Phillip?" Wes asked as he entered the barn. "Are you in here?"

"'Course . . . I am." Phillip staggered toward him. "Whaddaya . . . want?"

Wes frowned. "You're drunk."

Phillip stopped, pulled his chin back, and struggled to keep from swaying. "Wha' . . . if I am?"

"Brookstone cowboys aren't allowed to drink on the job. You aren't allowed to have liquor in the bunkhouse. Where'd you get it?"

Phillip laughed and shook his head. "I've always got a bottle. Not havin' a drink is . . . well . . ." He swayed again and caught hold of a stall gate just before falling. "Fella's gotta have a drink at the . . . the end of the day."

"Not here, they don't. And you've clearly had more than a drink." Wes shook his head. "Get rid of it. Any liquor you brought with you I want gone. Get rid of it immediately."

"Now wait jes a . . . jes a minute." Phillip's words were slurred, but he offered a grin as usual. "I finished it, but . . . why can't I have it?"

Wes closed the distance between them in two long strides. He took hold of Phillip's shoulders and gave him a fierce shake. "You can't have it because I need my men sober. If that's not possible for you, then you need to pack your gear and leave. We don't allow liquor on the Brookstone ranch."

Phillip's eyes widened. If possible, Wesley's words had sobered him. "You'd throw me out?" He blinked several times, as if the shaking had loosened something in his head.

"I'd throw you out, same as I'd throw any of the rest of them out. We have firm rules around here. I told them to you when I hired you on. If I can't depend on you to abide by them, you have to go. Even if you are my brother."

"Don't the res' . . . res'. . . ." He smiled. "Don't the res' of the men drink?"

"If they do, they do it in town on their

time and not mine." Wes pulled Phillip with him toward the door. "I'm going to put you to bed, and we'll discuss this in the morning. It's senseless to argue with a man who won't remember anything come daylight."

He'd no sooner gotten Phillip in bed and his boots off than the younger man was asleep. He hardly looked like more than a boy. With all the hard living and fights he'd no doubt been in over the years, Wes had figured it would change his appearance, but it hadn't. There was still something almost angelic in Phillip's expression. Their mother used to comment on it at times just like this. She'd sit beside her sleeping son and smile.

"For all his orneriness, there's really a good boy deep inside," Wes could almost hear her say.

Wes sat on the edge of the bed and pushed back the sandy brown hair that had fallen over one of Phillip's eyes. Where had he been all these years? Why had he forsaken his family? Wes knew there were issues in the past—things Phillip wouldn't even talk about. Their mother had tried and tried to get him to open up, but Phillip had always laughed it off or simply avoided the discussion. Maybe that was why he'd left. It definitely hadn't been for a lack of love, because no one had ever been as cherished and loved by their mother as Phillip had been. Wes couldn't even fault her for her favoritism, because he felt the same way. There was just something so loveable about Phillip that it was impossible to stay mad at him for long.

"Don't be angry with him. Pray for him instead." His mother's words echoed in Wesley's head.

Heaving a heavy sigh, Wes got to his feet. He pulled the blanket from the end of the bed and covered Phillip. He wanted to pray, but he wasn't sure God was even listening to him these days. It always seemed, when he tried to seek God in prayer, that the words just bounced back off the ceiling. He knew God existed—he truly believed that God did answer prayers. So why couldn't Wes shake the feeling that God was listening to everyone else but him?

———◆✦◆———

As a part of her routine, Lizzy went to visit her horses every night before retiring. Longfellow and Thoreau had come to expect this, as well as the treats she brought. Zeb had put together a rope pen on land owned by the railroad. It wasn't much, but it was better than keeping the animals on the train.

Smiling, Lizzy offered carrots, apples, and her love to her beloved horses. "How are you boys doing?"

Neither paused in their munching. The treats were far too compelling. Lizzy stroked their manes and continued to talk as if they might join in at any moment.

"I'm glad we brought you two back early, but I'm sorry you don't have a better place to rest. The others will be here soon. Uncle Oliver said August would have them back by nine, but as you can see, that time has come and gone."

She frowned. August should have been here hours ago. Ella too. What had happened to delay everyone? Lizzy gave each of the horses one last piece of apple and then headed toward the train to find her uncle. She hadn't gone two steps, however, when someone called her name in a whisper.

"Lizzy?" Ella appeared from the shadows. She led her black horse and glanced around like a thief avoiding capture.

"Hurry. Bring him this way." Lizzy led the way to the railcar where the horses were kept. She startled at the sight of Rupert, one of the wranglers.

"Hey, Miss Lizzy." Rupert limped toward her. He'd been severely injured years earlier, and the leg had never healed properly. "What are you doing out here at this hour?"

"Rupert, I need your help and your silence." Lizzy motioned over her shoulder, then looked all around them, fearing they'd be seen. "We need to hide Miss Fleming's horse with our own. She's leaving the farm, and it'll spell trouble for everyone if she's found."

He frowned. "No problem, Miss Lizzy. I'll see that he's in with the other blacks. He's enough like Miss Betty's horse that no one will ever notice."

Lizzy nodded. "Say nothing. I plan to tell Mother and Uncle Oliver after we're on our way."

"Yeah, I thought we'd be long gone by now. If August doesn't get here soon, we'll miss the midnight train."

"I know." Lizzy frowned and turned to Ella, who looked terrified. Lizzy felt bad for her. She was leaving the comfort of all she'd ever known, but not only that, if anyone found out before they got her safely out of town, it could cause no end of problems. "Come on, Ella. Rupert will see to your horse. I need to get you hidden away."

Ella nodded and fetched a bag from where it hung on the horn of her saddle. Rupert took the reins and led the horse down to another car before leading it up the boarding ramp.

"I'm going to hide you in the family car." Lizzy led Ella to the other end of the train. She hoped her mother was still busy with Agnes. She hurried to open the door and peer inside, then motioned Ella to join her.

Once inside, Ella paused to take a deep breath and steady her nerves. "It's such a dark night. I think I got a bit spooked. I thought I'd never get here. I had to ride out by myself for fear of being found out."

"Why? Where are August and the horses? They should have been here by now."

Ella's face paled, and her expression filled with fear. "I . . . uh . . . don't know exactly. There was some sort of trouble. I think it was with one of the horses. My father and Jefferson were both involved, and since they were both busy, I came on my own."

"That must be what has slowed August's return. Come with me." Lizzy crossed the car to the far side and opened a door. "This will be your room for now. There's a bunked berth. You can hide on top under the covers. Scoot clear to the back. No one will see you there, given the way it's positioned."

Ella pulled off the old felt hat she'd been wearing. Her hair was slightly mussed but styled as if for a party.

Lizzy couldn't help but smile. "Your hair is pretty, but it doesn't fit the rest of your ensemble."

The petite blonde looked down at her

costume. "Mara found this outfit for me." She bit her lower lip.

Lizzy could see her friend was exhausted and scared. "You're safe now, Ella. Come on, let's get you settled."

Once Lizzy had seen to Ella, she made her way outside just as the horses arrived. She smiled and started over to where the riders were halting the string of animals. August was nowhere to be found, but the sheriff was prominently leading the herd.

Uncle Oliver and Jason Adler welcomed the sheriff as he climbed down from his bay. Some of the other wranglers came out and began to converse with the Fleming men. Lizzy moved to her uncle's side.

"What are you saying, Sheriff? He's dead?" Oliver said, his voice pinched with shock.

Lizzy stiffened. Who was dead?

"I'm surely sorry, Mr. Brookstone, but it appears the poor man was kicked in the head and then trampled to death. Mr. Fleming and Mr. Spiby are following behind with the wagon and the body."

Uncle Oliver turned to her. "August is dead."

"August?" Lizzy looked at the sheriff.

The sheriff tipped his hat. "I'm mighty sorry, miss. Fleming sent his men to bring your horses back. He should be here directly to explain what happened."

By now most of the Brookstone troupe had gathered. Mother took Lizzy's arm as Uncle Oliver and the sheriff continued to discuss the tragedy. The Brookstone wranglers took the horses from the Fleming Farm men and began loading them on the train. Jason remained with Lizzy and her mother.

"If there's anything I can do," Jason began.

"What happened?" Mother asked. "Someone said August is dead."

"That's all I know, except they said he was kicked in the head and then trampled to death." Lizzy could hardly believe it.

"With horses there is always a danger," Jason declared. "I've been kicked myself. Very nearly broke my leg."

"Yes, I'm sure anyone who's around a horse for long is going to experience some sort of injury, but August handled horses in such a way that he rarely had any trouble." Lizzy shook her head. "In fact, some say August had a divine touch."

Jason looked doubtful. "Things happen to even the best of men."

"He was so young and such a dear man," Mother said, shaking her head. "How will we manage without him?"

"I'm sure the other men can handle the

horses," Jason said. "You've got a great team of people working for you."

"At least for the time being," Lizzy muttered.

Within a matter of minutes, Mr. Fleming and Mr. Spiby arrived in an old wagon. They had somehow arranged for a coffin. The wooden box no doubt contained the body of August Reichert. It seemed a foreboding sign, and Lizzy knew many in their troupe were superstitious.

Mr. Fleming was first off the wagon. He came to Mother and Lizzy and took off his hat. "Mrs. Brookstone, I'm so very sorry. We've brought your man back. My people did what they could to clean him up, but there wasn't much that could be done to make him presentable. I'm afraid the horses were brutal."

Mother shook her head. "How did it happen?"

The stocky man lowered his head. "We have a couple of green broke colts, and I'm afraid they got the better of Mr. Reichert."

"I've never seen a horse that August couldn't handle," Lizzy declared. The thought of August being killed by horses didn't make sense to her.

"He *was* talented," Mr. Spiby said, joining them. "I even offered to hire him away from you, although I'm ashamed to admit it now." He smiled, then gave his mustache a stroke with his index finger. "But accidents happen, and no one is immune to danger."

"That's true enough," Mother said, clinging to Lizzy's arm. "I appreciate that you've cared for him so completely." She turned to Lizzy. "Make sure Uncle Oliver pays them for the coffin and . . . anything else."

"Nonsense, Mrs. Brookstone," Fleming declared, raising his gaze. "It was my privilege to do this for the young man. I won't accept money, given the accident happened on my farm."

"Well, thank you so much for your kindness." Mother's words caught in her throat. "He . . . he was such a good man."

"Come on, Mother," Lizzy encouraged. "Let's go inside. We can't do anything more here."

"She's right," Jefferson Spiby said with a great deal of smugness. "You ladies shouldn't have to bother with such matters. You just leave it to us, and we'll see to everything."

Lizzy wanted to say something—anything—to show Spiby what she thought of his attitude, but she held her tongue. Leading Mother inside, a dozen questions raced through her head. Green broke colts were dangerous, that much was certain, but so too was it certain that August Reichert knew this and would have handled them carefully. Besides, what was he even doing with them? He was there to manage the new mares and the Brookstone stock. Why would he have been handling Fleming's colts?

"I can't believe the sorrows we've had on this tour," Mother said, sinking into the sofa.

Lizzy leaned against the wall. Her mother looked so fragile. There were lines in her face that hadn't been there this time last year. "Mother, I don't mean to add to our troubles, but there is something I need to tell you. I hope you'll understand."

"What is it?"

Lizzy knelt beside her. "You can't say anything to anyone about this."

"Is there anything I can do for you ladies?" Jason Adler asked from the doorway.

"No." Lizzy huffed and went to the door, blocking his entry. "We just need some privacy for the moment."

Jason looked apologetic and shook his head. "I'm sorry to have disturbed you."

Lizzy immediately regretted her harsh tone. "No, I'm sorry for snapping at you. It's just a lot to take in."

"I completely understand. If you have no need of my services, I'll go see how I might help your uncle. I believe we're arranging for the funeral home to manage the body and ship it back to his family."

Lizzy thought of Mary Reichert. She was August's sister and until this year had been Brookstone's sharpshooter. She would be devastated. She had quit the show in order to marry her childhood sweetheart, and their wedding was in less than a month. August's death would probably postpone it.

"Thank you for your help, Jason, but we'll be just fine." Lizzy waited until he'd gone, then closed the door.

"What's going on?" Mother asked, eyeing Lizzy suspiciously. "What do you need to tell me?"

Lizzy sat down beside her mother. "Ella Fleming has run away from home. She's hiding in the spare room." She pointed toward the tiny cabin.

"But why?"

"You saw Jefferson Spiby and the way he acted. He's even worse when no one is around. Ella is being forced to marry him—some sort of financial arrangement. She's begged her father to release her from the agreement, but he won't hear of it. He plans for them to marry at Christmas, because Ella turns twenty-one in January and can speak for herself then."

"But interfering in a family matter isn't wise, Lizzy."

Lizzy looked at her mother's weary expression. Perhaps she should have waited to tell her. No doubt the news about August was only serving to bring back the pain of losing Father.

"I know it's not, Mother, but I felt strongly about this. I believe God would have us help her. She was in danger—I can't say exactly what might happen to her if she marries Mr. Spiby, but she's terrified. She planned to do whatever she had to in order to avoid marrying him."

"But where will she go now?"

"Eventually she wants to go to Chicago to live with her sister. But for now, I thought she could stay with us. We'll keep her hidden until it's time to take everyone back to Montana. I figure she can stay in our car, and I can bring her what she needs. We'll just have to keep everyone else out of here. At least until after our show in Kansas City."

Mother glanced at the door to the small sleeping room. "Very well. Since you feel so strongly about this, I'll trust that it is the right thing to do. I've never known you to act in a rash manner. Should I go speak with her?"

Lizzy smiled. "That might reassure her."

Mother nodded and got to her feet. "Does she know about August's death or her father being here?"

"I don't think so. She knew something was going on at the farm, which was why she set out by herself to get here. I'm sure she'll be very sorry to hear about August."

✧═ EIGHT ═✧

The St. Louis showground was packed to overflowing, as most of the Brookstone performances were. Lizzy led Longfellow through his paces as usual. The crowd was completely aghast at her maneuvers aback a galloping horse. Several women in the audience fainted, which wasn't unusual. It happened with such regularity during their tour that Uncle Oliver always gave a warning before the show. It only served to further excite the audience.

It seemed silly that anyone should faint doing nothing more than watching. It was different if they were asked to participate in the show. She remembered once last year when Mary Reichert was still shooting for the show. She had asked for a volunteer, and a giant, burly fellow quickly accepted. He came to the arena floor, and Mary made him stand with an apple on his head. She aimed her rifle and put a bullet straight through the center of the apple. The crowds went wild, and the man passed out. Lizzy could understand why the stress of that situation might cause someone to faint, although the man quickly recovered and promptly asked Mary to marry him. She declined.

Lizzy brought Longfellow to the far end of the arena, quickly adjusted some straps on her saddle, then put him back into a full gallop. With Longfellow in motion, Lizzy did a rump spin and then a backward somersault onto the horse's neck. In one fluid motion, she whirled back around, slipped her feet into the straps, and stood. The audience went wild with applause and cheers.

Longfellow reached the end of the run, and Lizzy slid back into the saddle and maneuvered the horse back to their starting position. She slipped her right foot through the drag loop and gave the gelding a couple of pats on the neck. There was just one more trick, perhaps the deadliest. She urged Longfellow forward while giving the crowd a wave. Without pausing, she appeared to fall backward and slip over the left side of the horse, bringing her left leg straight up in the air as she did. With her right foot securely anchored in the strap's hold, she raised her hands over her head to complete what some called a Cossack drag. It all happened at once, so the audience couldn't be sure that it was intended. There were gasps, more fainting no doubt, and then silence as Lizzy rode upside down, her head hanging right beside Longfellow's front legs.

With her long hair nearly dragging the dirt, Lizzy gave a wave, and the crowd jumped to their feet in raucous applause. She smiled to herself, caught the horn, and pulled back up onto Longfellow's neck. She freed her foot and did a simple saddle spin, ending in a shoulder stand.

"Isn't she amazing?" Uncle Oliver called out from behind his megaphone. "Let's hear it for Elizabeth Brookstone and her valiant steed, Longfellow!" The crowds went wild.

Lizzy righted herself and led Longfellow out of sight of the audience. She positioned her feet for the final stand and flag wave. There had been a couple of minor accidents with earlier performances, but overall the show had gone very well. She breathed a sigh of relief, remembering this was the next to last show of the season.

The other performers were taking their final bows. The sharpshooting girls raced around the arena on horseback, shooting their guns in the air to further stir up the audience. As if they needed any encouragement.

Next, the girls who did Roman riding circled the arena side by side. Each of the three girls had two horses apiece and stood astride their team. After they made one full circle, they joined two teams together, and the two performers stood astride the center horses, one in front of the other. For their final move, the third team joined them, and while one of the girls managed all six horses, the other two climbed onto either side of her. With a firm grip on a harness that ran under her jacket, each of the side performers stuck out their free arm and leg to create a star pattern. The cheers were deafening.

Brookstone's other trick riders preceded Lizzy into the arena, doing vaults and twists as they circled and waved to the audience. Finally, Lizzy rode out standing and waving the American flag. The small band provided by the arena broke into "The Star-Spangled Banner," and everyone began to sing. It was the perfect end to the evening.

Lizzy rode her horse from the arena. Zeb took the flag and offered them both praise while Lizzy slid off the buckskin.

"Longfellow, you were amazing! Such a good boy." She gave him a hug. "You're all done for the year."

Rupert took the reins from her. "They loved you tonight."

Lizzy laughed. "Indeed they did." She gave the horse one more rub of affection. "I'll use Thoreau for the last show," she told Rupert. "Longfellow's earned his rest, although I know he won't see it that way." She made her way over to the costume seamstress. "I managed to tear my blouse, Agnes." She pointed out the ripped shoulder seam.

"No problem, dearie. I'll have the girls pick it up for washing and then mend it on our way to Kansas City. It'll be ready for the performance."

"Thanks, you're the best."

Lizzy made the rounds, thanking everyone for helping with the show. It was something her father used to do, and Lizzy didn't even think about what she was doing until she was halfway through the performers and crew. It felt right to offer the others praise. Her father had always been so encouraging, and Lizzy knew it had always blessed everyone.

"You did a mighty fine job out there, Miss Lizzy," Thomas, the oldest of their wranglers, told her.

"Couldn't have done it without you, Thomas. No one person is responsible for our success, as you well know. You boys are the very heart of this show."

The old man beamed with pride, just as Lizzy knew he would.

"Praising someone for a job well done costs you nothing, Lizzy, but the returns are tremendous. People need to know they're appreciated," Father had often told her.

Oh, Father, why did you have to leave us?

Exhausted, Lizzy made her way to the bright red Brookstone train. The men would soon be loading the animals for the next leg of the trip. Mother and Agnes would see to all the other girls, and with them busy, Lizzy wanted to check on Ella before going to Uncle Oliver's office to count the ticket sales.

"Did everything go all right?" Ella asked when Lizzy opened her door.

"It went very well, although I ripped my blouse."

"I'm a good seamstress," Ella said, perking up. "I could repair it for you."

"Thanks, but I've already mentioned it to Agnes. She handles all the costumes." Lizzy began unbuttoning her blouse. "I have to change my clothes and then do some bookwork. I'll be back soon. Mother or I will bring you something to eat, however. We always have a snack—well, it's more like a full meal—after the show."

Ella smiled. "I really appreciate all the help you and your mother have given me. I don't know what I would have done without you. I've been afraid, but you've both been so kind. I'm especially blessed by the way your mother prays with me."

Lizzy felt a momentary sense of guilt for not having done the same. Sometimes prayer just skipped her mind.

"I'm just glad we've seen nothing of your father or fiancé. It seems he hasn't considered you might have come with us. Especially given he saw the train off."

"I'm praying it won't even occur to him. Hopefully, he'll just think I've gone to Margaret's. She knows nothing about what I've done, so even if he goes to her, she can't tell him a thing."

Lizzy considered the future for a moment. "After the last show in Kansas City, we'll dismiss the performers and head home for a brief break. I think you should stay with us. Our ranch house is large, and you could stay there until you think it's safe to go to your sister."

"When is the performance?" Ella asked.

"Three days from today." Lizzy shook her head, and her brow furrowed. "Why do you ask?"

"Well, I'm anxious to be far from my home. There's still a chance it might occur to Father that I snuck off with the show. I won't rest until we're a long way away."

"Your concerns are exactly why I want you to come home with us."

"I'd hate to put your family in any more danger than I already have. I doubt Father would ever go all that way to find me, but he might hire someone." Ella bit her lower lip.

Lizzy patted her arm. "It'll be all right. If he comes to Montana, he'll be on Brookstone land—with Brookstone people. They won't allow him to take you."

Ella looked up, her face betraying her anxiety. "What if he comes to Kansas City?"

"Well, we've managed to keep you hidden from everyone else. No one in the show knows about you except Rupert and Mother. I would trust either of them with my life and know they'll keep your secret. We'll be just fine. You'll see."

Lizzy left her and quickly changed out of her performance clothes and into a simple wool skirt of brown plaid paired with an old white blouse. She combed through her long brown hair and knotted it into a bun at the back of her neck before making her way to the entertaining car, where Agnes's sewing room was at one end and Uncle Oliver's office at the other.

Mother was adding finishing touches to a buffet of treats. She smiled when Lizzy came into the car. "You did such an amazing job tonight. I tell you, I still feel my heart skip a beat when you go into that death drag."

Lizzy crossed the room and kissed her mother's cheek before snagging a couple of cookies from the platter she held. "I learned from the best."

Mother nodded. "Your father made it look so easy. Oh, how I miss him." Her eyes dampened.

"I do too. Especially after the shows." Lizzy pushed aside her grief, just as she had every day since her father's passing. "I'm going into the office to work on the receipts."

"Jason's already hard at it. Uncle Oliver sent him to get started."

Lizzy frowned. "He's letting him handle the money?"

"I suppose he feels Jason is trustworthy. He does have an interest in seeing the show succeed," Mother reminded her.

Sighing, Lizzy grabbed another cookie, then headed for the office. If Jason was going to be in charge of the books, then she wasn't going to stick around.

"Mother told me you were managing the show receipts," Lizzy said, looking in on Jason, who sat at her uncle's desk.

"Come in," Jason said, jumping to his feet. "Two sets of eyes are always better than one. I've started counting the coins. I've put them in stacks of ten dollars. Why don't you double-check them?"

Lizzy took a seat despite wanting to turn around and leave. "Very well." She started on the stack of nickels nearest her.

"I saw part of your act tonight. I was completely terrified for you." He grinned.

She couldn't help laughing. "You needn't be. It's all controlled chaos. My father was good at using each act for maximum effect."

"Yes, he was, but it's your talent and skill that makes the show. That's why we can't lose you. You have to see that they come to watch you."

"They come for the show in full. I'm only one small part of it. I don't make an entire show by myself."

"Perhaps not, but you are the star performer. I've been reading through the mail. Most of the letters are for you." He lowered his voice. "There were at least three dozen proposals of marriage in the last batch alone."

"Yes, I get that a lot," Lizzy admitted. She finished with the first stack of nickels and moved to the second. "I have no idea why a man would propose to a total stranger. He has no idea who I am or what I want out of life."

"It would be nice to know those things," Jason said. He looked up from the table and met Lizzy's gaze. He smiled.

She had to admit he was a handsome man.

His eyes were the color of sapphires and seemed to sparkle as much as the gems themselves. His face reminded her of chiseled marble sculptures she'd seen in museums.

"I would very much like to know who you are and what you want out of life," he said.

Lizzy grew uncomfortable. "I can't give you those answers, Mr. Adler."

"Can't or won't?" His smile never wavered.

"I can't." She shifted and pushed the stack of nickels aside. "I don't know the answer myself."

"It might be fun to explore the answers together," he said, jotting down some figures.

"Why are you here?" She hadn't meant to be so blunt, but now that the question was out, she was glad she'd asked it.

Jason leaned back in his chair. "Because I'm thirty years old and need to decide what I want for my future."

Lizzy shook her head. "And you plan to do that working around a wild west show?"

He shrugged and picked up a stack of dollar bills. "I had to start somewhere, and this pleased my father. I've been working for him in some capacity since I graduated from university. He's allowed me to take part in any and all of his businesses to see if something strikes my fancy." He put the money back down and leaned forward. "Now that I've answered your question, perhaps you'd be so good as to answer one of mine."

"I'll try." Lizzy had no idea what he might ask but figured it was only fair.

"What do you want for your future?"

"We already discussed that. I don't have an answer for you."

"But you have decided you don't want to stay with the show, so you know at least that much." He cocked his head slightly. "If you left the show, what would you do?"

"Pick up with my life at the ranch."

"And you like living on a ranch in the middle of nowhere?"

Lizzy laughed. "Who says it's in the middle of nowhere?"

"Your father, for one. Your uncle, for another."

"You knew my father?"

"Of course. He and your uncle visited my parents at their New York house several times. When they did, I was also there." He chuckled. "Your father said the ranch was perfectly situated in the middle of absolutely nothing."

Lizzy smiled. "I remember him saying that."

"Well, given where you grew up, I would think you'd enjoy experiencing some different places before you settle down to one."

"I've experienced a great many places with

the show. We've been to every corner of the United States and most every state in between."

"But that's just in passing. You should try staying for a time—living in one of the larger cities like London or even New York before deciding to lock yourself away on a ranch in Montana."

"I suppose it could be interesting to try, but my heart is in Montana."

"Is there someone special there who holds it?"

Lizzy grew uncomfortable at his prying. She got to her feet. "I'm afraid, Mr. Adler, that I'm more worn out than I realized. If you'll excuse me."

She left without waiting for his response. He was so refined and well-mannered that she knew he'd never demand she stay.

Many of the performers were starting to arrive for the evening meal, and Lizzy had no desire for company. Mother caught her attention and held up a plate. Whether it was for Lizzy or Ella, she didn't know, but Lizzy nodded and walked over to her.

"I thought you might want to take this with you back to our car," Mother said without hesitation. "I knew you would be much too tired to stay here."

"Thank you. I'm exhausted."

"Oh, I nearly forgot. One of the local

businesses brought us root beers. I put several in the icebox in our car."

The idea of a cold root beer appealed very much to Lizzy. "Thank you. I think that will make my night complete." She took the plate and headed to the door that connected to the family car.

Jason stood just outside Uncle Oliver's office, watching her. "I'm sorry if I offended you."

Lizzy shook her head and tightened her grip on the plate. "You didn't. I'm just overly tired. Good night."

He opened the door for her, but Lizzy didn't acknowledge the gesture. She had to get away from him. She had to get away from all of them and sort through her thoughts.

She passed between the cars, carefully managing the door to the family's private refuge. Once she was inside, Lizzy let out her breath. She hadn't even realized she'd been holding it.

Why had Jason's questions bothered her so much? The last thing she wanted was to explain herself or the past to him. Perhaps that was all it was. Then again, perhaps it was because his questions were the very ones for which she had no answers. Hearing them aloud only served to drive home the point that she was completely uncertain about her future.

She glanced down at the plate in her

hands and thought of Ella. She went to her tiny cabin and knocked before opening the door a crack. "I have some food."

"Come in."

Lizzy left the door open to allow the light inside. Ella had to be careful about even lighting a candle for fear someone might see the light glowing under her door or from her shaded window.

"We always have food after a performance, and it's always delicious. Mother has been cooking up a storm. There's a tidy little kitchen at one end of the female performers' sleeping car, and she makes some of the most amazing things." Lizzy sat on the edge of the berth and set the plate on the mattress between them. "There are all sorts of cookies and melted cheese toasts and little biscuits baked with sausages in them. Oh, and there's cold root beer in our icebox."

"Yes, she told me about that and brought me one." Ella held up the bottle. "I was supposed to tell you in case she forgot."

"I'm going to have one myself," Lizzy said, then sighed.

"What's wrong?"

"Nothing, really." Lizzy shook her head and smiled. "Mr. Adler was just asking me a lot of questions. Personal questions that I had no answers for."

"I think he likes you very much," Ella said. "Perhaps he wants to court you."

"I'm afraid you may be right."

"Is that such a terrible thing? He seems nice and he's very pleasant to look at. Falling in love might be a nice change of pace."

"True enough, but I'm not interested in falling in love."

"Have you ever been in love?"

The question was asked innocently enough, but it felt as if Ella had punched Lizzy in the stomach. Why did everyone want to know the intimate details of her heart? Why did people she barely knew feel they were entitled to ask such questions, much less receive an answer?

The look on Lizzy's face must have revealed her feelings. "Please forgive me," Ella began. "I didn't mean to pry. It's far too personal a question, and I meant no disrespect."

"I know that, but . . ." She let the words trail off as she considered Ella. There was no harm in confiding in her. Ella had, after all, confided in Lizzy. So much so that her very freedom depended on being able to trust Lizzy. Lizzy picked up a piece of toast. "I have been in love. Unfortunately, I think I still am."

"Why unfortunately?" Ella clapped a hand over her mouth.

"It's all right. I don't mind talking to you.

There's this guy back home. He's the ranch foreman, so you'll meet him."

Ella lowered her hand. "And you love him?"

Lizzy toyed with the toast. "I do. I've loved him since I was just a girl and he was a young cowboy working for my grandfather. He's always just seen me as his little sister, though."

"Well, what have you done to help him see you otherwise?"

Lizzy considered that for a moment. "I told him I loved him, but he married another woman."

"Oh, how awful. Especially since you still love him."

Lizzy shook her head. "When he married, I was determined to never think of him again. I did pretty well at it. I focused on the show and avoided him as best I could. I thought I was getting over him, but then his wife died a couple years back, and I realized I'd never stopped loving him. I know that sounds awful. I would never have done anything to interfere in his marriage. And I swear I didn't covet him while he was wed to another."

"I believe you," Ella replied.

"I begged God to take away my feelings for him."

"But now he's single again, and you still love him." Ella looked at Lizzy. "What are you going to do about it?"

Lizzy got to her feet and shrugged. "Nothing. I have no desire to marry him or anyone else."

———————◆•◆•◆———————

Ella tossed and turned in her sleep. She dreamed she was running through a thick forest of trees. It was dark and cold, and she couldn't see. She didn't know what she was running to or from, but the sense of dread and overwhelming danger hung all around her.

She thought she saw a light just ahead and rushed from the trees toward what would hopefully be sanctuary. An old but pleasant-looking house appeared, and from it spilled welcoming light. Her legs felt like lead as she moved toward the refuge. But when she was within a few feet of safety, Jefferson appeared from the shadows.

"Where are you going, my dear?"

Ella stopped and backed away. Her legs were just as heavy in retreat as they had been in her desperation to reach the house. "Stay away from me."

Jefferson laughed. "You're my wife, Ella. You should know better than to try to leave me."

"You killed the wrangler," she accused.

He laughed all the more. "He saw too much."

"What? What did he see?" She glanced over her shoulder and found herself on the edge of a cliff. Below was nothing but blackness. In front of her, Jefferson continued his advance.

"It doesn't matter what he saw. He's dead. You don't want to join him, do you?"

She looked once again at the abyss. "If it means you can never touch me or hurt me, then yes."

She turned and stepped off the edge, feeling herself falling and falling. Jefferson's laughter echoed all around her.

Ella awoke with a start. Darkness engulfed the room, and for a moment she couldn't remember where she was. Then she felt the rocking movement. The Brookstone train car. She was running away, with no idea where she would end up.

She really had stepped into the abyss.

᚛═ NINE ═᚜

Things in Kansas City were bad from the beginning. The show was well attended, as it was a side entertainment to the large American Royal show given each year. Lizzy generally enjoyed getting to be around other horse and cattle people, but the large show tent had issues with their electricity, and several surges caused bulbs to explode, startling the horses and performers. Not only that, but tent performances always required altering the tricks in order to avoid ropes and stakes and tent poles.

Uncle Oliver was also not himself. Lizzy smelled alcohol on his breath prior to the first act. Mother had mentioned that he'd taken to drinking quite heavily at night before bed. After Father's death, he'd moved out of the family car and set up with the other men in the men's sleeping car. Mother felt certain he had not done it out of propriety, as he stated, but rather so that he might be able to drink without being observed by the womenfolk. They both figured it was his way of dealing with his grief over the loss of his brother. However, he'd never before compromised the show in such a way.

Thankfully, the performances were awe-inspiring enough that the people didn't seem to mind the emcee slurring his words and weaving a bit on his feet. But Lizzy was gravely concerned, and that took her focus away from the act, and she banged her face against her saddle during one of her maneuvers. She had momentarily seen stars and wasn't sure that it hadn't loosened a molar or two. But the show had to go on, and she pushed through the pain and finished her trick.

Thoreau seemed annoyed by the problems and people. It was as if he sensed Lizzy's anxiety, and their timing and responses to each other were just not what they needed to be. To add further frustration to an already trying evening, a fall thunderstorm came up during the last quarter of the show, setting everyone's nerves on edge. Thankfully it was short-lived and not much more than a brief rainstorm with sporadic lightning and thunder. Nevertheless, it made the horses fretful.

"I'm so glad this night is done. And glad this tour is done," Lizzy said, handing Thoreau over to Thomas. She stroked Throeau's head. He was still pretty worked up. "You did a good job, boy. It wasn't your fault that I was out of step." She hugged the animal's neck, then turned to Thomas. "You might need to walk him extra, Thomas."

"I'll take the long way down to the big pen. It's quieter there, and he'll calm down soon enough."

"Looks like it rained enough to make things muddy," Lizzy commented as she caught sight of some water puddles.

"Yeah, we had a gulley washer there for a few minutes, but the storm moved through so fast, there wasn't much time to worry about it. Even though it's muddy, I think the animals have been glad for the freedom of the pen rather than bein' cooped up in their stalls."

"I'm sure you're right." She gave Thoreau one more stroke. "I'll be down later with their treats."

It had been arranged to corral the animals in a large pen well away from the performance tent. The entire area was surrounded by stockyards, and a multitude of pens and people were everywhere. The stockyards in Kansas City moved millions of animals through the city each year, rivaled only by those in Chicago. This, coupled with the annual horse show, gave everything the feel of a three-ringed circus.

Even so, Lizzy knew it would do their animals good to have a couple of days out of the confines of their train stalls. Especially given that they would be headed to Montana afterward, and the trip would take several days, possibly longer if there were problems on the line. And it seemed there always were problems of some sort. Lizzy never liked to have the horses on the train for long hours, and when they planned the tour, they always scheduled stops along the way, like Fleming Farm, where they could take a day or two for the horses to rest and feed off natural pasture. Of course, here they would only have hay, but at least they wouldn't be tightly confined.

"Miss Brookstone, I must say you performed exceptionally well," Jason Adler said, coming to join her.

Lizzy rubbed her cheek. It was starting to throb. "Thank you."

"Your uncle has called a meeting in the entertainment car. I told him I would make sure you knew about it and escort you there."

A sigh escaped her lips. "Very well. I need some ice first."

"Ice? Are you hurt?" He stood back, and his gaze traveled the full length of her body before coming back to rest on her face.

Lizzy placed a hand over her right cheek. "I hit it kind of hard, and it's starting to hurt. I'm sure it's just bruised, but I want some ice to stave off swelling."

"I'll arrange for it after I get you to the car. Are you certain you aren't injured anywhere else?"

"No, I'm fine. I just—"

"Miss Brookstone!" A man with a derby hat and three-piece suit jumped in front of Lizzy. "I've never seen anyone like you. I was completely overwhelmed by your beauty and your talent. I've written you a poem." He waved a piece of paper. "I'm dying of love for you!"

Lizzy forgot about all about her cheek as the man fell to one knee, hat in hand. "Please say you'll marry me. I can provide well for you. I have my own home—it's small, but we'll sell it and buy another. We'll buy however big a house you want."

"My good man, you will contain your enthusiasm and refrain from further embarrassment to yourself. Miss Brookstone is soon to be my wife," Jason declared.

The man looked as though Jason had punched him in the face. For a moment, Lizzy wasn't even sure he could breathe. He looked at her with a forlorn expression, then slowly got to his feet and put on his hat.

"I should have known someone as wonderful as you would already be promised." He looked at Jason. "In another time, I might have called you out for a duel." He shook his head and let his gaze travel back to Lizzy. "I shall live the rest of my life in the memory of this night and what might have been." He folded the piece of paper and put it in his pocket. Lizzy wondered if he might use it on another ladylove at another time.

"Be off with you, sir, or I shall dispose of you myself." Jason possessively took hold of Lizzy's arm, and the man gave her one last look, then turned and walked away. By the slump of his shoulders, she felt certain he was completely heartbroken. She knew very well how that felt.

Jason led her toward their train cars. The stockyards in Kansas City had multiple rail lines, and their cars had been positioned at one of the farthest points. Lizzy was actually glad for Jason's help navigating the yards, especially given there were a great many people—mostly men—milling about.

"Thank you for your help back there," she murmured. She didn't want to encourage him and intended to set him straight. "Although I can't advocate lying."

Jason chuckled. "Lying? Whatever are you talking about?"

"You know very well what I'm talking about. That part about me soon being your wife." Lizzy stopped, forcing Jason to stop as well. "I'm not trying to play games with you, Mr. Adler. I'm not looking to marry anyone, and I don't want you to have the wrong impression of me. I just lost my father, and my mother needs me at this time. I want to return to the ranch and heal from my loss. I hope you understand."

She saw a look of regret cross his face. He nodded. "I apologize, Miss Brookstone. I was thoughtless and hope you will forgive me."

Lizzy nodded. "Of course."

"Friends?" he asked.

"Yes. I'm happy to be your friend." She paused a moment, then looked up at him. "I wonder if you might be willing to do me a service?"

"Anything." He smiled. "And I assure you there will be no strings attached to my response."

"Thank you. It's just that I'm worried about my uncle. He's drinking—that much was obvious tonight. Mother says it's due to his grief over Father. Since you're working with him closely and in the same car with him at night, I wonder if you might try to keep him . . . from the alcohol."

"It won't be easy. Despite his own rules about the workers drinking, your uncle seems to have no trouble sneaking alcohol aboard. I will do whatever I can."

"I know it's not my business to tell my uncle what he can and can't do, but I'm very worried about him. Mother is too. When he was younger, Uncle Oliver drank a lot. My father encouraged him to give it up, and he did. But now, with Father's . . . well, it's apparently more than he can stand."

"I'll try to be available to him, but I can hardly dictate rules to him."

"Thank you. I appreciate it and know it will add comfort to his days."

"Your father's loss is no doubt deeply felt

by all of you." His words were sincere and his expression sympathetic. "I know it has to be very hard for you."

Lizzy stiffened. "I get by. I have fond memories of my time with him, and I must go on for the sake of my mother. She needs me, and I want to be a comfort to her."

"Ah, Lizzy Brookstone, but who will be a comfort to you?"

"I appreciate what everyone has done this year," Uncle Oliver began. "We've had a very successful season, even with the misfortune that has seemed to follow us."

He had sobered up a bit, and Lizzy breathed a sigh of relief. She glanced across the room to where her mother sat. Their eyes met, and Mother gave her a smile. It would seem all was well.

"Here you are," Jason whispered, handing Lizzy a cloth-wrapped piece of ice.

She pressed it against her cheek. "Thank you."

All around the car, the performers and crew sat listening to Uncle Oliver's closing address. Every year her father and uncle spoke to their people and praised them for a job well done. They would tell them about the plans for next year and when they should arrive at the Brookstone ranch in Montana to begin training for the show.

"All of you have performed exceptionally well, and I am proud of each and every one of you. I know my brother would be too." He paused a moment, and Lizzy could see his eyes well with tears. "Mark will be missed, but he was determined that the show go on, and so next year we hope to be even bigger and better. Mr. Adler has plans to make the Brookstone Wild West Extravaganza the most sought-after show in America—possibly the world."

Everyone clapped and looked toward Jason. He gave a little nod of acknowledgment before Uncle Oliver continued.

"The performers and crew will head home tomorrow. Mrs. Brookstone will accompany those of you going back to our ranch." He looked Mother's way and smiled. "After I'm done talkin', you'll each get your salary and travel money for your train tickets. Those heading back to Montana for the winter will depart at seven o'clock tomorrow evening. Feel free to enjoy a night on the town, but make sure you're back here by five tomorrow for loading the horses."

Uncle Oliver grew serious. "As you know, we lost not only my brother, but also our head wrangler, August Reichert. Lizzy and I will go to Topeka tomorrow to visit with the Reicherts before we head back home."

This was the first Lizzy had heard about this, but she was glad Uncle Oliver had thought of it. She had wondered if they should do something more than just ship the body back. She knew her mother had sent a lengthy telegram, but even that seemed too inadequate. August and his family were good friends of the Brookstones, and it seemed only right that they offer their condolences in person, even if it was too late to attend the funeral.

"Mr. Adler will also accompany us, and he has decided he will winter with us in Montana so that he might understand every aspect of the show. He will be with us next year as well."

Several of the female performers beamed at Jason. They were clearly pleased to know he'd be around. Lizzy wondered if her earlier comments would make Jason change his mind. She sincerely hoped he hadn't planned to come to Montana for the winter in order to woo her.

"Now, I'm going to let you all get to the party you're anticipating. Mrs. Brookstone has prepared us a feast." He motioned over his shoulder at the table. It was covered to capacity with plates of food. "I've been informed that some of the local vendors have provided us with barbecue, and I, for one, am looking forward to that."

Most of crew cheered at this comment, then grew silent, as they knew their boss would pray a blessing on the bounty.

"Let's offer thanks." Uncle Oliver bowed his head. "Father, we thank You again for Your protection this evening and Your loving-kindness to us throughout the year. We don't understand why we lost Mark and August, but we trust that You know best. We thank You now for this food and pray a blessing on each person as they travel to their various locations. Abide with us as we abide in You. In Jesus' name, amen."

There was no hesitation or waiting to be invited to chow down. Everyone was on their feet and heading to the buffet before Uncle Oliver could even wave them forward. Lizzy wasn't surprised when the youngest of their female performers, Debbie and Jessie, came to Jason and encouraged him to sit at their table. Lizzy let him be dragged away without protest, although he threw her a look that suggested he wished she would intercede. She was tired and had no desire to pretend to be jealous or otherwise desirous of his company. Instead, she put together a large plate of food and quietly slipped back to the family car.

"Ella?"

"I'm here," the young woman said, peeking out the door of her room. She had dark half-moons under her eyes. No doubt she wasn't sleeping well. Lizzy wasn't sure she would sleep well either, if the roles were reversed.

"We've had a development in our plans that will affect you, and I think we have to explain to my uncle and Mr. Adler about your situation," Lizzy said, placing the food on the tiny bedroom dresser.

"What's happened?" Ella's eyes were wide with fear.

"I don't think it'll be a problem, so please don't be upset." Lizzy sat on the edge of the berth and motioned for Ella to do the same. "Uncle Oliver feels we should pay our condolences to the Reichert family, and I think it's the right thing to do. They live on a farm outside of Topeka, so tomorrow we'll take the train there."

"What about me?"

"Well, I've been thinking about that. Mother is heading back to the ranch, but I think it's best if you stay with me. In fact, it might work to our advantage. If your father decides to check out whether you've gone to Montana with the show, he won't find you there. I'll speak to Mother later tonight, but for now, I figure Uncle Oliver will have the family car unhooked from the rest of the cars and then send everyone and everything else to Montana. It'll be easiest that way, and we can follow from Topeka in this car. Jason Adler plans to come with us, so it'll be the four of us, and since there are four small bedrooms in this car, it will suit us well enough. Although I could bunk with you if it made you feel safer."

"Are you sure they won't mind? I don't want to be any trouble. I could make my way from here to Chicago . . . if you helped me. I'll just need you to sell some jewelry for me."

"No. Not unless that's truly what you want to do. I'm sure by now your father has contacted your sister. I truly think you'll be safer to stay with us."

"Then, if your mother and uncle approve, I will do that. I just don't want to put anyone out on my account."

Lizzy shook her head. "It's not a problem. In fact, I want to talk to you about your own riding experience and whether you might like to join the show."

"What? Join as a performer?" Ella sounded completely stunned.

Laughing, Lizzy got to her feet. "You've ridden all of your life and have your own mount. You told me you and your brother used to play around with Roman riding and various tricks. I think you could probably learn to do what I do with relative ease. If you're of a mind to."

"It would be wonderful to learn your tricks, Lizzy. I so admire what you do." Ella's voice was animated. "It would be so exciting to perform for an audience. Do you really think your uncle would let me be part of the show?"

"I think he might, especially once he realizes that I intend for you to replace me."

Ella found sleep impossible that night. She tossed and turned, and with every creak or outside noise, she sat straight up, clutching her covers to her chin. Would it always be like this? Would she spend the rest of her life in fear of being hunted down and forced back to Kentucky? Was there never to be any peace?

She thought of the fact that her father was party to a murder, and it soured her stomach. Did her mother know? Did Robert? Jefferson had said it wasn't his first killing. Ella shuddered. How could he speak so casually about life and death? She'd known his reputation for cruelty but realized that she'd assumed it was exaggerated.

"Lord, I'm so afraid."

She forced herself to lie back down, but she couldn't bring herself to close her eyes. Maybe she should have made her presence known when Father and Jefferson came to the train with August Reichert's coffin. The sheriff had been there, and all the Brookstone people. Maybe she should have declared the truth she'd overheard.

Shaking her head, Ella knew it would have made no difference. No one would have believed her.

"God, I feel so alone. Please help me," she whispered. "Please give my spirit rest and show me what to do."

She hated knowing that August had been murdered and wished she'd never overheard her father and Jefferson. She didn't want to know the truth. Knowing it meant keeping it hidden from Lizzy, who had done nothing but offer friendship and help from the start. Would Lizzy still want to help if she knew what Ella was keeping from her?

⊹⹀ TEN ⹀⊹

Well, I must say this is a big surprise," Mr. Brookstone said, looking at Ella. "I didn't say anything to Lizzy before, but your father sent a man to us in St. Louis. He was asking if you had somehow managed to slip away with us. I assured him you hadn't, but now I see otherwise."

"I didn't want you to know for exactly that reason," Lizzy explained. "I didn't want you to have to lie."

"And I certainly didn't want to cause problems for you with my father." Ella looked from Oliver Brookstone to Jason Adler.

"I don't know what the legal implications might be." Lizzy's uncle looked to Jason. "She's nearly of age and certainly isn't a child."

"True." Jason nodded. "I don't see why it should be a problem. You didn't know until now about her being here, so as Lizzy said, you didn't lie."

Ella knew they were risking a great deal, going up against her father and Jefferson. "I never thought about any legal implications. If you think it best, I'll leave."

"No!" Lizzy was adamant. "We all know what will happen if they find you. You'll be forced to marry that abominable man. We must keep Ella safe."

"Of course," Mr. Adler assured them. "I cannot abide the idea of a woman being forced to marry against her will. We'll deal with any trouble when it comes."

Lizzy's uncle nodded as well. "Given the situation, I'm happy to do my part. Although

I suppose it will burn our bridges with your father and his horses."

"We've got two good mares now," Lizzy interjected. "We can breed them to Morgans if we want a pure line. Besides, there are other Morgan farms."

Her uncle nodded. "I'm sure we'll get by just fine." He smiled at Ella. "I appreciate you both being frank with us and telling the truth of the situation."

Ella grimaced. She hadn't told them the half of it. She still hadn't admitted to Lizzy that she knew Jefferson Spiby was responsible for the death of August Reichert. And now she'd have to face August's family on top of everything else. The nightmare, it seemed, had no end in sight.

"Thank you so much," she said. "I promise to do whatever I can to earn my keep. I'm a capable seamstress and happy to lend a hand."

"Agnes will be glad of that," Mr. Brookstone said, nodding. "Although she won't be with us in Montana until late January."

"I plan to teach Ella my tricks," Lizzy interjected. "She's spent her entire life around horses and knows them as well as I do. She's even done Roman riding and a few tricks of her own. I think she'll be the perfect person to replace me."

"Replace you?" Lizzy's uncle looked appalled.

Lizzy pushed back her long, dark hair. "Yes. I think it's about time, don't you?"

Mr. Brookstone shook his head. "I don't think we'd have much of a show without you, Lizzy."

"Then we need to build the show around Ella and the others."

"You have yet to even see her perform," Jason Adler said, sounding skeptical.

Ella didn't want any of them to worry. "Mr. Adler, I understand your concern, but I assure you that I'm capable and willing to learn. You should be able to tell my value or lack thereof by the time the show sets off again in late February."

"She's right." Lizzy pulled back the drapes covering the train window. "Oh, look. I believe we've arrived in Topeka."

Ella could feel that the train was slowing. She wished Lizzy had told her uncle and Mr. Adler everything the night before, but Lizzy had assured her it was better to do it today, just before they reached Topeka.

"Mother gave Ella her mourning veil," Lizzy said. "She thought it might provide some privacy. If Ella wears my black cape and the veil, no one will be able to tell who she is. Then, if you escort her, Uncle Oliver, just as you would have Mother, nothing will appear out of order."

"That makes sense." Oliver Brookstone nodded. "Your mother always was a smart one."

"Then Mr. Adler and I will follow behind," Lizzy finished.

Ella appreciated all the extra effort they were going to. She was touched that they cared so much about her plight. She only wished their support would allow her stomach to stop churning.

She hoped the men could be trusted not to ask her too many questions. The last thing she wanted was to explain what she knew about August's death. She felt selfish in her silence, but her desperation to escape a hopeless future seemed more important than a murderer going to trial. Besides, most of the men in their county, including the law officials, were obliged to her father. Even if she had *seen* Jefferson kill August, her father and Jefferson had enough friends to keep the matter from ever coming to light. The Flemings could do no wrong. Even if it involved murder.

———◆◆◆———

Mary Reichert's pale expression and reddened eyes told Lizzy what she already knew would be true. Her friend was devastated by the loss of her only brother.

"Lizzy, I can hardly believe he's gone," Mary murmured. The man beside her put his arm around her as she continued to speak. "As for the suggestion that he was killed by those colts . . . well, I simply don't believe it."

"Neither do I, Mary," Lizzy admitted, looking across the room at her uncle. "None of us do."

"She's right," Uncle Oliver declared. "But I can't imagine what really did happen, and Fleming's people seemed to know nothing. They said they simply found him that way."

All gazes turned to Ella. The poor young woman shook her head and looked as if she might burst into tears at any moment. "I'm so sorry."

Mary's grandfather, Oscar Reichert, spoke up in his thick German accent. "Our August vas a superior horseman. He vould not be trample."

"He vould not," his wife, Hannah, agreed.

Lizzy had known this family most of her life. Mary's father had once worked with Uncle Oliver and Lizzy's father in Buffalo Bill's Wild West show. Though all three men were superior in their horsemanship, Wilhelm Reichert was also a master marksman. A talent he passed down to his daughter. It was said that the only woman better at shooting than Mary was the famous Annie Oakley.

"Our Vilhelm, he died performing," Mr. Reichert said, shaking his head. "He broke his neck ven he fell from de horse."

Lizzy remembered the accident that had claimed the life of Wilhelm Reichert and injured her father. They had been working together with a team of four horses. Lizzy's father held the reins while straddling the center two. Mary's father would make a flying vault to join him. The trick started out just fine, and Mr. Reichert made it to an upright stance atop the horse. But he'd no sooner gotten there than the animal stumbled and hit the horse beside him. This in turn upset the rest of the team, and the horses began to rear and fight Lizzy's father for control. The men were thrown beneath a tangle of hooves. Mr. Reichert died instantly from a broken neck, while Lizzy's father suffered a back injury bad enough that he had to return to the ranch to recuperate.

"Horses are a danger," Uncle Oliver said, shaking his head. "Anyone who works with them knows as much. Still, I find it hard to believe August would put himself in such a position that he couldn't escape trouble."

Everyone nodded, then fell silent.

"Ve're mighty sorry for your loss too,"

Hannah Reichert finally said. She took her husband's hand and turned to Lizzy. "I'm sure it's hard for your mama to lose her husband, and you, your vater."

"Thank you." Lizzy straightened and gave a nod. "It hasn't been easy for Mother, which is why she didn't feel up to coming with us. I think she knew how sad you would be and didn't want to add to it."

"So much sorrow," Mary said, wiping a tear from her eye with the back of her hand. "At the funeral yesterday, I thought I would cry myself out, but it seems I have a never-ending supply of tears."

The man beside Mary was her fiancé, Owen Douglas. He quickly pulled a handkerchief from his pocket and pressed it into her hand.

"Thank you, Owen." Mary dabbed her eyes. "I won't rest until I know what happened to August and who's to blame."

Lizzy knew Mary and Owen had been promised to each other almost since childhood. Owen's family owned the farm next to the Reicherts', and Mary and Owen had grown up the best of friends. After a time, it was just assumed that the two would marry.

Mary and her brother had grown up on this Kansas farm. When their mother died in 1879 giving birth to her third and final child, Katerina, Wilhelm had taken his grief and hit the road, leaving his three children to be raised by his parents. Eventually his ability with horses and guns put him in good standing with Buffalo Bill Cody, and Wilhelm was hired to perform in the same wild west show that employed Lizzy's father and uncle. The influence of Lizzy's godly parents helped Wilhelm deal with his grief, and eventually he returned to his family for visits. That was when Lizzy and Mary had first met.

Hannah Reichert got to her feet. "Our dinner vill be ready shortly. You must excuse me. Mary—you go bring in de clothes, ja?"

Mary nodded. "I'll get them now."

"I'll help," Owen said, getting to his feet.

Mrs. Reichert nodded and headed for the kitchen.

"Let me help with the food," Lizzy said, standing. Mrs. Reichert stopped and turned.

Ella stood. "Me too."

"No. No. You are our guests," Mrs. Reichert said, gesturing for them to sit back down. "Our Kate vill be here soon, and she can help."

Lizzy crossed the room and took the old woman's arm. "But guests can help too. Please show us what we can do."

Lizzy followed Mrs. Reichert to the kitchen. The old farmhouse was pretty much unchanged from the first time she'd come here. It was nothing elaborate—a square, boxy house with two stories. The living room constituted the first third of the house with the dining area in the center room along with the stairs that led up to the bedrooms. The kitchen was located in the back third, with a curtained-off area that could be used for bathing.

The kitchen table was laden with food. It dawned on Lizzy that most of this must have been for the funeral. She saw various desserts—cakes, cookies, and a few pies. There were a couple of casseroles as well, which Mrs. Reichert uncovered.

"Ve have lots to eat. It's good you came. Ve cannot eat it all ourselves." She went to the oven and opened the door.

The aroma of Mrs. Reichert's German cooking made Lizzy's mouth water. Her own mother was handy in the kitchen, but this was a special treat that Lizzy experienced only occasionally.

"With all this food, you're still cooking something special?"

"*Wir haben Krautspaetzle,*" Mrs. Reichert announced, then shook her head. "I mean, ve are having . . ." She paused with a frown, not certain of her next words. She shrugged. "Krautspaetzle. Sauerkraut, noodles, and sausages. Mr. Reichert asked me to make it. He doesn't like some of de food our neighbors bring."

"It smells heavenly. I can hardly wait, Mrs. Reichert. You make the best German food I've ever had. Ella, you're in for a treat."

Mrs. Reichert smiled. "Danke. You are kind to say so."

"Well, I mean it."

Mrs. Reichert laughed. "If you two vant to help, I vill let you set de table. Lizzy, you know vhere to find de dishes. Dey are der—same as last time." She pointed across the kitchen. "I'll varm up de casseroles."

Lizzy went to the cupboard and began pulling out dinner plates and handing them to Ella. It seemed little ever changed on the Reichert farm.

Mrs. Reichert had just managed to squeeze the two casserole dishes into the oven when the back door opened in a gust of wind and in blew Katerina—Kate, to her family. She was dressed in a dark gray suit with only a hint of white blouse peeking out from beneath the fully buttoned jacket.

"Oma," she declared and went to kiss her grandmother on the cheek. They conversed momentarily in German before Kate noticed Lizzy and Ella. She smiled and switched to English. "There's a storm coming from the west. I'll let Opa know." She went to Lizzy. "I didn't know you'd be here."

"We wanted to give our condolences in person." The two women embraced. Lizzy pulled back to get a better looked at Mary's younger sister. "It's so good to see you again. I feared it might be a long time before we came to the farm again, since Mary quit the show."

Kate smiled. "It's wonderful to see you too." She looked past Lizzy to where Ella stood.

"This is Ella," Lizzy said. "She's a friend." She thought it best to keep explanations to a minimum.

"It's nice to meet you." Kate turned back to Lizzy. "Will you be with us several days?"

"No. Just a few hours. We have to get back home," Lizzy explained. "Mother went on ahead with the crew, but there's a lot of work that needs our attention when we get back, so we can't stay."

Kate frowned. "Well, I suppose we should make the best of our time together." She pulled off her gloves, then reached up to take the pin from her hat. "Let me go change, and I'll help get dinner on the table." She hurried from the kitchen.

Mrs. Reichert went back to tending the food. "Our Kate, she verks at de school in Topeka. She's a good teacher and de children like her."

Lizzy hadn't heard that Kate was actually teaching. The last letter she'd received from Mary had come just before they'd headed out on tour. At that point, Kate had just received her teaching certificate from a college in Emporia.

"And what of Mary?" Lizzy asked. "Is she working too?" She could hardly wait to see Mary in private. She wanted to talk to her about August.

"No. Owen, he doesn't vant his vife to verk." Mrs. Reichert wiped her hands on her apron. "It's not good for de vife to go off to a job vith other people. She needs to keep her home."

Lizzy smiled. "I'm sure Mary will be good at keeping a house. She's a very hard worker."

"Ja, she is."

Kate soon returned, and the trio made short work of getting dinner on the table. By the time they sat to eat, Lizzy could hardly contain her excitement. She found herself chattering to Jason about the meal. "You have to try the red cabbage—it's pickled. Oh, and the ham-wrapped figs. They're so good."

Jason gave her a bemused look. "Uh, I've traveled extensively and enjoyed German food . . . at its source."

Lizzy shook her head. "I doubt any of it was as good as what Mrs. Reichert makes."

Everyone laughed at this.

She dug into the meal, determined to forget her frustrations and concerns about the show and their troubles. She didn't want to think about their financial woes or the loss of her father or Mary's brother. She just wanted to relax and enjoy the company of good friends and good food. But unfortunately, watching Owen's attention to Mary served as a reminder of Wesley.

Was he still at the ranch? There was no reason to believe he wasn't, but one never knew. He might have decided to move on. People did. She felt sad at the thought that he might not be there waiting for her. Missing her as much as she missed him. One thing was certain—she was determined they were going to talk. He was going to tell her once and for all what she had done wrong—why he had put up a wall between them. He owed her that much.

No, he doesn't. He doesn't owe me anything.

She glanced around, almost afraid her thoughts had been heard. No one else seemed the slightest bit concerned. They were too busy eating and talking. Amazingly enough, Jason was praising Mrs. Reichert for her impressive food.

Lizzy forced thoughts of the past and future from her mind and enjoyed the meal.

Rumbles of thunder brought up conversations about the weather, which in turn led to the farm. Crops had been good that year, and Mr. Reichert was ahead of schedule readying the place for winter. It was inevitable that they should discuss Mary and Owen's wedding. Lizzy knew that the celebration was set for November.

"We have to have the farms in order before we get married," Owen said.

Mary frowned and ducked her head. Only Lizzy seemed to notice. It had to be hard to continue planning for a wedding when you had just buried your brother.

"De verk is never done," Mr. Reichert said, shaking his head. "But ve try."

Owen continued to talk about his plans for the farm after he and Mary were wed. His parents had been gone for several years, and it would be nice to have someone in the house again, he said.

"Hopefully before long, there will be children," he added, grinning.

"May you have a dozen!" Uncle Oliver said, raising his glass of apple cider. Thunder rumbled again, this time a little closer.

"I'd be happy with a dozen," Owen declared.

"Lots of help for de farm verk," Mary's grandfather added.

The more they talked about the wedding and the family the young couple might have, the more uncomfortable Mary grew. When the meal finally concluded, Lizzy pulled her friend aside.

"Can we go somewhere and talk?"

"I'd like that very much." Mary looked at her grandmother. "Oma, I'll clean everything up, but first, if you don't mind, Lizzy would like to speak to me privately."

"Of course. You girls go ahead. Kate and I can gather de dishes."

"I'll help too," Ella offered.

"Dat storm is blowin' up fast," Mr. Reichert announced as he stepped away from the window. "This autumn ve been havin' quite a few thunderstorms lately. Some years are like dat." He grabbed his hat. "Ve best put your hired carriage in de barn in case it comes a-hailing."

"I would imagine you're right," Uncle Oliver said, giving Jason a glance.

Jason got to his feet. "Allow me."

Owen rose too and went to retrieve his hat while the old man opened the front door. "Ve'll be right back, ladies," Mr. Reichert called.

Mary took Lizzy's arm. "Come to my room." She all but dragged Lizzy up the stairs.

Once they were safely away from everyone else, Mary made her announcement. "I can't marry him."

"I wondered about that." Lizzy gave her a sympathetic smile. "Is it because of August?"

"In part, but that's only a very small part." Mary plopped onto her bed and patted the thick feather tick. "Sit and I'll explain."

Lizzy sat beside her friend. "Go on."

"I don't know where to begin. I suppose I could start with the problem and work my way back." She frowned. "I'm supposed to marry Owen in just a few weeks, but the closer the wedding gets, the more I realize I can't. Owen and I have always been the best of friends, and I know he cares for me. But, Lizzy, I don't think either of us is in love."

"Maybe you're just confused because of all that's happened."

"No, I've felt this way for, well, years." Mary got up and began to pace the small room. "I'm twenty-four and old enough to know my own mind, and I know that I don't want to be Owen's wife. He's like a brother to me. A brother . . ." Her face contorted, and tears came to her eyes. "Oh, my poor brother. Lizzy, I'm sure there's more to this than a simple accident. Perhaps someone spooked those colts, and August was caught in the middle."

"That could be. It's a puzzle why August was anywhere near the Fleming colts in the first place. He should have been readying our horses to bring them back to the train."

"That's why this doesn't make any sense. August knows it would never be acceptable to handle another man's horses. Something happened, and the people who know about it aren't talking."

"I doubt they ever will. But whatever the cause or reason, our knowing won't bring August back."

"But my brother wasn't foolish, and I can't help but think someone else had a hand in this."

Lizzy thought back to August's confrontation with the Fleming grooms. The Fleming men had been severely punished for the incident. Would they have sought revenge? "August did tell me about an incident our first night there. He wanted some liniment for one of our horses, but the Fleming grooms got rather heavy-handed about the matter and made August leave the stable. The employees were later whipped. Quite severely, as I understand it."

Mary's eyes widened. "That's it, then. Someone wanted revenge."

"And forced August into a dangerous situation with green colts? That doesn't make sense. Who would do such a thing, Mary? The whipped men were hardly in any condition to force August to do anything."

"I don't know," Mary said, shaking her

head slowly. Tears streamed down her cheeks. "But someone does. Someone knows more than they're saying, and I intend to find out who that someone is and learn the truth."

"But how?" Lizzy had already been thinking about the situation herself, and she could think of nothing.

"I'm going back to Montana with you. I'm going to rejoin the show. Your father and uncle told me I'd be welcome back anytime. Maybe one of the men who worked with August has some idea what happened. One of them might have even been responsible." She stopped and shook her head. "Oh, I don't know why I said that. I'm so sorry. Those men are all good men."

"It's all right." It wasn't anything Lizzy hadn't already considered. They'd picked up a couple of new men to help after Father died. They really didn't know all that much about them, and maybe they were no good. Of course, they hadn't acted out of line—at least not that Lizzy knew.

"Maybe Ella Fleming will think of something that might help me, since it happened at her farm." Mary shrugged and wiped her tears with the hem of her gown. "I don't know. But what I do know is that I can't sit here and do nothing. I have to try. I owe August that much."

"But what about Owen?"

Mary drew a deep breath. "I have to tell him the truth. If he's honest with himself, he'll know calling off the wedding is the right thing to do." Thunder sounded, making Mary shiver. She went to her window and looked out. "I hate storms. Why can't we just have some peace and quiet?"

"Owen does care deeply for you, that much is evident."

"He does care, and we'll go on caring about each other. But not as man and wife. I can't do that to him. It wouldn't be right." Mary came back to where Lizzy sat. "Look, I'll go and—"

A knock sounded on the bedroom door.

"Who is it?" Mary called.

"It's Kate."

Mary looked at Lizzy. "Say nothing."

"Don't worry."

Mary smoothed her gingham dress and squared her shoulders. "Come in."

Kate opened the door. She wore a worried expression. "Owen is looking for you."

A sigh escaped Mary's lips. She looked at Lizzy as if for affirmation. Lizzy nodded. Mary turned back to Kate. "Tell him I'll be right there."

Kate looked suspicious of her sister's attitude but turned and left without another word. Lizzy got to her feet as Kate disappeared.

"You're doing the right thing. I'll let Uncle Oliver know you plan to rejoin the show. He'll be thrilled. You truly were a cornerstone of the Extravaganza."

"Well, if I was one, then you were the other three." She smiled and gave Lizzy an unexpected hug. "I'm so happy at the thought of returning. If only August were still alive. Everything would be perfect then. We would all be together again."

Lizzy hesitated. "Actually, I'm thinking of leaving the show."

"Please don't." Mary's eyes searched Lizzy's face. "Please. I need you to help me."

"I don't know. Mother needs me too."

"But she'll have others at the ranch to help her through. Oh, I know how selfish that sounds. Please just stay with the show long enough to help me. We must get justice for August."

Lizzy could see Mary's distress. "I'll help get justice for him. I'll do whatever I have to in order to help you find the truth."

"Thank you, Lizzy. Thank you so much!" Mary hugged her again as the thunder grew louder. "I need to find Owen and tell him. Pray for me."

Lizzy smiled as Mary headed for the door. "Always."

⋄⟩꞊ ELEVEN ꞊⟨⋄

Ella wanted nothing more than to run from the Reichert farm and not look back. She'd hardly been able to bear Mary's tears, nor the sorrowful expressions of her grandparents. Her father and fiancé had ended the life of their beloved August. Ella knew this for a fact yet couldn't bring herself to be honest about it.

What good would it do? She went to the window and stared out, seeing nothing. *How could my speaking up change anything? August would still be dead, and there would still be little chance of Jefferson ever standing trial for what he's done.*

"You seem reflective," Jason Adler said, coming to stand beside her. "Are you regretting your decision? Perhaps missing your family?"

Ella stiffened and crossed her arms. "I do miss my mother, but I'm more worried than anything else."

"Worried?"

She met his sympathetic gaze. "My father and fiancé don't easily give up. I never meant to put Lizzy and her family in harm's way, and I certainly never considered that there might be legal issues. I only wanted to get away from the farm and make my way to my sister's house. Lizzy doesn't think that's wise, however."

"Given what you've told us, I don't think it is either." He gave her a smile. "I come from a land where arranged marriages have been the way of things since the beginning of time. I've never agreed with such arrangements—at least not without complete cooperation from both the bride and groom."

Ella found comfort in his words. Perhaps she had a friend in Jason Adler. "Thank you for being willing to keep my secret. I'll turn twenty-one in January, and then legally I'll have the right to speak for myself. Meanwhile, I need to make my way as best I can."

"And after that, you intend to trick ride in the show."

This made Ella smile. "The very thought thrills me to the core. I know you might think that's silly, but I love the idea. I know I'll be able to learn the tricks and do them well."

His smile broadened. "I say, you have the brave nature it will require."

Ella looked back out the window. She didn't know about having a brave nature. She didn't feel there was a courageous bone in her body right now. If there were, she wouldn't be suffering such horrible dreams and fears.

"I suppose only time will tell," she muttered under her breath.

———◆—◆◆—◆———

Mary Reichert had always been one to
speak her mind. She supposed that was what
bothered her so much about Owen. She'd
never tried to hide the truth from him. She
had always answered his questions honestly
and tried to share her heart and dreams for
the future without altering them to spare his
feelings. But in the last year she'd done little
but avoid the truth.

She'd tried so hard to fall in love with him.
She'd spent time planning for their wedding
and talking about their plans for the future,
but she could never find any joy in the idea
of either one.

She saw Owen waiting in the front room
with the others and knew she couldn't avoid
the conversation any longer.

She motioned to the door, and he nodded.
Together they slipped out onto the porch as
a light rain began to fall. In the west the dark
clouds of the thunderstorm grew ever closer,
making the air seem heavy.

"I think it's going to the north, if you're
worried," Owen said.

"I'm not worried about the storm."

He pushed his hand through his black hair.

"Then what, Mary? I know you're grieving, but it's something more. You've been this way for weeks, even before August."

Mary looked at him and nodded. "I've really tried, Owen. You know that. You know that I love you—but not like a wife should."

His shoulders slumped. His expression emptied of emotion. "Yeah. I know."

"There is no other man, save my brother and grandfather, who I've ever loved as much as you. But . . . we're like brother and sister. You have to admit you feel the same way. I've seen it in your eyes after a kiss."

He leaned back against the porch rail and nodded. "I just figured love would grow."

Mary moved closer to him. "But we already have bushels of love between us. It's just not a romantic love. It never has been."

"Maybe it's better that it's not." He looked up, and Mary gazed into his green eyes. "Maybe folks put too much stock in romantic love."

"I don't think so. I think God intends for husbands and wives to feel romantic toward each other." She smiled. "I think if you're honest with yourself, you'll admit you want that kind of love—that passion."

For several long moments, Owen said nothing. Mary watched him turn and look out at the storm. A flash of lightning cut across the sky, and thunder followed within seconds. The wind picked up, and the rain fell a little harder.

"I guess the storm is coming our way after all," he murmured.

She touched his arm. "Owen, we will always be friends, but I don't think that would be true if we married."

"No. I don't suppose it would be. I just hate being alone. Since my folks passed on, that farm feels so empty. I thought a wife and family would make it feel like home again."

She forced him to turn and face her. "It will be home again. You'll find someone— probably sooner rather than later." She smiled. "You're a very handsome man, you know."

He gave her a sad smile. "Just not handsome enough to win you."

"That's hardly fair, Owen. Should I say I'm not pretty enough to win you?"

He shook his head. "No, Mary. You're right, and I know it. I know we're better off this way, but I still can't help feeling like someone has knocked me off the fence. I've been planning to marry you for well over twenty years. Probably longer, if I'm honest with myself."

"Well, now you have to make a different plan. Good thing the crops are in, huh?" Her smile widened, and she breathed a sigh of relief when he smiled as well.

"I suppose you'll rejoin the wild west show."

"Yes. That's what I plan to do. Like I told you, I don't believe August's death was an accident. I think someone intentionally put him at risk from those colts. Lizzy said some Fleming employees have reason to be angry with my brother. Maybe angry enough to want him dead. I intend to find out who they are."

"And how do you suppose to do that?" Lightning flashed again, followed by thunder, but it was evident the heart of the storm was moving to the north just as Owen had predicted.

"Ella will know who they were, but after that, I don't know how to go about proving one of them had a part in it," Mary admitted. "And it's possible that they had nothing to do with it. It could have been someone else who had it in for August."

"And it could have just been an accident."

She shook her head. "I don't believe that. It doesn't add up. August knew better, and he wouldn't have put himself in harm's way. Not unless there was a very good reason, and I need to know that reason."

"And you think someone will just up and tell you the truth?" Owen shook his head. "That's not likely."

"I figure if I'm part of the show again, I'll have a better time of it than on my own. I'm going to Montana with the Brookstones. That way I can ask my questions and listen in on conversations without seeming overly pushy for answers. Then there's that Fleming woman. August was killed at her place. I don't know what her story is, but she might have some idea what happened or who I can ask for more information. If nothing else, she can give me the address for her family, and I can write and ask my questions."

"And you really think they'll just provide them? I mean, if they were the ones to blame for his death, they're hardly going to admit that."

"No, I don't suppose they will." Mary crossed her arms. "But I have to try. August didn't deserve to die that way, and I feel obligated to dig for the truth."

"What if you never learn the truth?"

She met his gaze. "At least I'll have tried."

He nodded, and for several long moments silence hung between them. Finally, Owen rubbed his jaw. "Looks like things are calming down. I think I'll head on home." He touched her shoulder. "We're still friends, right?"

"Always." She put her hand over his. "I will always be your friend, Owen."

"And you'll let your grandparents know?"

She smiled and nodded. "Yes. Will you tell the pastor, since I'll be heading out with Lizzy and the others?"

"Of course. I'm sure word will get around quick enough."

He studied her face for a moment, then without another word headed down the steps and off to the barn. It was still raining, but he didn't even seem to notice.

Mary heard the door open behind her and turned. It was Kate. Her sister frowned as she saw Owen's retreating figure.

"Where's he going?"

"Home."

"But why?" Kate asked. "It's not that late, and it's still raining."

"It'll stop soon enough." Mary hugged her arms to her body. There was a distinct chill to the wet autumn air.

"Did you two have a fight?" Kate asked.

"Not exactly." Mary met Kate's curious gaze. "We just finally admitted that we can't marry each other."

"What?" Kate was clearly shocked.

"I can't marry my brother, and that's all I feel toward Owen. And he was finally honest enough to admit he lacks the same passion for me." Mary let her arms relax. "I love him, but only as a brother and a friend. I just can't marry him with nothing more to offer."

For several minutes they stood in silence. When the barn door opened and Owen led out his saddled horse, Mary gave a wave.

"Hopefully I'll see you next year!" she called.

"I'll be here," he said, then climbed into the saddle and headed for the road.

"What do you mean, you'll see him next year?" Kate asked.

Mary felt as though a tremendous weight had been lifted from her shoulders. "I'm rejoining the show. I'm leaving with Lizzy and the others tonight."

"What?" Kate took hold of her. "Do Oma and Opa know?"

"No, but I intend to go inside and make my announcement. I figure I might as well break the news about everything at once."

Kate still held fast to Mary's arm. "I can't believe you're just going to leave. We only just lost August, and now you."

"I'm sorry, Kate. I miss the show, and frankly, if it's possible, I want to find out what really happened to August. Surely you can't begrudge me that."

"I don't begrudge you anything." Kate let go and stepped back. "But I'll miss you. It was lonely around here without you."

Mary smiled. "You'll find plenty of things to keep busy with now that you're teaching.

Who knows, you might even end up moving to Topeka."

"No. I don't want to live in the city." Kate bit her lip and looked away for a moment. "Mary?"

"What?" She'd never seen her sister act this way. It was almost as if she were embarrassed.

"I wonder . . . that is, if you wouldn't be offended . . ." She couldn't seem to spit out the words.

"What are you talking about? If I wouldn't be offended by what?" Mary could see the hesitation on her sister's face. "Just ask me."

"I know it may be in bad taste, but I wondered if you mind if I . . . well, I'd like to seek out Owen . . . for myself."

Mary couldn't help a giggle. "Wait. You're sweet on Owen?"

Kate seemed to relax as she nodded. "I've been in love with him for ages. I just didn't let anybody know because I knew he was your intended."

Mary took Kate in her arms and hugged her. "Oh, that would be an absolute answer to prayer, little sister. Owen won't have to go far to look for love, and I won't have to worry about losing you to some city slicker."

"Do you mean it?" Kate asked, pushing away. "You really won't be offended or feel awkward? I mean . . . what if we married?"

"It would be wonderful. Even better if you could persuade him to fall in love immediately and take our wedding date and save him from a lonely winter."

Kate blushed. "That would be pushing things rather quickly, don't you think?"

Mary shrugged. "Maybe. But I have a feeling that once you set out to win his heart, things are going to move fast."

Wes waved to the engineer as the train pulled away, leaving the Brookstone Wild West Extravaganza's red railcars behind. They had a special arrangement with the railroad at Miles City, and the cars would be left on a siding there for the winter so repairs and re-painting could be done.

It was good to see the show's work crew again. Most of the men were longtime ranch workers, and Wes was good friends with them. He noted a couple of strangers, but old Thomas made short work of introductions.

"Wes, this is Judd and Richard. We picked them up shortly after Mr. Brookstone passed away."

Wes extended his hand. "Good to meet you men."

"They worked cleanup and helped with

the equipment. They're good healthy boys and not afraid of hard work," Thomas said.

"Well, we have plenty of that." Wes made a quick assessment of the men. They were both muscular but definitely looked like city boys. "You two have any ranch experience?"

"No, sir," they replied in unison.

"I grew up in the city, but I love horses," Judd offered.

"Me too," Richard admitted. "I did help at a dairy once. I know how to milk and shovel manure."

Wes smiled. "We've got a couple of milk cows and plenty of manure. For the most part it's horses and cattle that you'll be working with. I can use good hands, but the hours are long and dark in the winter. Cold too. Either of you afraid of that?"

The two men exchanged a look, then returned their attention to Wes. "No, sir." Again, the reply came in unison.

"Good. The cows will start calving in January, and we'll need everyone out there helping. Thomas and the others can show you around once we get back to the ranch. Right now we've got to get these cars unloaded, and that means everything. We strip 'em and leave only what's nailed down."

"I'll put them to work, boss," Thomas said.

Wesley smiled. He was at least half

Thomas's age, but the old man had called him "boss" since the day Wes took the foreman position after old Gus died.

Before the men left to start unloading, Phillip joined them.

"Oh, I have someone I want you fellas to meet as well." Wes put his hand on Phillip's shoulder. "This is my brother, Phillip. He joined us a little while back."

Thomas shook the younger man's hand while the other two sized up Phillip. They weren't that far apart in age.

"Good to meet you, son," Thomas declared. "I've been friends with your brother for a long time now. He's a good man."

Wes felt as if Thomas were questioning whether Phillip was the same. Phillip only grinned and nodded, then looked at the younger two men.

"Wes!" Mrs. Brookstone called from the family car. She waved, then allowed one of the men to help her down the steps.

His heart caught in his throat at the sight of her black gown. She was in mourning. He'd thought many times about how different the winter would be without Mark to advise him. He'd even thought about how the ranch would be run, but he hadn't thought much about Mark's widow. She looked so small and pale in black.

Wes frowned. "Phillip, you go on with Thomas, and he'll put you to work. I need to tend to some things before we can head back to the ranch."

"Sure thing, Wes."

Wesley watched the group of men head off as he walked to where Rebecca Brookstone stood waiting. Thomas was already talking to the trio of younger men about their duties. Phillip seemed to be listening intently—or at least Wesley hoped he was. He'd been good at tending to his assigned duties these last days, but he never volunteered to do anything more than what was expected. Wes had talked to him about how people—especially those in charge—liked to see their employees go the extra mile.

"It never hurts to offer to do more than what's expected of you," Wesley had told him. "There's always extra work to do."

"Then why not just ask someone to do it?" Phillip had replied. It made no sense to him that people would just wait around to see if he might volunteer to do more. He was there to work a job and do what he was told. After that, he expected his time to be his own.

Phillip was twelve years Wesley's junior and was born after his mother had lost half a dozen other babies. Because of that, he was spoiled and doted on. He'd always been such a sweet-natured child, however, that even Wesley didn't mind the extra attention Phillip had received.

"You seem mighty deep in thought, Wesley."

He noted Mrs. Brookstone's kind but tired expression. "My thoughts are all over the place these days." He smiled. "Did you see that man who headed off with Thomas and the others?"

"I did. New hand?"

"My brother."

"Phillip, right?" she asked, her gaze following his toward the group of men.

"Yes." He was surprised she remembered. Wes continued watching his brother. "I haven't heard from him in years, and one day he just showed up. I hired him on, but I don't know if it'll work out or not."

"We have to give folks a chance to prove themselves. Sometimes they just don't realize what they're good at."

He turned to face her and smiled. "Mr. Brookstone was always telling me that. I can't tell you how sorry I am that he's gone." There, the subject was now open.

She lowered her gaze and nodded. "I miss him so much. Life won't be the same without him."

"I've thought a lot about that and about the ranch. I hope you know I'll do whatever I can to make sure things run smoothly."

She smiled, but it was a sad sort of effort. "I know you will."

"Wes," a voice called out. He turned to find Rupert limping toward him.

Rebecca Brookstone put her hand on Wes's arm. "You've got a lot to do. Come have supper with me tomorrow night. I want to talk to you about several things." She headed off before Wes could respond.

Rupert tipped his hat at Mrs. Brookstone as she passed him. "Well, you look fit as a fiddle," Rupert said to Wes, grinning. He thrust out a stack of papers. "Oliver wanted me to give you these. It's the inventory list of what we started out with."

Wes looked through the papers quickly. This was the routine when the show returned. "I'll have a better look tonight. Just make sure the boys put everything in the arena first so we can check it off the list."

"Will do, boss."

Wes folded the papers and tucked them inside his shirt. "How's the leg?"

"Hurts like the devil, but it's better up here where it's dry. That damp air just sets it to aching somethin' fierce."

"I don't doubt it."

Rupert frowned. "You heard about August, I suppose."

"Yes. Oliver sent me a telegram." It was hard to believe the young man was gone. August had been so good to work with, and Wesley had hoped he might be able to teach Phillip a thing or two.

"We could hardly believe it. Still not sure what to think. It wasn't likely for a horse to get the better of that boy." Rupert shook his head.

"No, you're right there. August was never lax when it came to horses. Even if he was handling the gentlest of animals, he knew better than to let his guard down." Wes didn't want to ask about Lizzy, but he couldn't help wondering. "Uh . . . how'd the rest of the troupe take the news?"

Rupert shrugged. "It was hard on everyone. Especially since we'd already lost Mark."

"I'm sure his loss was terribly hard on everyone, especially Mrs. Brookstone and Lizzy."

"She's a tough one, though," Rupert said, nodding and scratching his bearded chin. "Ain't never seen a woman quite like her."

Wes smiled. "Mrs. Brookstone has always been the epitome of strength."

"That she has, but I was talking about our Lizzy. She stepped into her father's shoes as best as anyone could. She never even stopped to shed a tear or miss a show. She's quite a gal."

Wesley could imagine Lizzy shouldering her father's responsibilities. She would want to protect her mother. She was always trying to bear burdens that didn't belong to her.

"I've got a feeling a lot of things will be changin' now that Mark's gone. I know Mrs. Brookstone plans to quit the show."

Wes wasn't surprised by this. "I'm sure it's been really hard on her. We expected her to return home with the coffin."

"She wanted to, but Mark made her promise she'd stay on. Made Lizzy promise too. They both put up a fuss, but he said it had to be that way. The show must go on."

Wesley nodded. "No doubt he was worried about the financial aspects." He wondered what Lizzy's plans were for the future. If her mother was quitting, perhaps she would as well.

"Oh," Rupert said, "Oliver said to tell you that, barring any railroad complication, they would only be a day or so behind us, but he didn't want you to wait here on his account. He said to leave horses and tack, and they'll ride out to the ranch."

"I'll arrange for his horse and Lizzy's."

"You'll need two more. One for Mr. Adler, and then Miss Fleming's horse." He looked around and pointed. "That black that's being unloaded over yonder belongs to Miss Ella Fleming."

Wes was puzzled by this new development. "I don't understand. Who is she?"

"She's a pretty little thing. Ran away from Fleming Farm. Nobody knew about it but me and Mrs. Brookstone and Lizzy, although I 'spect by now Oliver and Mr. Adler know about it well enough. So it'd be best not to say anything about the young lady. I think they're afeared her pa might try to hunt her down and force her back."

Wes couldn't imagine what kind of intrigue Lizzy had gotten herself caught up in this time. "All right, I'll make sure the black stays. And what of this Mr. Adler? You aren't talking about that old man the brothers saved on that hunting trip years ago, are you?"

Rupert shook his head and chuckled. "Nope. It's his son. He's supposed to learn all about the wild west show and help with the management."

This took Wesley completely by surprise. "Why in the world would Oliver need his help?"

"I don't rightly know," Rupert said with a shrug. "I heard some talk that Oliver sold Mr. Adler some shares in the show, but I couldn't say for sure that's true. It was just rumors and such."

"Well, I suppose that would make sense. If Adler has an interest in the show, he might feel the need to send his son to familiarize himself with the workings." Wes didn't like the sound of that. It was never good news when folks outside of a family business came in and had their say.

Rupert didn't look overly fond of the idea either. "Like I said, there's gonna be changes."

TWELVE

The next night, Wes sat across from Rebecca Brookstone at supper. He wondered what she wanted to discuss with him.

After he offered grace, she picked up the platter of chicken. "I'm glad you're here to run things, Wes. Mark put great store in you, and I know Oliver feels the same." She gave Wes several pieces of fried chicken, then put a single piece on her own plate. Next, she dished out mashed potatoes. She nodded to the gravy. "Help yourself. Biscuits will be out of the oven in a few minutes." She added potatoes to her plate, then put the bowl on the table. "What's the talk about winter?"

Wes poured gravy on his potatoes. "Some of the old-timers think there's going to be a lot of snow and cold temperatures. I laid in extra hay, since we didn't have but two cuttings."

"That was a good idea. Better get extra grain too."

"I'll see to it." He sampled the chicken. Mrs. Brookstone could fry up chicken better than anyone.

"Oh, the biscuits!" She hurried for the kitchen before Wes could even rise to help her.

When she returned, she held a plate of biscuits. They were golden brown, and the aroma was enough to make Wes groan. "Don't tell Cookie, but I've missed your cooking, Mrs. Brookstone. More than just about anything or anyone."

She smiled and took a seat. "That's kind of you to say."

"It's true. Not even my mother made chicken this good."

She put her napkin on her lap. "I'm so glad you're enjoying it." She paused for a moment, then continued. "Wes, one of the reasons I wanted to talk to you in private is Lizzy. I'd like us to be frank."

Wes swallowed the lump in his throat and reached for a biscuit. "What would you like me to say?"

"It's more about what *I'd* like to say. I'm worried about her."

He relaxed a bit. "Worried about her? But why?"

"Wesley, she's not herself. She's trying so hard to be strong for me . . . for everyone."

"I can imagine that. She's always thought she had to be the nail that holds things together," he said, reaching for the butter. "You can't convince her she's not."

"No." Mrs. Brookstone smiled and chose a biscuit of her own. "You're right on that point. But . . . this is different. Lizzy has convinced herself that she needs no one. I saw it start when she lost her grandparents. Then, when you married Clarissa, she hardened herself a little more. When Mark had his heart attack, she was as worried as I was, and when the doctor told us he didn't hold out much hope for her father to recover . . . well, she was the stalwart support I needed. Even Oliver fell to pieces. Which brings me to another issue. He's drinking." She shook her head, and there were tears in her eyes. "We can discuss that later. I don't know what's going to become of either of them. Oliver is dealing with his grief by numbing the pain and Lizzy by ignoring it."

"What do you mean?"

"I mean she's carrying it all inside. She's always leaned toward that tendency, but this is worse." She eased back in her chair and fixed him with a motherly gaze. "She hasn't been herself since her father died. She never wants to talk about what happened, and she's never shed a single tear."

"Never?" Wes was surprised by this. He'd seen Lizzy cry bucketfuls when her grandparents died. She'd even broken down over the death of animals. She'd always been tender-hearted.

"Not once, not even when she's been alone at night and everyone has gone to bed." The older woman wore all her sorrow on her face. "I'm really worried about her, and I think you may be the only one who can help her."

"Me?" Wes shook his head. "Why would you suppose that?"

She wiped her eyes and picked up her fork. "Because she cares deeply about you and what you think. She always has. You know that." She stared down at her plate, moving her food around.

Wes felt that same strange tightness in his chest that came when he dwelled too long on Lizzy Brookstone. "But that was when she was a child."

Mrs. Brookstone raised her head and met his gaze. "She's not a child anymore."

"I'm so glad we're on our way home." Lizzy sat on the train with Mary and Ella. Her uncle and Jason were sitting in the seats on the opposite side of the aisle. "I've missed the ranch more than I can say."

Mary giggled. "The ranch or the ranch foreman?"

Lizzy pretended to brush lint from her traveling jacket. "I'm not even going to acknowledge that question. It doesn't deserve an answer."

This only made Mary laugh all the more. She elbowed Ella Fleming. "Wesley DeShazer is the ranch foreman, and he's very handsome. If Lizzy isn't willing to own up to her feelings for him, then you might want to consider vying for his attention. He's one of the kindest souls you'll ever meet. Not at all rough and smelly like a lot of cattlemen."

"Stop it," Lizzy said, rolling her eyes. She caught sight of Jason Adler glancing her way and knew she needed to change the subject. "Ella knows some trick riding and Roman riding from when she was young. I think she's going to be easy to train to take my place."

Jason leaned across the aisle. "Don't forget, you've given us your word that you'll stay on for at least one more year."

"Lizzy's a woman of her word," Mary said in her defense, but she couldn't keep from smiling. "But Wes might have something to say about it . . . especially if you keep trying to woo Lizzy."

"Who is this Wes?" Jason asked.

"He's the ranch foreman," Uncle Oliver replied. "Lizzy's been sweet on him for years."

"Honestly, you are all impossible." Lizzy got to her feet. "Wesley is our foreman, and he married another, and she died," she said, looking at Jason. "When I was young I looked up to him. Now I'm just looking forward to some dinner." She stormed down the aisle toward the dining car, hoping they'd all leave her to eat in peace.

Of course, that wasn't to be.

"Please forgive me," Jason said, joining her in the dining car.

"Table for two?" the waiter asked.

Lizzy shook her head. "For one."

"For two," Jason insisted.

The man nodded and showed them to a table for two at the far end of the car. There was a partition between their table and the rest of the car due to the serving station. The waiter pulled out a chair for Lizzy and waited. She thought for a moment about leaving, but her stomach rumbled loudly enough that she was certain everyone could hear. Finally, she took her seat, and Jason did likewise.

They placed their orders and received

192

water and bread before Jason leaned forward. "I'm sorry, but I had to speak to you. We are friends, after all."

Lizzy did not want to talk about Wes. Especially not to a man who so clearly wanted to court her himself.

"What is it you wish to discuss?" She placed her napkin on her lap. "If it's related to the show, you should probably speak with my uncle, and if it's personal—I don't want to talk about it." She picked up a piece of bread and began to butter it.

"It's your uncle."

Lizzy put aside her walls as a frown formed on her lips. "What is it?"

"He's somehow managed to procure several cases of liquor in Missouri. I didn't know about it, however, until last night. Apparently he arranged for them to be shipped back with the others but didn't tell them about it. He's having it held for him in Miles City."

Her stomach seemed to sour, and the bread she'd so eagerly buttered was no longer appealing. She put it on her plate and met Jason's gaze. "I don't want to know how you learned this. Just tell me what we should do about it."

"I have no idea. That's why I felt we should discuss it."

He looked as unhappy as Lizzy felt. She

glanced out the window, but darkness obscured the world beyond the train. "When my uncle was much younger, he drank something fierce. My father got him to stop drinking, and we all hoped it would never again be a problem." She looked at Jason, whose expression was sympathetic.

"I'm sure the loss of your father—his brother—was deeply felt. Perhaps he will mourn for a time and then realize the futility of what he's doing."

"I'd like to think that's possible, but I don't know." Lizzy thought of her mother and how worried she was. "We've had a rule against alcohol on the ranch for years. It was my father's way of helping Uncle Oliver. Father always said that while he wasn't opposed to the occasional drink, we couldn't have the stuff around because it would be too great a temptation for my uncle. He used the entire matter as a Bible study, showing me Scripture about not being a stumbling block for others."

"Surely we needn't avoid having a drink or whatever pleasure we enjoy because someone else might have a problem with it," Jason replied. "Must their problem become ours?"

She nodded. "We must care for one another and do what we can to encourage each other, especially those who are weak." Lizzy picked up her bread and took a bite. Focusing on spiritual matters always calmed her, even when she was defending her beliefs.

"But God does not expect us to forgo our own happiness because of someone else's weakness, right? I can hardly keep someone from doing what they choose to do. If your uncle wants to drink, that is his business. He is an adult and, I presume, a partial, if not full owner of the ranch, so whether or not alcohol is allowed is surely up to him."

"In Matthew eighteen, Jesus tells us, 'Woe unto the world because of offences! for it must needs be that offences come; but woe to that man by whom the offence cometh!'" Lizzy straightened. "In other words, there are going to be obstacles that lead us astray, because that's just part of the world, but it's going to be really bad for the person who causes them. Worse still for someone who knows another person has a problem and puts temptation in their path anyway. I won't be that person if I can help it. I won't turn a blind eye when Uncle Oliver gives in to his sorrow and drinks. It's easy to walk away and pretend that it's not my business, but it is. If we are to care for one another as the Bible tells us to do—if we are to love one another as Jesus loves us—then how can we turn away from a person in need?"

Jason seemed to consider her words as the waiter returned with their meals. Lizzy's senses filled with the tantalizing aroma of roast beef and vegetables. Her appetite was quickly returning.

"Am I to understand that you believe it necessary to avoid anything that might cause someone else to stumble?" Jason asked. "How can you possibly know what causes them to stumble? And how can you account for the entire world?"

She smiled. "I don't believe I have to account for the entire world. I'm not acquainted with the entire world. However, if someone comes into my life and I know that they have a problem, shouldn't I take care not to make that problem bigger? Even if I were not a Christian woman, would that not be the kind thing to do?"

"Shouldn't a person account for themselves? Am I not responsible for my own sin?"

"Of course, you are," Lizzy said. "But you are also responsible for loving others as Christ loved us."

"But He went to the cross and died a brutal death."

"Exactly so." Lizzy smiled and picked up her knife and fork. "So doing what I can to help Uncle Oliver not be stumbled by alcohol seems a terribly small effort, but a very useful one."

Jason was quiet for several minutes while

he pondered her words, and Lizzy ate. She couldn't help but smile at the memory of her father's teaching. She had never expected to use it in such a manner, but she was always glad to share the Bible with those in need.

Still, there remained the issue of the alcohol. If Uncle Oliver had shipped it to the ranch, his drinking would only continue. Perhaps she'd talk to Wesley about it. He might have an idea of what they could do.

"I wonder if I might change the subject," Jason ventured.

Lizzy looked up and nodded. "What would you like to talk about?"

"Next year's show."

She considered reminding him that such matters should be discussed with Uncle Oliver, but then took pity on him. "What about it?"

"I think it would be a great success for us to take the show to Europe. London in particular. The queen is very fond of wild west shows and has inspired much of England to share her pleasure in them."

"You told me we needed to economize. How would this fit in with your plans to put old men out of jobs and cut back on other unnecessary expenses?" She knew her tone was sarcastic, but she was still put off by his attitude that the older men working for the show were excess baggage.

"It would be tremendously well received, and we could charge more per ticket there. We could also perform in one spot for several weeks rather than move about. The biggest expense would be transporting everyone to England, but after that, we could make up for it by pasturing your animals on my father's estate."

"I see. But what about the rest of us? We wouldn't have our train cars to live in."

He smiled. "No, you would be comfortably cared for in our home. The workers would stay in servants' quarters, but your family and the performers would be treated lavishly. So again, the cost would be minimal."

"To us perhaps, but what about your father?"

"He would benefit from the popularity of the show and the sales. After all, he is a stockholder." Jason cut into his fish. "I can show you better on paper, but the money is there, I assure you, and I believe it would be a tremendous boon to the show."

Lizzy could see that he was serious. Maybe he was right. Maybe the trip abroad would breathe new life into the show, and maybe under his managing techniques they would see the Brookstone Wild West Extravaganza once again solvent.

"I think it would be very interesting to see Europe." She smiled at the thought of castles and beautiful lands that she'd only ever read about.

"You would have a remarkable time. I would show you around all the sights. London is full of beauty and history. I know you would enjoy it."

"I'm sure I would." Lizzy put down her fork. "But why tell me all of this? I have little say in the future of the show. Uncle Oliver is now completely in charge, and though my mother has inherited my father's part, she doesn't want to be bothered with any of the decision-making."

"Understandable. However, I believe your uncle is concerned about many things right now, and that, added to his drinking, might make it difficult for him to see the potential of my idea." Jason dabbed a napkin to his lips, then smiled. "I think he would listen to you. If you told him how much you wanted to do this, I think he would quickly agree."

Lizzy wondered if the idea of something bold and adventurous would help Uncle Oliver put aside his grief and look toward the joy of life again.

"I'll pray about it," she finally said, meeting Jason's blue-eyed gaze. "You might do the same."

"I wonder if you might answer some questions I have."

Ella looked at Mary and felt a rush of guilt. "Questions about what?" She already knew that Mary wanted answers about her brother's death, but Ella needed to stall for time and figure out what she would say. If only Lizzy's uncle hadn't gone off in search of Lizzy and Jason, she might have had an excuse to avoid the matter altogether.

"Lizzy said one of your father's employees had an encounter with August. It resulted in your father having the man whipped."

Ella breathed a sigh of relief. At least this was something she didn't have to lie about. "I don't know anything about that. Father never allowed me to know anything about his running of the farm. He said it wasn't appropriate."

The look of disappointment on Mary's face only added to Ella's feelings of guilt. "I had hoped . . . prayed that you might know something. Do you have any knowledge of the people your father had working there? I mean, you went riding a lot, from what Lizzy said. Surely you knew the groomsmen."

"Father had one particular groom . . . an elderly man . . . who generally helped me. My fiancé was the jealous sort and he didn't want any of the younger men near me. So

no, I don't think I know the man you're talking about. I heard nothing of anyone being
whipped . . . but then again . . . I wouldn't
have."

Mary sighed and sank back in the seat
and said nothing more. Ella watched her a
few moments, then closed her eyes as if she
were trying to sleep. She couldn't bear knowing how much pain Mary was in and not do
something to help ease her concerns.

*But I can't tell her the truth. I just can't. If I
did, they'd all expect me to stand as witness—to
confront my father and Jefferson.*

She sighed and drew her lower lip between her teeth. How could she ever hope to
make this right—to give Mary and the others
the truth?

⋄≈ THIRTEEN ≈⋄

Lizzy was happy when the train arrived in
Miles City. Everything was just as she'd
left it the previous February, but without
snow. Stepping from the train, she smiled.
The dry air and pleasantly cool temperature
brought to mind hours of riding Longfellow

across their property, drinking in the scenery and solitude. She would have a lengthy trip from town back to the ranch, but the others would be with her, and there would no doubt be plenty of chatter. It seemed the last few months had been nothing but noise and conflict. How she longed for hours of silence just to think and pray.

"I see our home away from home is waiting for us," Mary said, pointing to the Brookstone railcars.

Lizzy nodded. "They need to be repainted. I hope we can get the same artist as last time. He did such a good job."

"What a quaint little town," Ella said, coming to stand beside Lizzy and Mary.

"It's a wonderful town." Lizzy motioned down the street. "Let's do a little shopping while the menfolk get our things squared away." She went to Uncle Oliver and Jason. "The girls and I are going to pick up a few personal things at the store. Do you gentlemen need anything?"

Uncle Oliver shook his head. "I don't believe so. I arranged for a list in Missouri."

She thought of the liquor and wondered if that was what he was talking about. She forced a smile. "And you?" she asked Jason.

He returned her smile. "Thank you, but I managed to secure my needs in Topeka.

Although given the wild look of this country, I wonder if I thought of everything."

Lizzy laughed. "It is rather wild, but we have our comforts too. Don't worry, if you've forgotten something . . . you'll learn to live without it." She turned back to her uncle. "Where shall we meet you?"

"Just come over to the livery. Jason and I will have the horses ready," Uncle Oliver replied. "Don't buy too much stuff, though. I didn't tell the boys to leave us a wagon, just horses."

Lizzy gave her uncle a kiss on the cheek. "We won't buy out the store, I promise."

She felt relieved that Uncle Oliver was acting more like his old self. She didn't bother to bring up the question of how he planned to get several crates of alcohol home. Knowing there wasn't a wagon to use made her hope the alcohol wouldn't make it to the ranch at all.

She walked back to where the girls were waiting for her. "So did Mr. Adler propose?" Mary asked with a grin.

Lizzy looked at her, unable to hide her horror. "Why would you even think that?"

"Well, it's obvious he's sweet on you."

"Look, like I said before, I have no interest in him or anyone else. If you're looking for a beau, then by all means pursue him."

Mary laughed. "I just got rid of one fiancé. I certainly am not looking for another."

"Then don't try to sell me one." Lizzy hiked her skirt and picked up her pace to avoid a grain wagon.

Ella and Mary quickly followed, and they made their way into the nearest mercantile.

Lizzy stopped to speak to Ella. "I know your circumstances prevented you from bringing much and that you are limited on funds. I don't want you to worry about that. We have an account here, so just get whatever you need, and we can worry about settling it later. The sewing room at the ranch is full of fabric and notions, so we can make you some skirts and blouses or dresses, if you prefer."

"I don't want to add to what you've already paid out," Ella said, glancing around at the shelves of goods. "And I do have my jewelry. We can sell it. I don't want to be a bother."

"You'll be a bother if you need something at the ranch and don't have it." Lizzy turned Ella and gave her a little push. "Now, hurry. Uncle Oliver doesn't want us to dally."

A young man stepped up to the register from the back room. "Miss Lizzy! I heard you were back."

She smiled. "How are you doing, Barney? How's the folks?"

"They're all doing well. Me too. I graduated high school this year."

Lizzy could see the pride in his face. "That's wonderful, Barney. Do you have plans for furthering your education?"

He shook his head. "No. Mr. Levine said I could work my way up here. Said I'd be making twenty-five dollars a month in a couple of years if I worked hard."

"That's impressive, to be sure. Next thing you know, you'll be married."

The young man blushed. "I already know who I plan to marry, Miss Lizzy. I haven't asked her yet, but I plan to next summer."

Lizzy smiled. "I'm sure she'll say yes." She glanced over her shoulder. "I'd better get my shopping done, or the others will be ready to go and I'll still be dawdling." She hurried toward the selection of books before Barney could even reply.

Lizzy thumbed through the books, but nothing interested her. She turned her attention to items she thought would be useful, including a couple pairs of boy's long underwear. She hadn't told Ella how cold the winter could get and knew these would be welcome when they were training outside. Lizzy grabbed wool stockings and socks as well.

When she put her things down on the

counter, she spied a notice about collie puppies for sale.

"You want one, Miss Lizzy?" Barney
asked.

Lizzy thought about Christmas. Her
mother had always said that once she settled
back on the ranch, she'd like to have a dog.
A collie would be perfect.

"I do. I think I'd like to get one for my
mother for Christmas. Who has them?"

He chuckled. "My folks do. I can have
them save one for you. The pups are already
weaned and ready to go, but I think for you,
Miss Lizzy, we can hang on to one until
Christmas. You want a male or a female?"

"A male. Mother won't want to worry
about a female having puppies and such."

Barney nodded. "I know just the one I'll
save for you. Firstborn and a real sturdy fellow. He'll be a good watchdog. I can even start
training him to obey. You know, heel and sit
and lie down. Those kinds of things."

"Thank you, that would be useful, I'm
sure. I'm so glad you had the notice here."
Lizzy hadn't given much thought to Christmas yet, but it would be on them before she
knew it. "I suppose I should do some ordering
for Christmas, but Uncle Oliver wants to get
back to the ranch. We all do."

"That's all right. Did you have in mind

what you wanted to purchase?" Barney looked eager to help. "Are you buying for a man or a woman?"

She frowned. They would have Mary and Ella at the ranch as well as Jason Adler. But it was Wesley who concerned her most. "I've got quite a list, Barney."

He pulled a catalog from behind the counter. "Take this home with you. That way you can find whatever you want. Make a list and then get it back to me." He leaned forward. "The catalog too. We only have two."

Lizzy took the Sears, Roebuck catalog. "Thank you. This will definitely help."

"We might even have what you want on hand, but if not—I'll order it."

"How much time do you need if we have to order something?"

He straightened and puffed out his chest. "We're completely modern here, Miss Lizzy. If I send in the order, we can almost always have it in a month or so."

That didn't give her a lot of time, even if Miles City was completely modern. "Very well. I'll try to get back in a few days."

Ella came to the counter, her arms full of various items. She looked apologetic. "I promise I'll find a way to pay you back. You could always put me to work around the house. I could even sew for your mother."

Lizzy laughed and started helping her put the things on the counter. "Don't fret about it."

"This one of your new performers?" Barney asked.

Lizzy hadn't considered hiding Ella from the townsfolk. It had never even occurred to her, but now that the question had come up, she was hard-pressed to know what to do. The chances of Ella's father following her all the way to Montana were slim, but she couldn't help wishing she'd been more careful.

"Yes." Lizzy kept stacking the purchases on the counter. "Would you go ahead and tally these? Like I said, Uncle Oliver is in a hurry. Just put them on our account. Miss Reichert's things too." Mary had joined them at the counter with her meager selection.

"You don't have to do that," Mary said. "I brought the money I saved up. I can pay."

Lizzy was really starting to worry about Ella being seen and didn't want to argue about it. "We'll figure it out later."

Once things were settled at the store, Lizzy hurried the girls to the livery, where Uncle Oliver was just about to send Jason Adler to find them.

"If we don't get a move on, we'll lose the light. Sunset comes sooner this time of year." Her uncle handed her a saddlebag.

Lizzy stuffed some of Ella's packages

inside it, while Ella and Mary split the rest of the load in saddlebags Mary had brought with her. That accomplished, Lizzy went to Longfellow and secured the bags. Without any help, she got into the saddle and looked down on her uncle with a grin.

"So what are you waiting for?"

———◆—×◆×—◆———

Wes sat on the fence, watching his brother work with a new horse. Sandy Anderson, Wes's assistant foreman, had recently returned with a string of horses. They'd been purchased for using with the cattle, and most weren't saddle broke. Sandy was more than a little glad to learn that Wes had hired Phillip for such tasks so that the job didn't fall to him.

Phillip was delighted by the challenge. He lived to ride—wild or tame, it was all the same to him. He had been working long hours with each of the new horses, and though he'd taken minor injuries, nothing seemed to slow him down. He loved horses, that much was certain, and he was good with them. Wes had seen a lot of horsemen in his years, and most weren't concerned with breaking a horse in a gentle manner. They slapped the halter and bridle on, threw a saddle on their backs, and then rode them wild until they gave up the fight. Phillip, on the other hand, liked to take his time. He was that way about most everything. Wes had decided not to hurry him along. They had a little time, and he wanted to see what Phillip could accomplish.

"Looks like your brother is nearly as good at this as you," Thomas said, coming to stand beside Wes.

"I heard that, and I'll have you know," Phillip called out, "I'm better!"

"Yeah, well, just remember, this horse was already broke, just hadn't been ridden much," Wes countered.

"Trouble is, he's a bully," Phillip said, "but I'm a bigger one."

The men continued to watch as the horse, a beautiful bay, settled down and began to surrender to Phillip's demands. It wasn't long before the horse was trotting a circle around the corral.

"You've got him now," Thomas declared.

"There was never any doubt I would." Phillip slowed the animal to a walk. "It gets a little easier each time, that's for sure. This big boy just about broke my back the first time I climbed on him."

Thomas and Wes laughed. Wes jumped down from the fence. "Did you just come out here to watch Phillip, or did you need me for something?" he asked Thomas.

"Mrs. Brookstone sent me to tell you that Oliver and the others should arrive today."

He knew the others would include Lizzy. For a minute that old tightness in his chest returned. He'd pretty much avoided her for the last couple of years, but now Mrs. Brookstone wanted his help in drawing her daughter out, helping Lizzy get past losing her father. It wasn't a job Wes wanted, but it was also not something he felt he could ignore. The Brookstones had been good to him, and he owed them.

The dinner bell rang, and Wes breathed a sigh, but it wasn't one of relief. "I suppose we'd better go get our grub." He started for the bunkhouse. "Cookie doesn't like to have the results of his talents go cold."

"I'm gonna miss Mrs. Brookstone's meals," Thomas said. "Cookie fries and boils the life out of everything."

Phillip slid off the horse. He praised the bay, stroking his neck. "Save me some," he said, leading the horse across the corral.

Thomas and Wes made their way to the bunkhouse dining room. "How's Phillip settlin' in?" Thomas asked.

"Pretty good. There's been a little grumbling and roughhousin'. I think some of the boys thought I'd give Phillip special privileges or not make him toe the line, but I think they're starting to see that isn't the case. I figure if all goes well, everybody will be settled in by Christmas. Those new fellas you took on during the show seem to be working out well. Judd and Richard might be city boys, but they aren't afraid of hard work or getting dirty."

Thomas nodded. "Yeah, I didn't have any trouble with them on the circuit." He opened the door to the bunkhouse. "It's gonna be good to have everybody back home. Did you know Lizzy's thinking of quittin' the show?"

Wes shrugged. "It was bound to happen sooner or later."

"Well, after hittin' her head so hard in Kansas City, I think she got to figuring her time out there was gettin' shorter and shorter before something really bad happens."

"She hit her head?" Wes tried not to sound overly concerned. "How bad was it?"

"It made her see stars, that's all. She bruised a bit, but you know Lizzy. She used some of the theatrical makeup, and no one was the wiser—except for her ma and me. I told her she needs to get married and start a family. That's not nearly as dangerous." Thomas grinned. "Mr. Adler seems mighty interested in her, so who can tell what'll happen."

Wes tried not to feel worried by the old man's statement. He didn't like the idea of a man he didn't know getting close to Lizzy. If he was honest, he didn't like the idea of any man getting too close.

That evening the family gathered in the living room. Wes was touched that Mrs. Brookstone had invited him to join them and have dessert. She had made a wonderful apple cobbler and served it hot with fresh cream. Wes devoured two large servings during the casual conversation. Seeing Lizzy again had stirred something inside that he wasn't sure he understood, especially after he'd all but ignored her the last two years. He'd put a wall between them, but now he felt it crumbling.

"So you see," Oliver said, "Jason is important to our situation. His father has a vested interest in the future of the show, and Jason is here to learn every possible angle. He's also hoping to save us some money."

"Well, we're all going to be busy, for certain," Mrs. Brookstone said, speaking up for the first time. "Since I won't be returning to the show, we need to figure out who's going to take my place and then teach them how to manage my jobs. Also, Agnes mentioned to me that she might not return after next year, so in light of eliminating extra crew and saving money, I suggest we find someone who can come to the ranch in February, and I'll teach them how to handle cooking for the crew and managing the costumes."

"I think that's an excellent idea," Jason said, nodding. "The more crew jobs that can be combined, the better. Thinning the numbers will certainly help in the long run, and I find that people can generally take on additional duties with proper management of their time. The other important thing is teaching another person or two on the crew how to manage your position in case of illness or, as in the case of Mr. Reichert's . . . death. We've found this system very beneficial in our industries."

"You mentioned that should include performers as well," Lizzy said.

Jason nodded. "I think it should . . . don't you?"

Lizzy considered the question for a moment. Wes studied her. She was all grown up, that much was unavoidably true, but there was still something of the innocent tomboy he'd first known in her face.

"I do see the sensibility of it," Lizzy said. "And I think it could be managed. Ella knows some trick riding as well as Roman, and Mary can definitely teach some of the trick riders to shoot. I suppose we might all be able to do each other's jobs to a certain point. Of course, none of us will ever match Mary's marksmanship."

"Perhaps not, but in a crisis, having people familiar with her part of the act might allow us to fill in during her absence. Just as teaching Ella and the others how to do some of your tricks would allow the show to continue should you be unable to go on. I wouldn't expect them to do all of your tricks or come anywhere near to doing them as well, but having performers at the ready to take over in desperate situations could save the show."

"I agree. In the past, if someone was ill or hurt, we simply shortened the act and doubled up in another area, but this makes sense."

"Good," Jason said, beaming at her. "I'll count on you to do your part in helping the others learn what they need to know. Perhaps you could oversee it all, Lizzy. Better still, you and I could work out the details together. It might take long hours, but I'm sure you're up to the challenge." He winked, and she laughed.

Wes didn't like the suggestion of Adler and Lizzy spending all their time together. Adler was far too familiar, and he was always smiling at her. Who knew what he might attempt if they were alone?

Mrs. Brookstone started gathering the empty bowls and spoons. "Well, I'm afraid

Lizzy can't oversee it all, Mr. Adler. She will be needed to help with the ranch and, of course, to work on her own tricks for next season. Perhaps Mary could step in to take the job."

Jason's expression sobered, nearly making Wes laugh out loud. Good for Mrs. B.

"I'd be glad to help," Mary declared. "And once we figure out what we want each person to know, we can put together a training schedule."

"It's sure good to have you back with us, Mary." Oliver handed his bowl to his sister-in-law. "Since Teresa up and got married just before the last show, I was starting to fret about who our main shooter was going to be next year." He looked at Mary. "She was never as good as you, and the audiences were less than impressed. I had so many people asking me where you were and if you were ever returning."

"I'm glad to be back." Mary stretched. "But I have to admit that, at the moment, I'm completely done in. I hope you won't mind if I go on up to my room for the night. After I help with the cleanup."

"Nonsense," Mrs. Brookstone said. "I don't need your help tonight. You go ahead and rest."

Wes noticed that Adler was whispering

something in Lizzy's ear. Didn't he realize how rude he was being? Unfortunately, Lizzy didn't seem to mind.

"I'll help you with the dishes." This came from Ella Fleming. Wesley wasn't sure what to make of the tiny girl. She was genteel and pretty—like one of those fancy china dolls. He knew from Rupert that she was on the run from her family, but he didn't really understand why the Brookstones would put themselves in the position of facing an angry Mr. Fleming. Especially when they had done so much business with him.

Ella and Mrs. Brookstone headed off toward the kitchen, and Mary made her way upstairs.

"Jason, I want to show you a few things in my office before you retire," Oliver said, getting to his feet.

Adler frowned. He didn't look at all happy about this but said nothing. He stood and looked back at Lizzy, giving her a slight bow. "Shall we try for that ride in the morning?"

Lizzy shook her head. "I'm afraid not. Mother has several things she wants me to tend to. Maybe later in the day. We'll have to see how things go."

Wesley gripped the arms of his rocker. He didn't like that man. Didn't like him at all. Adler was all smoothness and refinement, and while he might be generally trustworthy, Wes didn't think it wise to turn his back on him.

"Well, that just leaves us," Lizzy said, looking at Wes. "Unless you intend to run off and avoid me like usual."

He looked at her and saw an expression that dared him to contradict the truth of her statement. "I wasn't planning on going anywhere. At least not yet."

Lizzy got up and went to the fireplace. She put another log on the fire, then turned to face him. Wes couldn't help but admire her. She had her long brown hair loosely tied back and wore a skirt and blouse. It was simple but perfect. She was beautiful. Of course, he couldn't tell her that. Their relationship was too strained right now. Then there was all that stuff her mother had talked about. It was best to go slow.

"I heard you got hurt in Kansas City." It was the first thing he could think of to say that wasn't overly personal. He looked for a bruise.

"I got banged up a bit, but not really hurt. I have a bruise on this side." She touched her cheek, then walked over to take one of the chairs near him. "How have things been here at the ranch?"

"Good. We've got quite a few animals to take to market yet. Then we're expecting most of the cows to start dropping calves in January. We have a few older cows we'll butcher next month. It'll keep us in meat all winter, along with a couple of hogs your mother arranged for."

Lizzy nodded but kept her tone aloof. "Did you see the new mares?"

"I did. They look good. It's no wonder they were all your dad could talk about last winter."

"Yes." She looked back at the fire and said nothing more.

Wes went to stand beside her. She didn't seem to notice, so he touched her arm. She startled and looked up at him. He felt bad that he'd surprised her. "Sorry." He paused. "I'm sorry too about your dad. It was the hardest news I've had to hear since I lost my ma."

Lizzy nodded and got up. She moved closer to the fire and held out her hands. "And Clarissa?"

He looked down toward the flames, embarrassed that he hadn't thought to mention her. "Of course. But your pa was special."

"Yes, we all miss him." She turned her back to the heat and shrugged. "But everyone dies sooner or later. My concern is Mother. She's taken it very hard. Father was her whole world."

"Yes, I know. We had supper together last night."

"I don't know how it's going to be for her, being back here. Father was such a presence. I can almost see him." Lizzy's voice softened. "He's really just everywhere."

"I'm sure it's really hard for you. I know you'll miss him very much." Wes studied her face. It was like finely chiseled marble, cold and void of emotion.

Then Adler cleared his throat. Wes and Lizzy looked toward the sound at the same time.

"I hope I'm not interrupting anything." Adler smiled and fixed his gaze on Wes.

Lizzy moved away from the fire. "If you'll both excuse me, I'm going to see if Mother needs any more help, and if not, I'm going to bed." She left the room, with both men watching her.

When she was out of sight, Wes looked Adler over from top to bottom while Adler did the same. It was like assessing an obstacle and trying to figure out the best way to deal with it. Wesley didn't like that Adler would be staying in the house but knew it wasn't his place to speak against it.

Wes gave a slight nod. "Evenin', Mr. Adler."

The Englishman returned the gesture. "Good evening, Mr. DeShazer."

Wes headed out of the house, barely remembering to grab his hat on the way out the door. He didn't like Adler's smug attitude and familiar handling of Lizzy. He didn't like his plans for remaking the show and figuring out ways to manage it.

He just didn't like the man.

As he neared the bunkhouse and headed for his own cabin, Wes ran headlong into his brother.

"Whoa there, big brother. You het up for a fight?" Phillip asked, laughing. "You look like someone stole your prized saddle."

Wes pushed Phillip aside. "It's nothing. I'm tired and headin' for bed."

"Hope nothing isn't still bothering you in the morning." He stressed the word *nothing*.

Wes stopped and turned to face Phillip. He started to give him an earful, then released a heavy sigh. This wasn't Phillip's fault. "Good night."

FOURTEEN

For three days, Lizzy did very little. She offered to help around the house, but Cookie's wife, Irma, took care of most of the household duties and wouldn't hear of it. Lizzy read a little and went for a couple of rides but unfortunately had to take Jason Adler with her on most of them. Because she didn't want to ride out alone with him, she asked Mary and Ella to accompany them. She knew that didn't please Jason, but she'd made her feelings clear, and if he didn't like it, that was entirely too bad. The rest of the time she spent trying to familiarize Ella with the ranch and house.

Mother quickly lay claim to Mary and Ella. She taught Ella how to wash clothes and cook, and enticed Mary to bake some of her grandmother's favorite German recipes. The three women worked well together, and Lizzy found herself unneeded in the kitchen.

"You need to learn how to run the ranch," Mother told her more than once. "For all these years you've paid it little mind. Now, with your father gone, I need you to help me in this."

Lizzy knew it was just an excuse to put her and Wes together, but at the same time, she hoped to make this place her home after retiring from the show. She imagined a good life, just her and Mother—and Uncle Oliver when he was home from the show. It would serve her well to know the details of how the ranch operated. She had a working knowledge of the various duties that were performed throughout the year, but no firsthand experience. What little time she had been in residence, she was always training for the next show. And back then, Father had been alive and Uncle Oliver sober. There had been no need for her to know how the ranch operated.

Walking around the yard, Lizzy paused to look at the massive log house. It was nothing fancy, but she loved it. She had made so many memories here, and even now, in the early morning, she could hear voices from the past.

"I think we need a porch," Mother had said, standing arm in arm with Father.

"Whatever would we do with a porch?" he'd asked.

"We could hang a swing from it and then snuggle up on chilly evenings and talk about the future," Mother had replied.

But the show had taken up so much time, and the porch was never built. Maybe it could be now. Of course, that would cost money, and Jason would probably think the idea unreasonable. But Lizzy didn't, and while Jason might have something to say about the show, he didn't have any authority over the ranch. Maybe she'd talk to Wes about it.

That only served to remind her of her next duty.

"So what's planned for today?" Mary

asked, coming to join her. "Another romantic ride?"

Lizzy grimaced. "No. I'm hoping Jason will be otherwise occupied. Uncle Oliver has taken to bed with a bad cold, but Mother said he still planned to meet with Jason about the show's schedule for next year. Meanwhile, I have to learn the business of running a ranch."

Mary looked at the house and nodded. "I suppose there's a lot to do before winter, and I suppose too that winter comes much earlier here than in Kansas."

"It does," Lizzy agreed. "I was just remembering how Mother always wanted a porch on the house. I thought maybe I could talk to Wesley about getting one put on. Of course, it might only make her sad." Lizzy frowned. "She wanted it so she could sit with my father and talk."

"Maybe you should ask her."

Lizzy considered the long, rectangular home for another moment. There were chimneys at either end of the house, and in back was enough chopped firewood to keep them warm throughout the snowy months to come. It seemed silly to consider a porch when winter was nearly upon them. "Maybe I will," she murmured.

"So what else is on today's agenda besides learning ranch business?" Mary asked.

Lizzy turned from the house and started across the yard. "I promised Ella a lesson at ten. That's why I'm wearing my performance skirt." She ran her hand down the side of the bloused leg. Her split skirts were specially designed to be banded just below the knee where they met the boot. The looseness of the leg gave her a lot of freedom without being roomy enough to cause any entanglements. "But before then, I must speak with Wesley."

"So you'll be thrown yet again into your father's footsteps, whether you like it or not."

"It's not a matter of not liking it. I just don't know that I'm qualified. I suppose I already know a good deal about the ranch. At least as far as the cow calendar, as Father used to call it." She smiled at the memory. "But as for the bookwork and other such details, I know nothing."

"And Wesley's the one you have to work with."

Lizzy glanced at Mary, who kept in step with her. "Yes."

Ella came from the house and gave them a wave. "Where are you two headed?"

Lizzy tried to sound less discouraged. "I'm off to see what I must learn to keep this ranch running smoothly."

"Who do you see for that?" Ella asked.

"Wesley." Lizzy frowned. "Wesley will have all the answers."

"Pity that," Mary teased, then took hold of Lizzy's arm. "Look, now that he's a widower, why don't you make him see how you feel about him?" Her expression was all innocence, yet she knew very well how Lizzy had loved Wes. Ella knew it too, given their conversations on the train.

"Just so you both know, it doesn't matter how I felt about Wesley before. Now it's just business. I don't plan to marry—ever." Lizzy buttoned her heavy work jacket as a sharp wind cut across them. She didn't know if her friends believed her. She wasn't yet convinced that she believed herself. What she did know was that she never wanted to go through what her mother was going through. If that meant closing off her heart, then she'd just have to find a way.

"But Clarissa died two years ago," Mary declared. She looked at Ella. "That was Wes's wife. She died after getting thrown from her horse. Just like my father . . . well, not exactly. She didn't break her neck, did she, Lizzy?"

Ella sucked in her lower lip. She looked like she might break into tears.

Lizzy knew Ella's emotions were delicate. No doubt leaving her family for the first time, and under such dire circumstances, weighed on her. "Let's not talk about such sad things."

"We're all dealing with our griefs," Mary replied. "They won't go away simply because we stop talking about them. I would think you'd have learned that by now."

"Yes," Lizzy agreed. "But I must put that from my mind and go learn the affairs of the Brookstone ranch. Sorrow and grief won't help me in this." She sighed and pulled up the collar on the coat. "If either of you need me, I'll be in the bunkhouse office. Mary, you might help Ella better understand about the show. Tell her about our routines and how we'll all come together in February to train and get everything lined up. Or even teach her how to shoot."

"Sure, I'd be happy to." Mary looked at Ella. "The more you learn, the more comfortable you'll be. For me, it's old hat."

Lizzy left them as Mary started to explain that she hadn't normally wintered at the ranch. Walking across the yard to the bunkhouse and barns, Lizzy did her best to stuff her feelings into all the proper places, where they couldn't get loose and cause her problems. She wanted to talk things out with Wes—wanted to know why he'd made it his job to keep out of sight the last two years—but at the same time she didn't want him to think she was trying to get too close.

She glanced across the open pasture as the wind picked up again. There was a taste of snow in the air. The skies were gray, and the wind had turned cold. No doubt they'd soon be facing bad weather.

"Bad weather and bad memories," she murmured.

She stopped about ten feet in front of the bunkhouse and prayed for strength. She had hoped when they returned to the ranch that she'd find she no longer had feelings for Wes. She'd played it all out in her mind. Wes would come into the house for their gathering, and she'd look at him and feel nothing more than brotherly love.

But that wasn't how it had been. In fact, when Mother had asked him in for dessert, Lizzy had thought she might be ill. Her stomach did all sorts of quivering maneuvers, and a sort of light-headedness overcame her. She'd carefully positioned herself between Mary and Ella and thought everything would be fine, but then Ella went to retrieve something, and Jason took her spot. From that point forward, Lizzy was keenly aware of both men. Jason, because he wouldn't stop talking to her, and Wesley, because he looked so angry.

Now she'd have to face him alone. Well, that was just the way it had to be. She squared her shoulders. She'd certainly faced bigger obstacles in her life.

She marched to the bunkhouse door and walked in, knowing that the men would be out working—preparing for the storm and doing their routine jobs.

"Wes?" she called. The bunkhouse was a long, rectangular building with a kitchen to the left and living quarters in the middle. To the back were the dorm-style sleeping quarters, and to her right was the bunkhouse office. The door was closed. She started to knock.

Cookie called out, "He'll be right back. Some unscheduled supplies came in from town, and he went to see them properly stowed."

Lizzy turned and wandered over to the kitchen. It was nice and toasty here by the large cookstove. The grizzled old cook smiled at her, revealing several holes where teeth had once been.

"Best place to be on a day like today," he said.

Lizzy nodded and held out her hands to warm them. "How are you doing, Cookie? I'm sorry I haven't been out to see you before now. I hope Irma gave you that hot water bottle I picked up for you."

This only caused his grin to broaden. "She did. I used it last night. Helped my lumbago, and I'm fit as I can be this morning."

She chuckled. "So should I expect you and Irma to be kickin' up your heels in town tonight?"

"Grief, no. It's comin' up a storm. Don't you feel it?"

"I do." Lizzy sighed. "I was hoping for a few more days of nice fall weather."

"Bah, you know how things are up here. It could snow a foot today and be gone tomorrow. Don't be gettin' all disappointed. Ain't winter yet."

The door to the bunkhouse swung open and Wesley walked in. He seemed to fill the room, and Lizzy felt her breath catch. He caught sight of her and immediately stopped. A fierce wind blew in and froze Lizzy to the bone.

"Close the door, you fool!" Cookie yelled.

This seemed to shake Wes back into the moment. He did as Cookie ordered, then looked at Lizzy again. "I figured you'd come see me sooner or later. Your mother told me to expect you." He sounded matter-of-fact.

Lizzy had let her guard down talking to Cookie, and now just the sight of Wesley set her heart aflutter. Why did she have to love a man who clearly didn't love her? Why did she have to love at all?

"Yes," she said, trying her best to sound businesslike. "Mother wants me to be aware of all that's going on with the ranch. She said Uncle Oliver is bound to be much too busy, and since it was Father's interest anyway, the duties fall to me."

"Are you trying to step into your father's shoes?" Wes asked. His tone was even, and there wasn't a hint of what he was thinking in his expression.

Lizzy nodded. "As best I can. Someone has to."

Wes looked like he might say something, but then he just nodded. "Well, come on in." He opened the office door and stepped inside.

Lizzy hesitated. She glanced back at Cookie, who was coming toward her with a cloth-covered plate. "What's that?" she asked.

He pulled back the dish towel. "Buttermilk biscuits and jam. He didn't eat this morning, and I figure if you take this in there and have one, maybe he will too."

She took the plate. "I suppose I can try, but he never listens to me."

Lizzy followed Wesley into the office and found he was already sitting behind his desk. He watched her in that casual way of his—seemingly uninterested, while at the same time taking in every detail. She'd seen him deal with snakes the same way. She felt her cheeks flush and put the biscuits in the middle of the desk just to ensure his focus would be on something other than her face.

She reached for a biscuit. "I hope you don't mind, but I'm hungry." Without waiting for his approval, she plopped down in a chair and started munching.

"Thought you might like some coffee to wash down those biscuits," Cookie said, following her in with a couple of mugs.

Lizzy happily accepted and smiled at the coffee's milky hue. "Thank you for remembering that I like cream in my coffee."

"It's the other way around, isn't it?" Cookie teased. "You like a touch of coffee in your cream."

Lizzy smiled and nodded. "You know me too well."

"I should hope after all this time that I do." Cookie put Wesley's cup beside the plate of biscuits. "Now, you just holler if you want anything else."

"I didn't want this," Wes said sarcastically.

"Well, that's too bad," Cookie replied with a chortle, "'cause you've got it now, and I'll be offended if you don't eat and drink what I've served." He left and closed the door behind him.

For just a moment, Lizzy waited in silence, trying to figure out whether she should tease Wesley or just get down to business. She wished things could be lighthearted between them. It seemed so terrible that such a good friendship had to be compromised by the past.

"I'm glad we have you, Wesley. Father said you were by far the best foreman he'd ever had. He said he would have been proud to call you his son—that if God had blessed him with a son, he would have wanted him to be just like you." Lizzy put down her cup and placed the half-eaten biscuit beside it. "My mother also puts great stock in what you think. She has admired your abilities for years."

As she talked, Wesley watched her without attempting to comment. There was no hint of pride in his expression for the praise she offered, but when she spoke of her mother, she saw a softening in his face.

Lizzy continued talking, desperate to fill the silence. "Mother is very wounded over losing my father. He was her very best friend, and she will never be the same. However, I'm hopeful that with your help and mine, she will be able to find happiness here at the ranch again. I know she wanted to come home to be near his grave, but also to be in the place she thought him happiest."

"If he was happiest here, why stay with the show?" Wes asked, then looked surprised, as if he'd never meant to be caught up in the conversation.

Lizzy shrugged. "That's easy enough. He did it for Uncle Oliver. My uncle hates ranch life—always has. Uncle Oliver was born to perform. He loves to make pretty speeches and promote the show. If he hadn't been injured so many times, he'd still be out there, performing on horseback." She tried to look relaxed. "My father put Uncle Oliver's desires ahead of his own. He promised his mother they would always look after each other."

"Oliver was five years your father's senior. If anyone should have been looking out for anyone, it should have been the reverse."

"That's probably why Uncle Oliver is having such a difficult time with Father's passing. He's drinking again. Did you know he bought several crates of alcohol and brought it back here?"

Wes frowned. "No, I didn't know that. I knew your mother was concerned about him drinking."

"Well, whatever we can do to keep him from getting that liquor is going to be to the betterment of everyone. I heard an unexpected shipment came in today. Was it by any chance for Uncle Oliver?"

Wes nodded. "It was."

"I was afraid of that." She picked up the

biscuit and nibbled at it. There had to be a way to keep Uncle Oliver from receiving the alcohol. She supposed she could just take it and dispose of it somewhere. But where, and how could she manage huge crates by herself?

"What do you want me to do about it?" Wes asked.

She glanced up to see him watching her. She swallowed. "I want you to help me take the crates away from here and get rid of them." She fully expected an argument, but instead he nodded.

"I can do that, but you don't need to be involved. I'll just load it up and drive it out of here."

"No. If you do it alone, he might get mad and try to fire you. If I do it, then he'll be angry, but he'll get over it."

"I'll take care of it," Wesley insisted. Then he gave a wry smile. "He's not going to fire me. Like you said, he hates ranch work."

Lizzy decided it wasn't worth the fight. "Thank you. I have to do whatever I can to help Uncle Oliver stay sober. It's bad enough that he even took another drink, but that he's been drunk several times is going to make this even worse."

"It's really not your responsibility. He'll most likely just find more liquor."

"That's true, but Mother hopes to convince

him otherwise, especially now that he has a bad chest cold. He might listen to her. He respects her and loves her like a sister. She plans to sit down with him and talk about Father. Maybe if he talks about how much he misses his brother and how hard losing him has been, then he won't feel the need to drink."

"And what about you?" Wesley asked. "Are you willing to talk about how much you miss your father and how hard losing him has been on you?"

Lizzy hadn't expected that turn and nearly dropped the coffee she'd just picked up. "I'm not seeking alcohol to comfort myself, so I'm not sure why you ask that question. Of course I miss Father, and it's been very hard to lose him." It was her turn to speak matter-of-factly—with no emotion. She raised her chin and looked Wes square in the eye. "Not that I believe you are overly concerned about my feelings. No doubt Mother told you to be concerned, but you needn't be. I'm just fine."

"Yeah, I can see that. Stubborn and closed up. I guess that equals being fine to you."

"You're one to talk. You wouldn't even speak to me for the last two years. Would you like to tell me how much you miss Clarissa? How difficult it's been for you to lose her?" Lizzy regretted the words the minute she said them.

Wes stiffened, and something hardened in his expression. "No."

She nodded. "Then I suggest we discuss ranch business and leave it at that. I hoped we could at least be friends, but in lieu of that, I'll simply be my mother's envoy."

She was surprised to see him shake his head and frown. "I don't want that, Lizzy."

"No? Then what do you want?" For a moment she thought he might actually tell her.

But then he opened the desk drawer and took out two large ledgers. He tossed them on the desk. "For the books to balance."

Realizing he wasn't going to let the conversation get any more personal, she reached for the book on top. "Then let's get to it. I'm fairly good at math." *It's understanding a man's heart where I fail.*

They pored over the ledgers for the next two hours. Lizzy could see that Wes had been careful to keep track of every detail. He had noted every transaction. From what she could see, the ranch was in good order.

She was about to ask him about riding into town with her when a light knock sounded on his office door.

"Come in," Wes called.

Ella opened the door and peeked inside. She smiled at the sight of Lizzy. "You said you'd give me a lesson at ten, so I thought

I'd come find you. I don't know much about the place yet, so I was hoping you'd show me where you want to work."

Lizzy got up. "We'll work in the enclosed arena. It looks to start snowing at any time." She looked back at Wesley. "I need to get to town soon—maybe once the threat of snow is past. I was thinking you could ride in with me."

Wes frowned and looked like he would refuse, but Ella piped up before he could answer. "I'll bet Mr. Adler would go with you." She smiled so sweetly that Lizzy wasn't sure if she was innocent of the suggestion or had done it purposefully to goad Wesley into agreeing.

"I can spare the time," Wes muttered.

⋆⟞ FIFTEEN ⟝⋆

Wesley didn't know why he'd just agreed to go to town with Lizzy. The last thing he wanted was more time alone with her. Thinking about her being alone with Adler, however, was more than he could bear to consider.

"I'm so excited to learn some new tricks,"

Ella said, stepping fully into the office. "Isn't it exciting that she's going to teach me, Mr. DeShazer?"

Wesley had been glad for the interruption, but at Ella Fleming's words, he felt a chill run up his spine. "Not particularly. It's dangerous."

Lizzy looked at him and narrowed her eyes, as she so often did when she was angry. If eyes could alight with flames, then Lizzy's would be blazing. Her feelings were evident, but maybe that was better than her pretense at having none at all.

"Ella is an experienced equestrian. She tried her hand at trick and Roman riding when she was younger. She wants to learn it again so she can perform and perhaps even take my place." Her words were clipped and hard.

"I like the idea of you quitting the show, but don't you think it's dangerous for someone like her to learn to do what you do? From what your mother said, Miss Fleming has been raised as a proper lady. Not just that, but in a refined Southern manner that would never allow for such things. A person needs a great deal of muscle and body control for what you do."

Ella responded before Lizzy could. "I appreciate your concern, Mr. DeShazer, but I know what I'm doing, and I didn't just do such things when I was a child. I'd try my hand at various tricks when I was out riding alone and knew I could get away with it. Lizzy has given me exercises to do in order to strengthen my muscles and gain additional balance. I practice them several times a day— faithfully. I want to learn all that I can. I'll need to be able to support myself, after all."

"I don't want to offend, but there are easier ways than this. It is, after all, 1900. A great many women work jobs, and the opportunities are far more numerous than ever before." He glanced at Lizzy for confirmation. The instant his gaze met hers, he regretted it. "I'm not trying to offend either of you."

"Well, for someone who's not trying," Lizzy said, taking Ella's arm, "you're doing a great job."

"Hey, Wes, do you have—" The voice fell silent as Phillip entered the room and nearly knocked Ella over. He reached out to steady her and grinned when she turned to face him. "I'm sure sorry for that. I wasn't lookin' where I was goin'."

Wes couldn't see Ella's expression, but his brother's left little doubt of his attraction to the pretty blonde. "Lizzy, Miss Fleming, this is my brother, Phillip. He's recently come to work for us."

Lizzy crossed her arms and looked at the ceiling. "Great, now there's two of you."

Ella smiled. "How nice to meet you, Mr. DeShazer," she said.

"Just call me Phillip. Everybody does, and I sure hope that the prettiest girl I've ever met would too."

"Phillip, you're in the presence of two very beautiful ladies. It's not polite to single one out, especially when the other is the ranch owner's daughter." He knew better than to point out Lizzy that way, but the words were said before he gave them thought.

Lizzy stepped up to Phillip. "That's quite all right, Phillip. I'm glad to meet you, and I believe people should be honest about the way they feel. I agree with you that Ella is very pretty, and I don't mind at all that you think her prettier than me."

Phillip went ten shades of red and shook his head. "But I didn't even see you, Miss Brookstone. I'm real sorry too, 'cause I think you're mighty pretty. But it's like dessert. I love cherry cobbler and I love chocolate cake. But I love them both for different reasons, and right now I'm really very fond of cherry cobbler." He grinned in his impish way.

Wes had seen that smile disarm even the angriest of opponents. Phillip was a sweet kid, and for the most part he could always talk his way out of trouble.

Lizzy laughed. Once again Phillip's charm seemed to work. "I'm very fond of cherry cobbler myself, so I completely understand. Please know that I am not offended in any way by anything you have said." She emphasized the word *you*, and Wes knew it was intentionally done to make sure he knew she was offended by him. As if concerned that he wouldn't pick up her subtle comment, she added, "I wish it could be so for everyone." She took hold of Ella's arm. "Sorry, but Ella and I have work to do."

"What are you going to do?" Phillip asked. "Is there anything I can do to help?"

"I don't think your brother would approve, and I learned long ago that when you step on his toes, there are repercussions." Lizzy looked at Wesley and raised a brow.

No one said a word for several long moments.

"Lizzy is going to teach me some riding maneuvers for the show," Ella interjected into the uncomfortable silence. "I'm going to trick ride."

Phillip grinned. "I break horses. I'm the best there is. You should come watch me sometime. I do my own trick riding."

Ella nodded. "Maybe I will, but for now

I have a lot to learn, and I'm anxious to get started."

"No more anxious than I am to be out of here," Lizzy said and pulled Ella toward the door. "I definitely prefer the company of horses."

Once they'd gone, Phillip looked at Wesley with a grin. "She's an angel."

"She's a girl who left her home under bad terms. Stay away from her," Wesley said, sitting back down.

Phillip plopped down where Lizzy had just been sitting. He grabbed a biscuit and made a hole in the side, then spooned jam into the hole, mashing it down into the center. When that was done, he pushed the whole thing in his mouth.

"Have some manners." Wesley shook his head and moved the plate to the far side of his desk. "What are you even doing in here? Don't you have enough work to do? Do I need to assign you more?"

Phillip nodded and swallowed before speaking. At least that was an improvement. "I have a lot of work, but I just wanted to find out if you have any extra boots that might fit me. Mine are plumb worn out, and they're startin' to cause me trouble."

"I don't suppose you have any money, although you seemed to have enough to buy liquor the other day."

Phillip ate another biscuit before answering. "I didn't buy that whiskey—it was given to me. But no, I haven't got a cent until payday."

Wes shook his head, then pulled out his wallet. He threw down several bills of his own money. "Go to town and get another pair. Make sure they're good ones."

"I'll pay you back real soon," Phillip said, grabbing the money. "Thanks for helping me out. I won't let you down, I promise."

Wesley nodded. "You may have to hold off a day or two. We're due a snow, and I don't want you getting stuck in town."

"I'll take the new bay. He needs the exercise and a good, hard run. I'll be back faster than a whistle, snow or no snow."

"Phillip . . ."

For a moment Wes considered telling Phillip to take Lizzy with him, then thought better of it. He didn't know why, but even the idea of sending her off with his brother bothered Wes.

He shook his head. "Be quick about it, and no liquor!"

Phillip left, and Wesley tried to focus on his work, but Lizzy was all he could think about. He hadn't meant to upset her. He wasn't even sure how things had gotten so bad. Should he go apologize? His mother had once said that if that question came to mind, there was a good chance you already knew the answer.

———◆◆◆◆◆———

"It's always good to practice first with the horse standing still and then with someone walking him around or leading him on horseback for control. Since Pepper is accustomed to you doing unusual maneuvers, he'll be easier to work with, but it's still a good idea to do some basic moves to start to remind him."

Lizzy looked the sleek black gelding over from nose to tail. "He's got a pretty long back. That makes it difficult for a lot of the tricks I do. We might do better to let you train on my horse and discuss what you want to do for the future. We have some other horses here that have been used for trick riding. I think in the long run, you'd be happier with one of them." She ran her hand over the black's rump. "I also have a smaller saddle that might be perfect for you. As you know, the saddles are very different. In fact, I've made quite a few personal changes and have pretty much created my own design. Come with me and I'll show you."

They left Pepper tethered to the gate and walked back to where several saddles were posted atop wooden stands.

"As you can see, these saddles are a little longer than the normal work saddle."

Ella nodded and ran her hand along the elongated horn. "This is longer too. I imagine that's a wonderful tool for tricks. I've had some rough moments and all because it was hard to get a grip on my horn. There were also times when I did tricks without a saddle, and sometimes I thought that was easier."

"I know what you mean. Sometimes I even perform a few tricks bareback. The crowds love it. But for the most part you'll use one of these saddles, so you should be familiar with them. If you decide you're serious about staying with the show, you'll want to have your own saddle made."

"My brother-in-law's family business is making saddles. He's part owner of Knox Saddlery. Maybe you've heard of them."

"Of course I have. Everyone knows Knox saddles. They're some of the finest."

Ella nodded. "That's how my sister and brother-in-law met. She was having a saddle made, and he came to our farm. It was all very romantic." She smiled and then sobered almost instantly. "I hope she's all right and that Father hasn't made it difficult for her. I never wanted to cause her pain."

Lizzy touched Ella's arm. "I know you didn't want to hurt her. That's why I suggested you come here. Maybe after Christmas or your birthday, you can send her a letter and let her know what's happened."

"I will. I've already started writing it." Ella paused and looked as if she were struggling to come up with the right words. "Lizzy . . . I really . . . that is, I hope you know how much I appreciate what you've done for me."

"I do. You're a friend, and you were in need. Goodness, given all that happened with August, I'd never have rested a wink if I'd known you needed to escape and I did nothing." Lizzy flipped her long braid back over her shoulder. "It's what friends do."

"I've never had that kind of friend. One who cared so deeply." Ella wiped away a tear. "I just want you to know how much it means. I sometimes lie awake at night and think of what must be going on back at home. I miss my poor mother. I know she must be beside herself."

"In time, you'll be able to write to her as well." Lizzy smiled. "Now, try to put it from your mind. We have a lot of work to do if you're going to perform in the spring." She knew that the best thing Ella could do for herself was concentrate on something else. "Come on, let me show you a few things about this saddle." She glanced at Ella. "Oh, I forgot to ask. How does that split skirt fit?"

"It's good. I had to take it in a little, but I

think it'll be fine. It's a little longer than I need, but given it tucks into the boots, I don't think it'll be too loose. If I can get some material, I can make my own."

"Good. Mother has a whole sewing room full of materials and supplies. She even has one of the latest treadle sewing machines. Father bought it for her for Christmas last year." Lizzy sighed. She could still see the love that had shone in their eyes as her mother thanked Father with a kiss. How would she ever go on without him?

Lizzy shook the memory from her mind and hoisted the saddle. It weighed about sixty pounds, and she wondered if Ella was even able to lift something that heavy. No doubt Wes was right—Ella had lived a pampered life and probably never had to saddle her own animal. Well, they'd deal with that later.

She carried the saddle to where Thoreau awaited her. She placed it on the ground, then retrieved the saddle pad. She gave Thoreau a cursory rub on the nose.

"How are you today, Thoreau?" She let him nuzzle the pad. "You're such a good boy that I thought you might like to show off a bit for Ella."

Ella joined her, and Lizzy decided to start the lesson. "I presume you are familiar with all the components of saddling a horse."

"Yes, but I rarely saddled the horse myself."

That answered that question. Lizzy nodded. "Well, you'll be doing it for yourself here. If Jason has his way about cutting costs, we'll probably be doing a great many things for ourselves. You'll have to build some muscle before you can hoist these heavy saddles, but in time you'll do just fine. I was saddling my own horse when I was just a child, so I know it can be done."

"I'll do it," Ella assured. "You can count on me."

"Good." Lizzy put the pad on Thoreau's back. "I always let him see what I'm doing so he doesn't get spooked. And I always come from the left. We do that with all the horses." She lifted the saddle and brought it within Thoreau's line of sight. "You can see how I've secured the right-side stirrup and girth strap up and out of the way. This makes it easier to put the saddle on the horse's back." She placed the saddle. "I always shake it a bit back and forth to make sure it's in the right position. After a time, you'll get a feel for it."

She went on explaining, and after she'd seen to the cinches, she picked up a breast collar. "I use this for extra stability, but some of the girls don't." She fixed the collar in place, then stood back. "You can see there are a variety of extra straps and handholds. Most of these I've added as I've developed tricks where I found I needed a better grip or more security in one place or another. You'll learn as you train, and you'll be able to see what works best for you."

Ella was an attentive student, and Lizzy had no doubt she'd be able to master most anything, given her willing spirit.

Lizzy turned to the open arena. This had been a surprise gift from her father two years ago. It was a rectangular building with equipment and storage rooms at one end and an open area for training hour after hour without worry of the weather. There was a bank of large windows at either end to let in the light and overhead lanterns that could be lit if needed.

"We always keep the horses working in a long oval in the center. You don't want to get too close to the side for several reasons. If the tour locations are fenced, then you could risk getting snagged during the run. If it's open, as many of the performance areas are, you could come in conflict with the audience. Of course, we generally set up ropes to keep the audience from getting too close."

"That makes sense to me," Ella replied.

"To make the tricks look best, we have to prove to the audience the element of danger, yet not look afraid. And we definitely don't want to *be* afraid, or the horse will sense that, and then you'll really have trouble. It's all about balance and rhythm, and once you have that, you'll go far. The appearance of the act is the most critical thing. My father taught me that. We're entertaining people, just like actors on a stage, only our performance is much more physical."

Lizzy took up the reins. "I'll show you a few very basic tricks. Then you'll practice these over and over in the days to come." She climbed atop the horse and guided him to the center of the arena. "I don't know what you know and don't know, so we're going to start from scratch."

"That sounds wise," Ella said, moving a little closer.

Lizzy stroked Thoreau's neck, then looked back at Ella. "First are the spins. I usually tuck the reins beneath the bridle's headpiece or throat strap, like this." She doubled the reins, then slipped them partway under. "This way they're out of the way but easy to grab if something goes wrong." She shifted her weight slightly. "I'll show you this sitting still, but all tricks will be done in motion."

"I understand," Ella said, watching intently.

"The most important thing I can tell you is that you have to keep looking up. Fix your eyes on a mark well in front of you. Where your eyes go, your body follows, my father always said." Lizzy smiled. "He incorporated that into a spiritual lesson as well. If we put our focus on the things of this world, that's where we're likely to end up. So he always admonished me to fix my eyes on Jesus."

"That makes sense to me."

Lizzy gave Ella a nod. "Father generally made the best sense in every matter, and in this case, with trick riding, it's imperative. Your body follows your eyes. If you look down while trying to perform a trick, you'll go down." She put her hand on her left thigh. "We're going to spin counterclockwise. Take your feet out of the stirrups, tucking your leg up and back. At the same time throw your right leg over the horse's neck. Use the horn to shift your weight, like this." She made the backward turn. "Then tuck your left leg again and put your right leg forward across the saddle and turn again using the horn." She did the action as she spoke. "Now you're facing forward again. In time, you'll be able to spin just using the horn and your leg muscles, and your bottom won't even need to touch until you're back in the saddle. It's all about continuous motion, and practice will make it look smooth."

"I used to do that when I was little," Ella

252

said, grinning. "I'm so glad I know at least something useful."

Lizzy laughed. "Well, just remember the placement of your hands, feet—well, really every part of your body is going to be critical to getting the tricks right. But I know you're going to take to this like a duck to water."

⬥━◆━◆⬥

That night at supper, Wes watched Lizzy and Jason from across the table. He hadn't wanted to come to dinner with the others, but Rebecca Brookstone had insisted. She wanted to talk to him about the crates that had been delivered and, it was discovered only recently, disappeared. Oliver was still in bed sick, but he'd been asking about them.

Wes knew he needed to apologize to Lizzy for his attitude earlier, but as the day wore on, more and more problems came to his desk to be dealt with. Before he knew it, it was suppertime, and the request from Rebecca came to share the meal with the family.

"I think that's marvelous, Lizzy. You have such a generous heart," Jason Adler declared.

Wes didn't know what he was praising Lizzy for, but just the fact that this stranger called her by her family's nickname irritated Wes more than he could say.

Mary shared a story about her brother.

Something from the early days, when Wes had been working with August on the show. She looked at Wes. "Do you remember that? I think the two of you were up all night, trying to figure out what had happened to the saddles."

Everyone suddenly looked at him. Even Lizzy's expression suggested interest in his reply. He tried to put aside his frustrations with Adler. "I do. It was a nightmare, and little did we know it was a joke being played on us by Mr. Brookstone—Lizzy's father." He gave a slight smile.

"He's exactly right," Mary declared. "August was mortified because he was new and it was his job to see the saddles were put on the train. When he couldn't locate them, he thought for sure he'd be fired. But Wes was so kindhearted and took pity on him. He took responsibility for the entire thing and assured Mr. Brookstone that any fault was his. I think August was completely devoted to Wes after that. I know I was."

"Wes has always been such an important part of our lives," Mrs. Brookstone said. "Mark said he'd never met a man he trusted more, outside of family."

Wes was uncomfortable under the scrutiny and praise, but he forced himself to give her a smile before refocusing on his plate.

Thankfully the conversation shifted again, and he was no longer the center of attention.

By the time the meal finally ended, Jason and Lizzy were agreeing with Mary and Ella to play a new card game that Jason intended to teach them.

"Why don't you come learn too, Wesley?" Mary asked.

"It's really just a game for four," Adler quickly said. "But of course, he could come and watch."

"No, I've seen quite enough," Wes muttered. His eyes met Adler's just long enough to convey his disapproval.

"Very well. Come, ladies. I think you'll enjoy this," Jason said, leading them away.

"We need to help Mother with the table and dishes, first," Lizzy said as she started to stack the plates nearest her.

"Never mind that." Mrs. Brookstone shooed them away. "Wes and I will manage it."

He hadn't expected to be volunteered but would have offered anyway. He got to his feet and started collecting plates even as laughter came from the opposite side of the house.

"You really should stake a claim on her," Mrs. Brookstone said as she took the plates from him.

"What?" He looked at her in surprise.

She chuckled. "You know you were her

first love. In fact, as far as I know, her only love."

"You couldn't tell by the way she acted with me earlier. I think she has lost any and all love for me."

"Well, you did go and marry another. That hurt her deeply. Then when Clarissa died, you continued to avoid and ignore Lizzy."

Wes started collecting cups and saucers. He never wanted to talk about Clarissa or Lizzy, but something about having this conversation with Rebecca Brookstone put him at ease. It seemed natural to share his feelings with Lizzy's mother.

"Lizzy was a child, and besides that, I always saw her like a little sister." He shook his head. "If not that, then as a good friend."

"I don't think you still feel that way toward her, not if you're honest with yourself. And if you're being honest with yourself, then you should give some consideration as to what she means to your future."

He felt his face grow warm. "I . . . uh . . . I don't think Lizzy wants me in her future. I think she's well past her childhood dreams and thoughts of romance with me."

Rebecca chuckled again and shook her head. "I wouldn't be so sure about that. She may say and do one thing, but I know my daughter. She'll do whatever she can to keep from feeling the fool again. If you do have feelings for her, Wes—desires for a future with Lizzy—then you'd better not dally. Jason Adler has made his intentions quite clear."

"No doubt he has. Seems to me he's a pushy sort of fella."

The older woman smiled. "You might say that."

They deposited the dishes in the kitchen, but before Wes could leave, Rebecca took his arm. "What happened to the crates of alcohol my brother had delivered to the ranch?"

Wes shrugged. "Well, I figured it had to be a mistake since we don't allow alcohol on the premises, so I took it back to Miles City and sold it to one of the bars. I figured that made the most sense and wouldn't force any of us to lie. I'd be happy to go tell Oliver about it right now, if you like."

Rebecca smiled. "That was pure genius on your part. Now no one has to acknowledge that Oliver would do such a thing, and we can pretend it was a simple mix-up. Oliver will dry out, and the urge for liquor will ease. At least that is my prayer."

"It won't be easy."

"No, perhaps not," Mrs. Brookstone replied. "One doesn't cease being an alcoholic, I suppose."

"No." Wes shook his head. "I'm sure the

desire remains. It was pure willpower and your husband's attentive care that got him off the bottle the first time around, as I hear it."

"Yes, that's true. Perhaps this time my attentive care will suffice to make him want to be sober." Her expression was tinged with sorrow. "But I know his pain, and it won't be easy."

"No, not for us or him. But God, on the other hand, will find this a simple matter." Wes tried to sound reassuring. "Like your husband used to tell me, 'Put it to prayer first and give God a chance. If He—'"

"'If He can't handle it, then you can give it a try,'" Rebecca interrupted. She smiled and nodded.

***

Ella woke screaming. She clamped her hands over her mouth when she realized what she was doing, but it wasn't soon enough to keep from waking Mary, whose room was next door.

"Ella? Are you all right?" Mary came into the room without even knocking.

The darkness shrouded them, hiding Ella's pained expression. She fought back her fear and steadied her nerves. "I had a bad dream."

"I gathered that." Mary came through the

dark to Ella's bedside and sat down beside her. "I've had my share of nightmares too. I think it's all the change and losing August. I'm certain it'll pass when you get used to being here."

Ella tried to ignore the rush of guilt that washed over her. "My father will be livid over what I've done. He'll never forgive me."

"Are you afraid he'll come here?" Mary's tone was surprised.

"I suppose I am. I know it's a long way, but you don't know my father . . . or Jefferson Spiby. They aren't used to having their demands denied."

Mary patted Ella's arm. "You don't have to be afraid here. There are enough ranch hands to fight off an army."

Ella drew a deep breath. Mary was right. There were a great many people here who would keep her from being taken by her father or Jefferson. "I'm sorry I woke you."

"It's not a problem. I just wanted you to know you weren't alone. I'm your friend, Ella." Mary got up. "I'll always be here to talk . . . if you need me."

She left, and only after the door was closed and Ella was alone again did Mary's words truly register. Ella felt even worse. Mary was offering her friendship, and Ella was lying to her. Well, not exactly lying, but certainly not telling her the truth. How could they be friends if Ella wasn't willing to be honest?

"But how can we be friends if I am?"

✦= SIXTEEN =✦

Snow came and went, and just as Cookie had predicted, it didn't last long. The cooler temperatures did, however. The chill remained a silent reminder that winter was on its way.

Thanksgiving had always been a favorite of the Brookstone family, but this year there was a sense of bittersweetness for Lizzy. She had done well to be strong and not let her feelings get the best of her, but it hadn't been easy. Her father had cherished Thanksgiving. He loved to talk about all God had done and why he was thankful. He had taught Lizzy to be thankful, but this past year she had forgotten.

How she could possibly be thankful when Father was gone and Mother was so grieved? Nothing would ever be the same on the ranch or in the show. How could she have a thankful heart when there had been so much sorrow?

"Is God only worthy of our love when He's giving us good things, Lizzy?" her father had once asked her after her granddad died. This had come after Lizzy had told her father how angry she was that God had taken her grandparents.

That question sat heavy on her heart now.

This year her father's absence was clearly felt. Even with everyone gathered for the holiday meal, including Cookie, Irma, and all the cowboys, there was a sense of sadness. Lizzy listened to her Uncle Oliver lead them in prayer and then speak about what he was thankful for, hoping she might find something to be thankful for herself.

"It's hard not to remember that Thanksgiving was a day my brother relished. He was always good at reminding us of the blessings we have. He could see the good in almost any situation. I remember once, in fact, when we were surprised by a grizzly. We were trapped on the edge of a mountain with very few choices. The sun was just coming up, and this bear seemed uncertain as to what he should do with us. I thought for sure we weren't going to make it out unscathed. Then the sun came up over the horizon. Mark smiled and said, 'Isn't this just about the prettiest day you've seen in weeks?'"

Everyone laughed, although Mother had tears in her eyes.

Uncle Oliver's eyes dampened as well. "Then, just as if we weren't even there, that bear ambled off down the mountain, and we sat there thanking God for His rescue and the beautiful morning."

"I remember," one of the cowboys said, "when we were out rounding up cows. Couple of 'em got stuck down in a gully. We were havin' the devil of a time gettin' 'em out of there, and I was cursin' and stompin' around. After quite a spell of finaglin', Mr. Brookstone managed to make his way to them, and when he did . . . well, that was when we found that patch of coal. Turned out to be a thick vein, and it has served us well. Even then, Mr. Brookstone said, 'God's blessings are often at the end of places where we're stuck and can't see any good purpose in being.' He offered up thanks for the cows havin' got stuck down there and us findin' 'em and the coal. Kind of made me look at life different."

Others shared similar stories about Lizzy's father. They had learned thankfulness or gratitude through him for a wide variety of reasons. Lizzy feared the stories would only make her mother sad, but instead she was smiling and nodding, even offering her own comments. From time to time she wiped away tears, but Lizzy could see that the stories did her mother more good than harm.

I wish they'd do the same for me. But rather than offer Lizzy joy, they only served to put pressure on a heart already close to exploding. More than once during the dinner, she felt herself choke up close to tears. Only her fears kept her from giving in.

If I start crying, I might never stop.

She remembered when one of the newborn foals had died. She'd only been a little girl and had cried her heart out. Wesley had been upset at her tears, because he didn't know what to do. At least that was what she figured as the years passed. He had given her a bad time of it, telling her that life on a ranch was going to be full of death and she needed to be stronger or she'd spend all her time crying. But Father had put his arm around her and reminded her that death was just a season of life. He told her it was just fine to cry—that God collected our tears—that when our hearts were broken, He understood and would comfort us.

But I don't feel that comfort now.

She looked across the table at Wesley and wondered if he remembered the way he'd treated her. No doubt he thought he was helping her be strong, or maybe he was just embarrassed by a little girl's tears and didn't know how to deal with her. A year later, Mary's father died in the wild west show. Lizzy didn't know Mary then, and while it was sad that her father's friend had died, it wasn't as heartbreaking to her as the foal's death had been. But then her grandmother died, and her grandfather the year after that, and Lizzy had thought her broken heart might never mend. It hurt so much to lose someone she loved. Again the tears had flowed.

When she learned Wes had married, Lizzy's lessons in loss and pain were complete. Or so she'd thought. She had never hurt as much as she had then, and she spent every night sobbing quietly into her pillow. She couldn't understand the situation at all. She was in love with Wes and knew he cared about her. Why hadn't he fallen in love with her?

It was after weeks of tears that she had decided they were getting her nowhere. Tears were for the weak. She vowed one night that no matter what, she would survive her pain by hardening her heart. At least where romance was concerned.

After that, she forced back any rush of emotions. She was committed to dealing with life in such a manner that it couldn't hurt her. The price? It also diminished the pleasure she took in life. Lizzy found that she never had as much joy in simple things. Happy times were pleasant enough, but the extreme feeling of delight was sadly absent.

However, by handling her sorrow in that manner, Lizzy was better equipped to deal with her father's passing. His death was a hard blow to bear, but she handled it with the same stalwart manner she'd dealt with other sorrows. It had solidified her resolve to have nothing to do with romantic love and hold all other feelings of love in a carefully controlled manner.

If I don't feel anything too much—either good or bad—then I'm better off. I can still enjoy the good times, but the bad ones can't hurt me like they once did.

Was that such a terrible way to deal with pain and loss?

"I say, I very much enjoy this Thanksgiving dinner of yours. I've never eaten so much," Jason said after the dinner concluded and they were all trying to find room for dessert.

"Don't you celebrate Thanksgiving in England, Jason?" Mary asked.

"We have days of thanks that we celebrate from time to time, but nothing like this holiday of yours. After all, you are celebrating a group of people leaving England to start a new life in America. I doubt very much the English people would want to celebrate that."

"We're celebrating God's mercy and provision," Wesley corrected. "It isn't about those people leaving England. It's about how God kept them alive and provided for their needs and how we should celebrate our thanks for how He's done the same for us."

"Wesley's right," Mother added. "We're very grateful for all the blessings we've had this year. It hasn't come without loss and sorrowful moments, but we're thankful for God's provision and mercy. We are very blessed."

Murmurs of *amen* rounded the table, but Lizzy remained silent.

After dinner, Wes and his crew declared themselves in charge of cleanup, and the others were dismissed to enjoy themselves by the living room fire.

Lizzy collected some treats for her horses and slipped out of the house before anyone could notice and stop her. Snow was falling lightly in tiny flakes that were hardly noticeable. They fell straight down in a slow, lingering descent. Without wind to kick it all up, it was calming and restful.

She made her way to the pen where Longfellow and Thoreau were huddled with some of the other performing horses, as well as some of the horses they'd retired from the show. She offered encouragement to each of the mounts but gave special attention to her own.

"You are such good boys," she told them

after giving them some carrots. She stroked their faces and scratched Longfellow behind the ears like he liked. "I am thankful for you. You work well with me and keep me safe. You also don't judge me or try to make me into someone I'm not. I'm definitely thankful for that."

"Aren't you cold out here?"

She grimaced. She was glad her back was to Jason Adler. She squared her shoulders and dropped her hold on the horses. "I wanted to give my boys some rewards." She turned and faced him. "What brings you out?"

"Why, you, of course. I didn't want you to be alone out here in the weather." He smiled in his pleasant way.

Lizzy shook her head. "Jason, I grew up here—as an only child, I might add. I often go off by myself. I like it that way."

"I am sorry." He looked rather worried. "I didn't mean to overstep."

Lizzy didn't want to offend him; she just wanted him to leave. "It's all right. I just enjoy some time alone."

"I can understand the need for reflection, but I hope you can learn to enjoy my company as well."

"I thought we decided you and I would be friends and nothing more."

"To start with." He stepped closer. "Lizzy,

I don't want to make you uncomfortable. That has never been my desire. I've enjoyed our friendship, but surely you know I would like to see it become something more. From our first meeting, I knew there was something special about you . . . that I wanted you to be a part of my life, my future."

"We will share a mutual future, since I agreed to participate in next year's show. Isn't that enough?"

"I suppose for now it has to be," he agreed. "I won't lie to you. I want more. I'm so certain of what I feel that I would get down on one knee and propose right now if I thought I would get a positive reply."

Longfellow nudged her neck, and Lizzy dug out two more carrots and returned her attention to the horses. "I really don't want to discuss this. I'm not looking to be anything more to you than a friend."

He moved up behind her and stood so close that she was penned between him and the fence. If she turned, she'd be in his arms. His familiarity made her angry, and for a moment she considered giving him a good shove. But her sense of propriety prevailed.

"Please step away. I don't appreciate you forcing yourself on me."

"That wasn't my intention."

He did as she asked, and when Lizzy

turned, she could see he looked embarrassed. "Jason, we should maintain a good relationship because we will be working together. But otherwise I have much too much to concern my thoughts and heart. My mother is still mourning my father's death, and Christmas will soon be upon us. I have a lot of work to do between now and the next show, so fairytale romances are not on my schedule."

"But I'd love to be your knight in shining armor. I'd love to fight off your dragons and carry you safely to my castle on my beautiful white stallion." He grinned in a way that made him look like a lovesick schoolboy. "Although I'll have to purchase one first. All my horses are blacks or bays."

His entire face was aglow with what Lizzy could only suppose was adoration. Sad that she couldn't give him even a glimmer of hope that she might one day return his feelings, Lizzy shook her head. "I'm sorry, Jason. I'm all grown-up and no longer believe in fairy tales."

"And what of happily-ever-after?" he asked softly.

She shook her head again. "Only after we leave this life. Only when we're safely in heaven in the arms of Jesus. Not here. Not where we so easily lose the people we love."

His brow furrowed. She thought he might challenge her, but instead he gave her a slight bow and headed back to the house. She felt both relief and sadness. She was glad he'd left her alone but sorry that she'd obviously hurt him.

Turning back to the horses, Lizzy contemplated what had just happened and wondered if staying another year with the show was wise. Ella was far more accomplished than Lizzy had dared to hope. She was younger too. It wouldn't be long before she'd be able to handle anything Lizzy threw at her. Surely Ella could take on the starring role and do it as well, if not better, than Lizzy. Of course, she had promised Mary she would help her learn the truth about August. That was the biggest thing that had influenced Lizzy's decision.

But if I must worry about being pestered by Jason at every turn, I don't think I can endure another year.

"You got a couple of beauties there," Phillip DeShazer said as he joined her at the fence. "Probably the best in the lot."

"I think so," Lizzy said, giving him a smile. "By the way, I want to thank you for taking my list and that catalogue back to Barney in Miles City."

"It was no trouble. I like doing things for folks."

"How are you settling in?"

"I like it here. I can see why Wes has stayed

on year after year. I always liked movin' around and meetin' new people. I never stayed long enough to get too bored. But I never met a family like yours either. Your ma is a real nice woman. Reminds me of our ma."

"She is first-rate, if I do say so."

Phillip was nothing like his brother. Phillip had a boyish charm and sense of innocence about him. She knew from things Wes had said in the past that Phillip was bound to have seen plenty of trouble in his life, but he didn't wear it in his expression or his attitude.

"You said you liked moving around. Where all did your travels take you?" she asked.

He shrugged. "Just about everywhere. Been to California and up the coast. Been to Texas and saw that coast too." He laughed. "I didn't go east of the Mississippi, though. I didn't figure they'd have as much use for my skills there as out here."

"You are amazing with the horses. I heard someone say that you've done exceptional work with that new string."

His expression grew thoughtful. "I've always felt a keen sense of understanding with horses. It doesn't mean they haven't tried to make me pay now and again. I've been thrown and kicked just like any other horse breaker. I guess I just feel I get along better with animals than humans."

Lizzy nodded. "I'm beginning to feel the same way. I don't seem to relate well to anyone anymore."

"Wes thinks a lot of you."

She met Phillip's dark brown eyes and shook her head. "Wesley thinks I'm a spoiled little girl sent to make his life a misery." She'd had enough of this discussion. She gave the horses one last kiss and turned to go. "It was nice talking with you, Phillip. If you ever need anything, just come find me."

"She said what?" Wes asked his brother.

Phillip grinned. "She said you think she's a spoiled little girl sent to make your life a misery."

Wesley knew he'd made mistakes where Lizzy was concerned, but he certainly never meant for her to think those things. Nobody was less spoiled than Lizzy. She was generous to a fault and never had to have the best of anything. He'd seen her give up her place at the table when company was overflowing the house. Give up her room and bed too. He'd seen her work with others in the show and put them in positions where they could outshine her. No, she wasn't spoiled. Nor did she make his life a misery.

He was able to do that all on his own.

"She's not spoiled, and I don't think that way about her." Wesley bent to throw another long on the fire. Phillip had come to visit at his cabin for a bit before heading to the bunkhouse for the night. "You want some coffee?" Wes asked. "Cookie always leaves me half a pot in the afternoon. The stove's cold, but I could put it over the fire."

"Nah, I ate too much and drank too much already. I'm full up." Phillip pulled his chair closer and stretched out his legs. "It's sure nice here. Almost like being a family again."

"It is. The Brookstones have always treated me like family."

"That Oliver Brookstone is a cutup. He was in the bunkhouse a couple of nights back and had us all in stitches with some of his stories from the old days."

Wesley remembered what he'd heard about Oliver still drinking. "Phillip, you haven't been bringing whiskey back to the ranch, have you?"

"No, sir. I do my drinking in town just like you told me to."

"I didn't tell you to drink at all. I'd rather you didn't. You know it's not good for you. It serves no purpose other than to dull your senses."

Phillip sobered and nodded, but his gaze never left the flames. "That's a purpose."

Wes knew there were years of pain inside

his brother, but he wouldn't talk about it, and any time Wes tried to get close enough to ferret out something of the truth, Phillip would push him away with a joke or a story about one of his humorous antics.

It seemed no one wanted to talk about anything . . . to anyone.

———◆◇◆———

"Oliver, I think we need to have a talk now that you're feeling better," Rebecca Brookstone said, coming into her brother-in-law's office.

"You know I've always got time for you, Becca." He rose and placed a chair by his desk. "What's on your mind?"

"You are." She sat and gave him a smile. "I've been very worried about you since Mark's death."

Oliver stiffened. "And I've worried about you."

"I know you have." She waited until he reclaimed his seat to continue. "Oliver, I know that you suffer from losing your brother. Even though you say very little to me, it's evident."

"I don't want to burden you with my feelings, Becca. Your loss was much greater."

"I didn't know loss could be measured. You loved Mark just as I did. He was your brother, and the two of you were thick as thieves. I sometimes envied that." She put her hand atop Oliver's. "My loss was great, but yours was too, and I know that perhaps it was made all the worse because we had to keep the show going. We weren't allowed time to mourn or even give Mark a proper funeral."

"It didn't seem right."

"No," Rebecca agreed. "It didn't. But we did what Mark wanted, and that's what matters. And, in thinking on that, I have to say something else."

Oliver shifted his weight, and his jaw tightened. He shook his head and looked away. "I think I know what you want to say. You're upset with me about the drinking."

She squeezed his hand. "I'm not condemning you. You were hurting, and you sought comfort in the old ways."

"I drank so I wouldn't have to feel the pain. But it was always there."

"Made worse by guilt, I'm sure." Rebecca straightened, and Oliver looked at her and nodded.

"I didn't want to hurt you or the others. I just couldn't stand to think about Mark being dead—about everything falling on my shoulders. The more I let myself dwell on it, the worse I felt. The worse I felt, the more alcohol appealed."

Rebecca nodded. "But it doesn't have

to be that way. You told me once that you have some ideas for the future, and I think we should talk about those now. It might help you continue on a sober path."

He drew a deep breath. "All right." He pulled open a drawer. "Let me tell you what I've done . . . and what I still want to do."

SEVENTEEN

I swear you'd think she'd never seen snow." Mary let go of the window sheer and turned back to Lizzy.

Lizzy had seen how animated Ella was when Phillip offered to teach her how to make a snowman. "I don't think it's the snow as much as the company."

Mary shrugged. "I suppose there's someone for everyone. Maybe one day I'll find mine."

"I don't think there's necessarily someone for everyone. God calls some people to be single. I'm beginning to think maybe that's His purpose for me."

"Hogwash." Mary came to where Lizzy was tightening the laces on her boots. "You and Wes were meant for each other. I knew that the first time I saw you together."

"Then someone forgot to tell Wes." Lizzy grabbed her jacket and made her way outside. The last thing she wanted to do was think about Wes. She and Ella were going to work on some of the more difficult tricks today, and it was important to maintain focus. "Ella, I'll be in the arena when you're ready."

"Just give us a couple more minutes, Miss Lizzy." Phillip bent to pick up a large snowball. "We're just about done. Got to put the head on and then find some things for his eyes and nose."

"And his mouth," Ella added.

"You could use coal." Lizzy motioned toward the bunkhouse. "The pail by the stove is usually full."

"Don't I know it," Phillip said, nodding. "I filled it. That's a good idea, though."

Lizzy smiled and watched as Phillip plopped the head atop the snowman's body. She could remember her father teaching her to make a snowman when they still lived in Illinois. Lizzy couldn't have been more than four or five. Father had been like Phillip. His nature had always been playful and infectious. Mother had even joined them, putting aside her normal chores to play. Lizzy smiled as she remembered the snowball fight her parents had gotten into. It had ended with Mother hitting Father in the head with a snowball. Father had fallen backward into a snowbank as if mortally wounded. It had frightened Lizzy and her mother. Both had run to see if he was still alive, and as they bent over him, Father had pulled them down into the snow with him. They had laughed until their sides ached.

"Lizzy?"

She looked up to see she was about to walk straight into Wes. She was still smiling, but that faded. "Morning, Wes."

"You getting ready to practice?" He pushed his Stetson back a bit.

"Yes. I promised Ella we'd work on some of the more difficult tricks today." She waited for his condemnation, but none came.

"Well, Cookie said you want to go into town to pick up some Christmas gifts. I'm planning to drive in to get supplies. I'm leaving in about ten minutes, and you're welcome to ride along."

She knew this was her best chance of getting to Miles City, but why did it have to be with Wes? She sighed and realized there was no way out of it. There was only another week until Christmas. The month of December had passed so quickly. If she didn't take the opportunity to go with Wes, she might not get another.

"Thank you. Just let me tell Ella."

Lizzy wasn't at all sure about this. She and Wes had worked together amiably enough on ranch business, but it had been hard to set her feelings aside. Try as she might not to love him, she couldn't help herself. Thankfully there was no chance of the feeling being returned, or she might have been in big trouble. With that thought as assurance that she'd be all right, Lizzy went back to explain things to Ella.

"I have to cancel our practice, but you and Mary can definitely work on some of her shooting tricks." Phillip was returning with coal from the bunkhouse. "I need to let Mother know what I'm doing. If you need anything from town, just let Wes know. He'll be out here with the wagon momentarily."

Ella nodded as she continued to pack snow to create a neck for the snowman.

Lizzy made her way back to the house. She found Mother in the kitchen, packing a basket of food.

"I'm going to ride to town with Wes. I have some things I want to pick up for Christmas."

Mother looked up and smiled. "I knew Wes was planning a trip in. I'm glad you can spare the time to go. It'll do you two good to have some time together."

"I don't know about that. I was thinking you could come with us." Lizzy spoke before thinking about how she'd ever be able to hide the puppy from her mother if she came.

"Goodness no. I've too much to do." Mother glanced toward the closed door to the dining room. "You probably shouldn't linger. Jason and your uncle are working at the table, and unless you want Jason going with you . . ." She let the words trail off.

"No, I would prefer not to be in the middle of things with him and Wes."

Mother handed Lizzy the basket of food. "I was going to send this with Wes so he'd have something to eat coming and going. There's plenty there, however, for you as well." She took her daughter's free arm and pulled her toward the back door. "Hurry along, now. You know how unpredictable the weather is this time of year."

"I do. Is there anything I can get for you in town?"

Mother shook her head. "I gave Wes a list for the kitchen, so I believe we're set." She kissed Lizzy's cheek. "See if you two can't clear up the past while you have nothing better to do. It's a long drive, and maybe God's giving you this opportunity where you'll be uninterrupted."

"I'm beginning to think you had something to do with all of this." Lizzy gave her mother a stern look.

Her mother just shrugged and waved her on. "You'd best go now."

Lizzy hesitated in the doorway. She didn't want to admit she was afraid of having so much time alone with Wes. They would have to talk about something, and there was no hope of walking away should things get heated.

By the time Lizzy left the house, Wes had the wagon pulled up and ready to go. Two strong Belgian geldings stood at the ready. Wes took the basket from Lizzy and put it in the back of the wagon under the tarp.

"Thanks for the grub, Mrs. Brookstone," he said, giving a wave.

Lizzy hadn't realized her mother had followed her outside. She gave Mother a wave, then climbed into the wagon without any help. Wes jumped up the opposite side and took the lines.

"It's clouding up, but if the weather holds, we should be back later this evening." He reached under the seat, pulled out a thick wool blanket, and handed it to Lizzy. "If it turns on us, we'll stay in Miles City." He released the brake, then snapped the lines. "Let's go, boys."

"Don't take any chances," Mother called after them.

Lizzy thought the entire trip alone with Wes was a big chance, but she did want to iron out the past so they could work together better. So many times she had made a comment about something from her childhood only to see Wes grow sullen. She wanted to understand why he had been so closed off with his feelings and thoughts these last few years. She understood why things had changed between them when Clarissa was alive, but why had he all but turned away from her these last two years? Was he afraid Lizzy would demand his love? Love that he could never give?

The first few miles of the trip were spent in silence. Lizzy had a dozen questions she wanted to ask, but sitting so near Wes made rational thinking impossible. She was still in love with him. She couldn't deny that—at least not to herself.

"Looks like some weather is moving in from the west," he murmured.

Lizzy looked out across the landscape. He was right. A dark bank of clouds lined the horizon, while overhead the skies were turning gray. They drove on in silence, but Lizzy was ever mindful of the weather. She remembered her father always admonishing her to be weather-minded.

"It's not like Illinois, Lizzy. The weather up here is different, and the distance to safety is farther. You always need to keep an eye on what's happening," he would tell her.

At the halfway mark, the wind picked up, and it began to snow. Grateful for the blanket, Lizzy wrapped it around her. She thought of offering to share it with Wes but knew there was at least one more blanket beneath the seat. If he was cold, he'd wrap up.

The snow came at first in tiny flakes. The wind blew it around them in a swirl of white, but it wasn't enough to stop their journey. It wasn't long, however, before it changed to a heavier assault with larger flakes. Lizzy hoped it would pass quickly and without any serious accumulation, but as the minutes passed, it was clear this wasn't the case. She knew they were in a dangerous situation when the visibility closed to no more than a few feet in front of the team. The blowing snow blinded them to any hint of the road.

"We're gonna have to take shelter and wait it out," Wes said. "Gus's Break is just ahead. We'll stop there."

Lizzy nodded. She had already thought of that place and figured it would be their best bet. Their old ranch foreman, Gus, had discovered the spot when he and Lizzy's uncle were making a better road to Miles City from the ranch. Positioned a short distance from the river, the hill and its rocky outcroppings made a nice place to stop if a person needed to rest or fix a wagon. The men hadn't built an actual shelter, but they had stored wood for fires and kept a variety of other useful tools on hand. It wasn't much, but it was better than trying to navigate in a blizzard.

"Take the lines." Wes handed them over. "I'm gonna lead them in."

Lizzy waited as he climbed down and took hold of the horse on the right. He pulled the team forward and then off the main road. The narrow trail wasn't too bad. Wes and the ranch hands had come this way when they took calves to market just two weeks earlier. They'd tramped down the path then, stopping at the resting place on their way back.

Wes led the horses in such a way as to bring the wagon close to the rocky outcropping where the best coverage could be had. "This is good." Lizzy barely heard his voice over the wind. "Set the brake," he said, coming back to the wagon.

Lizzy did so, then handed Wes the lines. She allowed him to help her down, given the icy buildup on the wheel and hub.

"I'll get the horses settled," he said with a nod. "You get a fire going."

She went to work without a second thought. The cowboys had left wood stacked under the rock ledge. She gathered several pieces and piled them close to the wagon. She found the wooden box where the men kept a number of helpful items and pulled a tinder box with matches and oily rags from it.

She looked around for the perfect place to make the fire and decided to clear the area where the tools were stored. There was the slightest rock shelf overhead, and it would give the fire a bit of protection. The wooden box was heavy, but Lizzy took her time scooting and rocking it along the ground. Next, she took the lid of the box and used it to shovel snow. Finally, she had a nice cleared spot and set the logs in place.

Despite the heavy snow, Lizzy soon had a decent fire going. Wes had positioned the wagon in just the right place, giving them protection from two sides, thanks to the way the hill was hollowed out. The wagon would block the wind from a third direction, and with the help of the tarp, they would do well enough.

While Wes finished with the horses, Lizzy went to the wagon and took out the basket of food. She placed it under the wagon not far from the fire. She returned to retrieve the blankets and a length of rope. Under the blankets was Wesley's rifle, so she brought that as well. It'd be good to have in case there was any trouble, although Lizzy couldn't imagine there would be. Not many folks were brave enough to endure the weather, and this road was only used to get from the ranch to the main road heading into town. She didn't anticipate anyone passing by.

Once she had gathered their provisions, Lizzy began to wonder what had happened to Wes. Icy snow stung her eyes, and she wiped her gloved hand over her face to clear her vision. She couldn't even see ten feet in front of her. The wind howled in her ears.

"Wes?" she called and pulled her hat down tighter.

Without warning, he appeared at her side. "Untie the tarp from the other side."

Lizzy did as he instructed despite her dislike of being ordered around. At a time like this, it would have been foolish to refuse. She unfastened the tarp ties and waited as Wes pulled the loosened edge over the wagon on the opposite side.

Seeing what he had in mind as he picked up some rocks, Lizzy quickly joined in without him having to say a word. They had to fight the wind, but eventually they managed a little lean-to tent. When it was complete, he crawled under and pushed out the snow as best he could. With that done, he spread one of the blankets on the ground under the tarp and motioned Lizzy inside.

"This should serve us pretty well," Wes said, stretching his legs just outside of the lean-to to knock the snow from his boots. "Fire looks good."

"I decided to move the box so I could make the fire there. It has a little more protection."

"Good thinking."

Lizzy was glad he was pleased. "I brought the basket. Oh, your rifle too." She motioned to where they sat just under the wagon.

"I'll get the coffeepot out of the box and melt some snow. Cookie told me he had the boys refill the coffee tin. You want some?"

"Yes, please." She was starting to shiver and wrapped the other blanket around her body.

Half an hour later, she sat nursing steaming coffee while the storm raged on. Until that moment, Wes had kept himself busy with one thing or another, but now he sat down with his own tin cup and gave her an awkward smile.

"Sure glad Gus and Oliver set this place up."

"It would have been even nicer if they had just built a range shack."

Wes chuckled and nodded. "That it would."

"Would you like something to eat? I've taken an inventory, and Mother has enough food here to feed an army."

"Food sounds good."

Lizzy pulled sandwiches from the basket. "They look like ham and cheese," she said, handing one to Wes. "There's more if you need it."

For some time they sat in silence, eating and drinking. Wes refilled their cups once, then accepted another sandwich and went back to concentrating on his food. Lizzy wondered how she could open the conversation between them, but she didn't have to wonder for long.

"Look, there's something I've been wanting to say for some time." Wes turned his cup in his gloved hands but didn't look up. "I've been kind of hard on you since you returned. I didn't set out to be that way, and I want to apologize. I've had a lot on my mind, what with Phillip showing up and all."

"He's a nice man. I know you've spent many years worrying about where he was. I'm glad he showed up." She was afraid to make too much of the apology and kept the focus on Phillip.

Wes glanced up. "Me too, but he's still full of trouble. He likes to drink."

She could see pain in Wesley's eyes and hear the regret in his voice. "He and Uncle Oliver have much in common, then. Mother says he's still sneaking drinks, although she's searched in vain for his supply."

Wes didn't speak, but neither did he look away. Lizzy wanted nothing more than to touch him but knew that was completely un-called for. Another awkward silence fell between them. Why couldn't she just say what was on her heart?

"I'm glad you've decided to quit the show," Wes said.

The show had long been a bone of contention between them. Wes didn't like her risking her life to entertain. Lizzy, truth be told, was ready to leave it all behind—well, almost.

"I told them I'd stay for one more year." She sipped her coffee.

"I heard that, but I thought you were training Ella to be your replacement."

This time it was Lizzy's turn to avert her gaze. "I gave a promise."

"To Adler?" Wes's tone was full of sarcasm.

Lizzy met his questioning gaze. "Yes, to him and to Uncle Oliver. Mary too, if you must know. She wants to find out what happened to her brother."

"Maybe so, but it seems to me that Adler is the one trying to keep you close."

"Well, no one else wants my company." Her voice was taking on a shrewish edge, and Lizzy forced herself to calm down. "Why is it of any interest to you, anyway? You've made it perfectly clear that you don't care anything about me." Why had she said that? She didn't want him thinking she was looking to win his love. Even if she wanted exactly that.

"Don't care? Are you serious? That's why I don't want you to return to trick riding. I care very much about you. I've always cared, Lizzy."

"So much that you married the first woman who came along just to get away from me." Lizzy immediately regretted her words. She put the cup to her lips but silently wished the earth would open up and swallow her whole. This wasn't how she wanted to start a discussion about Clarissa.

"She was alone in the world," he countered. "Her folks were dead, and she had no one, Lizzy. She would have been thrown to the wolves. You know that as well as anyone. A woman all alone in the world doesn't have a lot of options."

Lizzy shook her head. "She wasn't your responsibility, Wes. Mother and Father would have helped her if you'd told them. You knew that. You also knew how I felt about you." She hesitated to use the word *love*, but she was certain he still remembered her declaration.

"You were the boss's daughter and just a kid."

"I was eighteen, and my father loved you

like a son. He would have been happy to have you as one." She put down her empty cup, then pulled the blanket tight around her.

"I never meant to hurt you, Lizzy. I just didn't see things the same way." He turned and studied her for a moment. "By the time I realized . . ." He fell silent, as if he'd said too much.

"What happened to us, Wes? We were good friends—even after . . ." She hadn't meant to ask the question aloud, but now that she had, she knew it was the right thing to do. "I got past you marrying Clarissa, and I thought we had a good understanding. But you've hardly spoken to me since she died."

He sighed and poured himself another cup of coffee. He raised the pot in her direction, but Lizzy shook her head. She didn't want coffee. She wanted answers.

She felt awash in guilt. Guilt for something she didn't even understand. "What did I do wrong?"

His expression softened. "You didn't do anything. Although I did try to blame you."

She could see the regret in his expression. "Blame me for what?"

"Clarissa's death."

Her mouth dropped open. "You blamed me? But why? As I understand it, she punctured her lung when she fell from her horse.

Complications set in, and she died several days later."

"Yes, that's how it happened." Wesley's expression turned grim. "But you were the reason she was on that horse and the reason she fell. At least that's what I let myself believe. In truth, she was desperately trying to get my attention. It was easier to blame you. At least then I wasn't . . . I wasn't . . ." He heaved a sigh.

Lizzy had never heard anything about this. "You said I was the reason she was on that horse and fell. How can you say that?"

For several minutes he said nothing. Lizzy wasn't sure he was going to answer her. She'd never in her life imagined that he blamed her for Clarissa's death. Did others?

"Lizzy, I don't know what to say. The truth is, I didn't love Clarissa as I should have. I married her because she was alone and needed someone to protect her and not go on abusing her like her drunk father always did. I felt sorry for her, and she knew it. She wasn't in love with me either, but we both thought we could find love once we were married. It just didn't work that way. She was jealous. All the time she was jealous . . . of you."

"Of me?" Lizzy thought of the pretty blond-haired woman. "But why?"

He rubbed his jaw and drew in a deep

breath. "Because she knew how much I cared about you. For some reason, she thought it had to do with your trick riding. She figured if she started doing tricks on horseback that I'd care more about her than you."

"She tried trick riding?" Lizzy's eyes narrowed. "I never knew that."

"She convinced herself that my feelings for you were wrapped up in trick riding. That's why she fell from the horse. She was trying to do some sort of stunt. She lost her grip and slipped under the horse."

"I don't know what to say. No one ever told me."

"Because I didn't tell anyone what really happened. I figured it was better that way. I would have had a bad time trying to explain why my wife was performing stunts to impress me."

"I'm really sorry, Wes." Lizzy had never thought it possible that Clarissa had been jealous of her relationship with him. Lizzy had tried hard to bury her feelings for him after learning he was married. She respected the sanctity of marriage. God had joined them together, and while the truth of that devastated Lizzy, she hadn't wanted to cause Clarissa any pain. Lizzy's own pain had been enough.

The wind died down, and everything suddenly seemed quiet. Lizzy tried to think of what she could say or do. She couldn't even imagine Clarissa trying to do stunts. She wasn't at all athletic and, in fact, had a rather weak constitution.

"Look, Lizzy, I'm sorry for the way I've acted. It was never your fault. I know that. I felt terrible that I couldn't make her happy. I tried. I really did. I offered to pack us up and leave, but she didn't want that either. I'm not sure anything I could have said or done would have made her happy."

"Maybe that's just it, Wes. She had to find happiness for herself. Nobody can create it for you."

"Just the same, when she died, I felt like it was my fault. I kept hearing her tell me over and over that one day I would love her as much as I did you, because she was going to do all the things you did. When she died, I guess my guilt made me keep you at arm's length. I figured it was the price I had to pay."

Lizzy startled at his words. Had he loved her then? Did he still? She couldn't ask him for fear of the answer. If he told her he didn't love her—could never love her again—it would be more than she could bear.

But you're determined not to love him or ever marry, she tried to reason with herself. *It shouldn't matter what he thinks or feels now.*

You know the dangers of caring too much. You know the pain that will inevitably come.

But I can hardly go through life without friends.

Lizzy wrestled her thoughts in silence. The need for people to care about her argued with the part of her determined never again to feel the pain that came with loss.

After a long time, she gave up the fight. "Wes, can we start again? Can we go back to being friends?" The words seemed to echo around them.

He gave her a sad smile. "We've always been friends, Lizzy. Forgive me for letting my problems come between us."

She felt a weight taken from her. "Of course." Her voice barely sounded. "Forgive me for whatever part I had in all of this. Maybe I should have done more to make her feel a part of our friendship, done more to befriend her."

"It was never your fault, Lizzy. It was just easier to blame you than accept my role." He got to his feet. "I think the weather is clearing. We should push on and see if we can't get to town."

She crawled out from under the tarp and let the blanket drop. "I'll take care of all this. You get the horses."

For a moment he looked at her as if he

might say something more. But then, without another word, he crawled out and was gone.

She watched him go, and for the first time she understood something about Wesley that she'd never known. He had sacrificed himself and his happiness for Clarissa's safety and well-being. At eighteen, Lizzy had been too worried about her own feelings to really understand. Wes had come home married, and it had devastated her. She couldn't believe anyone would marry for less than love, and it wasn't until years later that she'd overheard her mother and father speak of Wes's sad situation. She had never imagined people married without being madly in love. But this knowledge had only hurt Lizzy more. Mother had said he married Clarissa because she needed him. Well, Lizzy needed him too. If only she had understood then what she knew now. Wes had seen the need and given up everything to save Clarissa from a worse fate. The truth only made her love him more.

A warning went off in her head. *If you love him more, it will only serve to hurt you more.* She frowned. How could she rid herself of her feelings and protect her heart? It wasn't Wesley's fault that she felt as she did. For so long she'd been angry because he refused to return her feelings, but now . . .

"It would serve me right." She began

gathering their things. How ironic it would be if Wes fell in love with her. Now that she was determined to love no one.

Wes nearly sighed in relief when they finally reached Miles City. The road hadn't been easy. Parts of it were drifted high with snow. The team was strong, however, and Wes had simply urged them on when the way was rough. The hardest part had been keeping to the road, since it and the land around them looked much the same.

The sun was nearly gone from the sky before they could see the town in the distance. Now, as they made their way down Main Street, most of the stores were closed, and the only places that showed signs of life were the saloons.

"Let's check with Clem and Eva Truman. I'm sure they'll let us stay at their place and save us the fee of a hotel," Wes said, guiding the horses in the direction of the older couple's house. The streets were in fairly good condition, making their journey to the other side of town easy.

"I haven't seen them in ages." Lizzy stretched. "I sure hope Mother won't worry about us."

"Can't be helped if she does. She knows that we're pretty capable." Wes looked at

Lizzy and gave her a slight smile. "I'm sure she'll be fine. We'll head out first thing in the morning if the weather looks good."

He brought the team to a halt in front of a small clapboard house. The place was lit up, leaving little doubt that Clem and Eva were home. "Why don't you go talk to them, and I'll get the team put up."

Lizzy nodded and jumped down from the wagon. As she headed up the walkway, Wes moved the horses down the street and back toward the livery. He climbed down, feeling tired and frozen. He made arrangements for the horses, then grabbed the basket of food from the back of the wagon along with his rifle and headed back to the Trumans'.

Wes thought back on his conversation with Lizzy. He'd never been honest with anyone about Clarissa's death. He hadn't even allowed himself to think about it. He'd been unable to bear the guilt, and it had been easier to tell himself it was Lizzy's fault. Even though he'd never really believed that.

He walked on, grateful that it hadn't snowed as much here. Despite the cold, he wanted to take his time and sort through his thoughts. Lizzy had asked if they could go back to being friends, but Wes knew now that he wanted so much more. He loved Lizzy.

When had his feelings for her changed

from that of a watchful big brother to one of romantic intentions? He thought back to when she'd first come back to the ranch after Clarissa's death. That was when it happened. He remembered seeing her standing in the barn, talking to one of the hands. In that moment, he had wanted nothing more than to take her in his arms and hold her. At the time, those feelings had only made him feel guiltier. He already knew that his friendship with Lizzy had made Clarissa feel the need to show off. Admitting his feelings for Lizzy was akin to having a hand in his wife's death.

Staring up at the Trumans' house, Wes felt a sense of sorrow as he remembered Clarissa just before she'd passed. He'd knelt at her bedside and held her hand.

"You need to fight, Clarissa. Fight to stay alive."

"There's no fight in me, Wes." She strained to breathe, and the sound of it caught in the back of her throat. The wheezy gasp chilled him to the bone. "There's never . . . been . . . any fight in me." She shook her head. "I'm so sorry, Wes. I did . . . you wrong."

"No," he tried to assure her. "We did what we had to in order to keep you safe."

"Not a good reason . . . to marry." She closed her eyes, and for a moment Wes thought she was gone. "You always belonged . . . with her. I knew that . . . but . . . didn't care."

Wes had never denied that he and Lizzy had a special connection, a relationship that went far beyond anything he had with Clarissa. But he never felt he belonged with Lizzy. She was just a carefree and adventurous child. She hadn't needed him like Clarissa had. Lizzy had a family who loved and protected her. Clarissa had endured beatings and starvation. She had no one. Wesley had truly believed that he was her savior.

He glanced heavenward. "Forgive me, Lord. You were the only Savior she needed, but I thought I could do the job." He heard Lizzy's laugh and looked at the house. His heart pounded harder at the full understanding that he wanted more than friendship with Lizzy. "I've wasted a lot of time, Lord, and I'm gonna need Your help if I'm ever gonna make this right."

⊰⋆⊱ EIGHTEEN ⊰⋆⊱

Lizzy opened her eyes and stretched. The intensity of the sun as it shone through the window actually made her feel hot.

She pushed off the heavy quilts Eva Truman had given her the night before and stretched again. She might have stayed there for a long while if not for all they needed to do that morning. That, along with having spent the night in town when Mother expected them home, added a sense of urgency.

Lizzy dressed and made her way downstairs, where she found Wes reading the paper in front of the fire. She paused for a moment, just watching him—imagining they were married and this was their home.

"Finally decide to wake up?" he asked, shaking her from her thoughts.

Lizzy hid her embarrassment as best she could and shrugged. "I guess I was tired. Where's Eva?"

He put the paper aside. "She had to go to her sewing circle, and Clem is at work."

Lizzy looked around the room for a clock. "What time is it?"

"Nine thirty."

"I'm sorry. I haven't slept that long in years." She went to the door to collect her boots. "We'd best hurry, or we won't get home at a decent hour."

"You can take the time to eat your breakfast. Eva kept it in the warmer on the stove."

She started to protest but realized she was starving. Her stomach even rumbled as if to remind her. "It won't take me but a minute."

After eating, Lizzy made her way to the store with Wes. They spent a minimal amount of time shopping, then went to retrieve the collie pup for Lizzy's mother.

"He's precious." Lizzy giggled like a little girl as the puppy squirmed in her arms and licked all over her face. He was all legs and nose, with the softest fur Lizzy had ever felt.

"I have a crate for you to put him in for the ride home," Mr. Daniels, Barney's father, said. "I'll put it in the back of your wagon."

"I'll give you a hand," Wes said, following him outside.

Lizzy looked at Mrs. Daniels and laughed. "I think he will cheer Mother considerably."

Barney's mother nodded. "We were sure sorry to hear about your pa's passing. Barney brought the news when the train arrived with the casket. It was a real surprise. Surprising too that you and your mother didn't come with it."

"We wanted to, but Father made us promise to finish out the show." Lizzy stroked the pup until he settled in her arms. She wanted to be angry at Mrs. Daniels's comment but knew it was a situation most people wouldn't understand.

"Will you have a funeral now that you're back?"

Lizzy frowned. She and Mother hadn't talked about it. "I honestly don't know. I suppose that will be up to Mother. We had a service with the show folk."

"Well, that's good. I know Wes arranged for the preacher to come out to the ranch when he was buried."

Lizzy hadn't known that, but then, she hadn't been willing to speak about her father and his death. She squared her shoulders and nodded.

"We're all ready to go," Wes announced as he and Mr. Daniels returned.

Lizzy handed Wes the puppy, which only excited the animal once again. "I have your five dollars." She reached into her pocket and retrieved the cash. "I believe that was the asking price for the puppy."

"I'd nearly forgotten," Mrs. Daniels said, taking the money. "Most of the others were sold off before Thanksgiving. Barney's enjoyed working with this little fella. Calls him Pup, but I know your mama will come up with another name."

"I'm sure she will, and I'm sure she'll appreciate all that Barney has taught him. This is going to make a wonderful surprise."

She and Wes made their way to the wagon. Wes held the puppy while Lizzy climbed up, then handed him over. Lizzy placed him in the crate. There was plenty of straw at the bottom so the puppy could snuggle down. Unfortunately, all he did was whine and bark in protest.

"That's going to be annoying," Wes muttered, taking up the lines. He gave them a snap. "Let's go home, boys."

They were on their way out of town when the sheriff flagged them down. Lizzy couldn't imagine what he wanted, but they had little choice but to hear him out.

"Wes, you got a few minutes?"

"Not many. We got stuck here overnight and need to get back to the ranch."

The sheriff frowned. "It won't take long. Just thought you could collect your brother."

"Phillip is here?"

"'Fraid so. He came riding in during the storm, lookin' for you two. Said Mrs. Brookstone sent him to make sure you weren't broke down in the weather."

"He must have ridden right past us." Lizzy could see by the way Wes clenched his jaw that he wasn't happy about this.

He set the brake and handed the lines to Lizzy. "I'll be right back."

She sat and waited. She wondered what had happened. What had Phillip done to get himself thrown in jail? Then she remembered what Wes had said about Phillip drinking.

Had he gotten drunk and started brawling? A lot of men did.

Wes returned with Phillip behind him. Wes pointed toward the livery. "Your horse and gear are down there. Do you have any money left to pay them?"

"No." Phillip's head was down and his voice was barely audible.

Wesley dug into his pocket and handed Phillip some change. "Go pay the bill and collect your things. I'll come park out front. You can tie your horse to the wagon and ride in back."

Phillip took off without a word, and Wesley said nothing as he climbed aboard and snatched the lines from Lizzy. He released the brake and turned the wagon around to head back to the livery.

"I'm sorry, Wes. Whatever's going on, I'm really sorry."

Wes shook his head. "He was drunk and disorderly and got himself thrown in jail. Luckily just to sleep it off. No one pressed charges against him."

"Well, at least that's good."

"None of this is good." He turned to her. "None of it."

The ride home was long and silent except for the constant displeasure of the puppy. Lizzy finally took pity on him and took him from the crate. The collie settled down in her arms and went to sleep almost immediately.

Phillip also slept most of the way, and Wes was in no mood to discuss anything. Lizzy tried a couple of times to engage him in conversation, but he made it clear that he wanted no part of it. Finally, she stopped trying. When the wind picked up, she snuggled the pup inside her coat and wished there were somewhere she could hide away as well. She hated the silence and being stuck with only her thoughts to ponder.

When they finally reached the house, it was late afternoon. Mother was the first to greet them. Her expression was filled with relief.

"I'm so glad you're home safe. When it came up with such a howling wind and snow, I sent Phillip to find you and warn you that it was coming your way. I figured he could outrun it, since it was just starting up. I guess he found you all right." She nodded to Phillip, who was climbing off the back of the wagon.

"More like we found him," Wes muttered.

"What?" Mother asked.

Lizzy shook her head. "Never mind." The puppy squirmed inside her coat. "I have something for you. It's your Christmas present, but it can't wait."

Mother gave her a strange look. "What

do you mean? We always wait for Christmas morning."

"I know, but I would have a hard time hiding this present." Lizzy opened her coat to reveal the puppy. A long nose came first and then the rest of his head. The collie gave a little yip to announce himself.

Mother's expression changed from confusion to absolute delight. "Oh, my!"

"You've talked about getting a dog once you were back on the ranch for good. I saw the advertisement in town when we came home. The Daniels family had a litter and held one for you so I could give it to you for Christmas." Lizzy handed the squirming pup down to her mother, then jumped off the wagon.

Mother laughed as the dog wiggled and began licking her face. "He's perfect. Thank you so much."

"What will you call him?" Lizzy asked. "Barney Daniels has been working with him to obey a few commands. He's just been calling him Pup."

"I don't know what I'll call him." Mother released the puppy and let him explore the ground around them. He didn't seem to know what to think of the snow. "I guess I'll have to ponder that awhile and see what name fits him best."

Lizzy embraced her mother and planted

a kiss on her cheek. "I hope he'll make you feel a little less lonely."

Mother nodded. "I'm sure he will." She hugged Lizzy close. "Thank you. I already know we'll be the best of friends."

———◆※◆———

Christmas morning was spent in the company of the entire staff and household guests. Mother had arranged gifts for everyone, even the newest ranch hands. She made certain that each man had a new pair of work gloves and two pairs of wool socks, as well as a bevy of baked goods that she and Ella and Mary had worked on while Lizzy was busy with ranch business.

Lizzy had gifted Mary and Ella with bottles of perfume and gave Jason and her uncle monogramed handkerchiefs. For Wesley, she had labored over the thought of a gift that wouldn't be too personal, but just personal enough to remind him of her. She settled on a pocket watch and had his named engraved on it. It seemed to please him. He presented her with a beautiful leather-bound volume of Longfellow's poems. It touched her deeply.

"Your Mother made the bookmark, but I put it in its place," Wes told her.

Lizzy immediately wanted to look at the passage he'd marked, but Jason spoke up.

"If I might," he said, pulling a slender box from his jacket pocket, "I have a gift for Lizzy as well."

Lizzy couldn't hide her surprise. Jason had gifted no one but Mother, and to her he gave a lovely music box. He told them he'd purchased a few things while in Kansas City, knowing he would spend the winter at the ranch.

"When I purchased your mother's present, I saw this and couldn't refrain from buying it. You might think it a bit extravagant, but I felt it so perfect for you, especially given my thoughts for the future."

Lizzy took the box and opened it. She gasped at the sight of a jeweled necklace. A large yellow topaz was set in gold and hung on a delicate gold chain.

She looked up to find Jason grinning from ear to ear. "I thought it complemented your eyes and hair. When I saw it, I knew you should have it."

"I, ah, I don't know what to say." Lizzy closed the lid. "It's much too expensive, and I cannot accept it." She looked to her mother for support.

Mother came forward and took the box to examine the necklace. Lizzy stepped back and caught sight of Wes across the room. His eyes were narrowed and his brow furrowed.

He put down his plate of food and left the house. Lizzy wanted to go after him but had no idea what she'd say to him. She thought she'd made it very clear to Jason that she had no interest in becoming more than friends, but his gift clearly suggested he still wanted things to be otherwise.

"Lizzy's quite right, Mr. Adler." Mother smiled and replaced the lid on the box before handing it back to him. "It's a beautiful necklace, but she couldn't possibly accept it."

Jason looked around the room. "It was only a token . . . a gesture of my appreciation that she is staying on with the show another year. I meant nothing else."

"Still, it's a very expensive and personal item." Mother took Jason's arm and patted his sleeve. "You were very thoughtful, but please understand. I cannot allow her to accept it."

The room fell silent, and Lizzy held her breath. If Jason protested, she feared it would spoil the Christmas spirit. The situation had already driven Wesley from the house.

Mother, however, seemed completely at ease. "Now, I want everyone to come with us to the barn. I have one final gift for Lizzy. It was something her father and I planned."

Lizzy felt her chest tighten. Father had been part of this gift. How wonderful. She could almost feel him at her side. She followed her mother to the barn, not even bothering to put on her coat. The winter chill didn't bother her at all. The thought of her father having planned this gift with Mother left her warm.

By the time they reached the barn, Lizzy was giddy with excitement. She knew the gift must be a horse. When her eyes adjusted to the dimmer light, she could see that she was right. Wesley stood holding the halter of a feisty buckskin colt. Phillip was nearby just in case Wes needed help.

"Merry Christmas, Lizzy dear," Mother said. "This fella was born earlier this year. When your father first saw him, he told me that he knew you should have him."

"He's beautiful." Lizzy stepped forward for a closer inspection. Her gaze met Wesley's, and she smiled. "I suppose you were in on this too."

He smiled, seeming to have forgotten the earlier matter. "I was with your father when he purchased him last January. He wasn't even a month old but was already the finest quarter horse we'd ever seen."

She marveled at the beauty of the colt. He was skittish, but Lizzy spoke softly. "It's all right, little fella. We're going to be good friends, I just know it." She looked at Wes. "Where did you get him?"

"Over in Billings. Remember last winter just after Christmas when we made that trip?"

"Yes. I wanted to go but had a cold and felt so lousy that Mother kept me in bed for a week." The colt's coat was the color of tanned deer hide, and his mane and tail as well as the lower half of his legs were black. He was regal in his stance, almost as if he knew how fine he was.

"I love him, and I love that you have kept this surprise from me." Lizzy gently touched the colt's black muzzle. She glanced at Wes and saw the pleasure he took from her joy. She'd never wanted to kiss him more than in that moment.

"He is a magnificent animal," Jason said. "What will you call him?"

Lizzy didn't even acknowledge him. Instead she offered Wes a smile. "Emerson. For Ralph Waldo Emerson."

Wesley shifted his grip on the halter. "I suggest you keep him for breeding." The colt was clearly getting agitated. "For now, however, I think I'd better put him back in the pen. He's going to start kicking up his heels."

"And I think we should go back to the house for more hot chocolate and breakfast," Mother declared.

Lizzy went to her and linked their arms together. "I quite agree."

The day passed in merriments. They sang Christmas carols, played games, and ate until they could hold no more. Lizzy wasn't at all sorry, however, when it was time to go to bed. She was exhausted from the day and fighting to keep her emotions in check. The gift of the colt had overwhelmed her. Knowing her mother and father had planned it since early in the year truly touched her heart.

Standing at her bedroom window, Lizzy gazed out into the dark night. "I miss you so much, Father. But today, it almost felt as if you were here with us." She drew a deep breath and pulled the curtains. She wasn't going to let her feelings take charge. She needed to be strong.

She walked to her bed and saw the book of poetry Wes had given her. She crawled into bed and snuggled under the covers before opening it to the place Wes had marked.

"'Memories,'" she read aloud, then continued in silence.

> Oft I remember those whom I have
>   known
> In other days, to whom my heart was
>   led
> As by a magnet, and who are not dead,
> But absent, and their memories over-
>   grown

With other thoughts and troubles of
  my own,
As graves with grasses are, and at
  their head
The stone with moss and lichens so
  o'erspread,
Nothing is legible but the name alone.
And is it so with them? After long
  years,
Do they remember me in the same
  way,
And is the memory pleasant as to
  me?
I fear to ask; yet wherefore are my
  fears?
Pleasures, like flowers, may wither
  and decay,
And yet the root perennial may be.

Something inside her stirred to life despite her desperate attempt to bury her heart. It wasn't really a declaration of love, but it was more than she'd had before. Dare she hope that love might still grow between them? Did she want it to?

She thought of the painful sorrow her mother had experienced losing her husband. Lizzy had always admired the deep love her parents had for each other. They always seemed so happy in each other's company. No matter how bad the situation, they always had each other. Now Mother was alone. Even Lizzy's company couldn't keep her from feeling Father's absence.

"How could I bear it if something happened to Wes?"

She tucked the book under her pillow and blew out the lamp. Settling back on her pillow, Lizzy stared out into the dark, letting her eyes adjust.

The muffled sound of her mother sobbing filtered through the walls. This was her first Christmas without Lizzy's father. Lizzy ached for her—wished she could go to her and take the pain from her so that Mother could have a decent night's sleep.

"Please, Lord, take away her pain. Help her to endure this sad time. I don't know how to help her, but I would give my life to make things right again."

Tears dampened Lizzy's eyes, but she refused to cry. She wiped her face with the sleeve of her nightgown and pulled the thick quilt up over her head. Then she did likewise with her pillow to block out the sounds. To block it all out so that she didn't have to feel anything.

Mary Reichert sat opposite Zeb and Thomas at one of the bunkhouse tables. She'd asked specifically to speak with them, knowing they had taken August under their wing and taught him what they could about working for the Brookstone show.

"Did he say anything to either of you when he came back to the train for the liniment that night?"

"Said there was some trouble going on at the farm," Zeb replied before taking a long drink of coffee.

Thomas nodded and swirled the contents of his mug. "Some fella there accused him of snooping around, and when August tried to tell him all he wanted was liniment, the man threatened him."

Mary perked up. "Threatened him?"

Thomas shrugged and put down the cup. "Yeah, told August he'd have to answer to Mr. Fleming if it happened again."

Her shoulders slumped. "But he didn't threaten August with physical harm?"

"Not that he said. Why all the questions, Miss Mary?"

"I think someone did my brother harm. I don't think he'd ever go near the Fleming colts, especially not after being warned about snooping. August wasn't the kind to cause problems. He told Lizzy what happened only because he wanted to make sure Mr. Brookstone knew where he'd gone when he left the farm. He wasn't seeking retribution for being driven out of the stable. I doubt he would have mentioned it at all if he hadn't been worried about his absence being noted."

"That seems about right," Zeb said. "Never knew that boy to buck authority."

"He wouldn't have. Nor would he have gone into tight quarters with those green colts if he hadn't been asked to. And if he was asked to, then someone at Fleming Farm did the asking—knowing full well the danger."

"Did anyone see him gettin' trampled by those colts?" Thomas asked.

Mary shook her head. "I don't think so. It's unclear. From what Mr. Adler recalls, someone said August was found that way—already dead—in the pen of the colts." She felt the words stick in her throat and found it impossible to go on without dissolving into tears. Getting to her feet, Mary forced a smile. "Thank you for answering my questions. If you think of anything else, please let me know. I think for now it's best I go practice my shooting."

"Would you like some help with the targets?" Thomas asked, pushing back from the table.

"No. I think I'd like to be alone."

⊶⊷ NINETEEN ⊶⊷

P rince, come," Mrs. Brookstone commanded the pup. The dog had quickly learned to obey and fell into step at her feet.

"You have him eating out of your hand," Wes teased as he led them into his bunkhouse office.

"Well, it has been nearly a month, and Barney did a good job of getting him started," the older woman said with a smile. "Prince and I are good companions. I couldn't have asked for a better Christmas present."

"I'm glad." Wes knew that her spirits had been considerably brighter since receiving the dog. "Especially given that everyone plans to take off at the end of next month."

"Which brings me to the reason I asked to see you." She took a seat in front of his desk, then snapped her fingers at the pup. "Prince, sit." He instantly obeyed. Rebecca Brookstone turned her attention back to Wesley. "I want you to go with them as head wrangler."

"What?" He hadn't anticipated this idea at all.

She raised her hand. "I know you love the ranch and prefer the work here to that of the show, but I'm concerned about Lizzy."

"Is something wrong?" He tried not to sound too worried.

"No, but neither do I want there to be. Oliver has taken Mark's death quite hard. He's sober now, most of the time, but that only makes him sadder. I fear once he's on the show circuit, he'll take to the bottle again."

"And you think I can keep him from doing that?"

"I don't know, but I know you care about him. Maybe just having a friend will help him remember his priorities. Regardless, I know Lizzy will need your support. Especially if Oliver does start drinking again." She paused and lowered her gaze to her hands. "Speaking of Lizzy brings me to another aspect of my request."

Wes and Lizzy had seen little of each other since Christmas. Wes had been busy with calving season, while Lizzy had been practicing daily with Ella for hours on end. He knew from Phillip that Lizzy often came to visit Emerson, but that generally happened when Wes was tied up elsewhere.

"Jason Adler intends to marry Lizzy."

This blunt announcement brought Wes back to the present. He knew Adler's intentions. They had been clear from the moment he first arrived at the ranch. "I know."

"Lizzy isn't in love with him and has

made it clear that she has no desire to marry him. Still he pursues her, and I fear that once they're on the road, he will continue to do so. I think Jason is a nice enough young man, but with the plans he has to take the show to England, I fear his persistence might wear Lizzy down. And that, combined with my concerns about what Oliver will do . . . well, it might leave Lizzy vulnerable."

"So vulnerable she'd marry a man she didn't love?"

Mrs. Brookstone shrugged. "Who can say? Lizzy hasn't been herself since Mark died. I just feel that if you were there for her, it would make all the difference in the world. I know you love her, Wes."

He wasn't ready to admit to his feelings aloud. So far he'd done good just to sort them out for himself.

"I'm not pressing you to admit your feelings," Mrs. Brookstone continued, fixing Wes with an understanding gaze. "That should be shared between you and Lizzy first. I just felt that I needed to speak to you about this while Oliver and Jason were gone, making final arrangements for the show."

The two men had taken off the previous week for Chicago. They would soon be back, however, and it wouldn't be long before the rest of the performers showed up to start their daily practice runs for the show's new routines.

"I have no idea what Oliver's condition will be when he returns. I hope he will refrain from drink, but who can say. I've already told Oliver that I think he should ask you to come on board. Jason has trimmed the number of men down considerably, and I fear that if you aren't there, things may take a turn for the worse. Jason doesn't know how much work it is to keep those animals in shape for their performances."

"I don't know why Adler thinks he knows better than Mark and Oliver when it comes to the show."

"Moneywise, I'm sure he will manage things better," the older woman assured him. "I truly believe Jason to be a good man with the show's best interests at heart. But I agree with you where the animals and their care are concerned. Jason is used to handling book-keeping, and I'm not sure he realizes the degree of work that goes into traveling with so many animals. But you do. You helped in the early years, and you know how difficult things can get."

"I do, and I know how pushy Adler is with Lizzy."

"So you'll do it?" Her voice was hopeful.

Wes couldn't give her an answer. Not at

that moment. He needed time to think. Maybe he could talk Lizzy into staying home. That would solve a lot.

"Who will run the ranch?" he asked.

"I will. Along with Sandy and Cookie and whoever else you tell me is competent enough to fill in for you. I can handle the bookwork, and the men can tell me what they need. We've got a good crew here—men who've been at this long enough to know what's expected and needed. And since Jason has eliminated jobs for some of the older men, they can stay on here and help. I can't bring myself to put them out completely."

Wes nodded. He'd hoped that would be the case. "I need to think on it, Mrs. Brookstone. I need to sit down with Oliver too. I think it ought to be his idea, asking me to come along. Don't you?"

She considered this for a moment, then nodded. "You're right, and I know he does intend to speak to you about it, so I'll leave it alone." She got to her feet. "Thank you for hearing me out. Prince, come." The pup jumped up and started wagging his tail as if they were about to head off on a grand adventure. "I don't usually advise men to think with their hearts, but I hope this time you will—at least in part." She gave Wes a smile, then left him to ponder all they'd discussed.

322

Since leaving Kentucky, Ella had awoken every morning concerned that her father and former fiancé would show up at the Brookstone ranch and demand her return. That fear overshadowed everything, even the longing she felt to see her mother again. But today was her twenty-first birthday, and Ella finally felt a sense of relief. She was certain now that no matter what else happened, she was safe from having to marry Jefferson Spiby. Safe from having to return home.

What continued to haunt her, however, was the knowledge that she knew what had happened to August Reichert. At least in part. She knew her father and Jefferson were responsible, and she still couldn't keep the nightmares at bay.

Every day she prayed for wisdom. Today was no exception. She opened her Bible to pick up her daily reading. She had marked her spot at Ephesians five and began to read. Verses fourteen through seventeen drew her attention.

Wherefore he saith, Awake thou that sleepest, and arise from the dead, and Christ shall give thee light. See then that ye walk circumspectly, not as fools, but as wise, redeeming the time, because the days are evil. Wherefore be ye not un-wise, but understanding what the will of the Lord is.

She wanted to walk in wisdom—to re-deem the time. Most of all, she wanted to understand what the will of the Lord was for her life.

"What should I do, Lord? What is Your will for me?" she prayed aloud.

Truth. The word seemed to echo in her soul. *Truth.*

She looked at the Bible verses again. *Wherefore be ye not unwise, but understanding what the will of the Lord is.* Ella bit her lower lip. Truth. She needed to tell the truth. That was God's will for her. She remembered hear-ing a sermon in their Kentucky church in which the pastor said that the truth would set you free.

"It could also cause the Brookstones to put me from this house and their company."

"Hey, Ella, are you ready?" Mary called from the other side of her bedroom door.

Ella frowned. "I'm getting dressed." She put the Bible aside and gathered her clothes. "I'll be right there."

She quickly combed and braided her hair, then threw off her nightgown, shivering from the chill of the morning. Never had she dressed so fast. She was still shivering when she made her way downstairs to breakfast. Everyone else was already seated and awaiting her arrival.

She offered them a weak smile. "Sorry I'm late. I was reading my Bible."

"Never have to be sorry for that," Oliver Brookstone said, smiling. He looked tired, but given he and Jason had just returned from Chicago, it was no wonder. "I'll share the verses I read this morning and then pray for our meal."

Ella settled into her chair. She was seated between Mary and Mrs. Brookstone and gave each a smile and nod while Mr. Brookstone read from the Psalms. After he prayed, Mrs. Brookstone reached for Ella's hand and gave it a squeeze. "Happy birthday, Ella."

The others joined in, wishing her well for the day with the promise of cake that evening. Mrs. Brookstone had even gone to the trouble to make Ella's favorite—pound cake.

She couldn't help but feel safe and loved. These people cared more about her well-being and happiness than her own family did. How could she not give them the truth?

Going through her paces later that day while Mary and Lizzy watched, Ella pondered how she would come clean and tell Mary what she knew. The truth would be hard to hear, but Ella knew it would help her friend move forward. At least she hoped it would. A part of her feared it would only cause Mary more grief. After all, few would ever believe that George Fleming and Jefferson Spiby had committed murder. And those who did believe it would be too afraid to do anything.

Ella felt a tightness in her chest. She loved the life she had here with the Brookstones. She had worked harder than she'd ever worked at home, but there was also a greater satisfaction in her accomplishments. She'd grown stronger in the last few months and now had little trouble saddling her own mounts or performing the various tricks Lizzy gave her to try. She'd even managed to renew her love of Roman riding using the Brookstones' horses. All in all, she was delighted with the way her life had turned out. What if the truth changed all of that?

"It's not like I know exactly what happened," she whispered to Pepper as she leaned low over his neck. She saw Lizzy and Mary at the other end of the arena. She liked both women very much and didn't want to lose their friendship or her place in the show by admitting what she knew.

Nothing I say will bring back her brother.

That thought constantly stayed at the forefront of Ella's mind. Confessing wouldn't change the fact that August Reichert was dead, nor did she believe it would make a difference in seeing justice done for him.

"You're better at those Cossack drags than I am," Lizzy declared as Ella brought Pepper to a stop in front of her and Mary.

Ella slid off the horse and gave him a generous hug. "He's such a good horse. He always anticipates my every move." She glanced at Mary and noted that she was wiping her eyes with her handkerchief.

Lizzy's gaze followed hers. "Mary's having a rough day. She's talked to everyone who was with us on the show, but nobody has any answers for her regarding August."

Guilt washed over Ella in waves. "Would it matter so much if she knew what really happened?" Her voice was barely a whisper, but despite that, Mary's head snapped up.

"It would matter a great deal." Mary came to where Ella and Lizzy stood. She looked at Ella. "My brother deserves justice."

"What if there was no justice to be had?" Ella hadn't meant to get drawn into this conversation, but now that it had happened, she knew she'd have to continue.

Mary gripped Ella's shoulder. "You know something, don't you?" Her tone was accusatory.

Ella swallowed the lump in her throat. "I

". . . I can't. . . ." She bit her lower lip. How could she admit to knowing all these months? Especially when she had no proof except what she'd overheard.

"Ella, if you do know something, you must tell us," Lizzy urged.

Tears slid down Ella's cheeks before she could stop them. She had always been given to crying when under pressure.

Lizzy put her arm around Ella's shoulders. "Come. Let's sit down."

She led Ella to the bench in the tack area. Ella sat, and Lizzy and Mary took their places on either side of her.

Mary took Ella's hand. "I'm sorry for snapping at you. It's just, well, you know how this is for me. I've tried so hard to find answers regarding my brother. Please—if you know something—help me."

Ella couldn't bear her pleading. "It won't help."

"Let me be the judge of that," Mary said, squeezing her hand.

"Ella, I know you've been living in fear of what your father and fiancé might do if they find you," Lizzy began, "but you are twenty-one now. You don't have to worry about that anymore. They can't force you to return home."

"You don't know my father. You don't know Jefferson. They are powerful and cruel."

"Did they have something to do with my brother's death?" Mary asked.

Ella's words caught in the back of her throat. She felt the room closing in and knew she had no choice but to tell the truth.

"Please," Mary begged, "I must know what happened."

Doing what she could to compose herself, Ella drew a deep breath and nodded. "I've wanted to tell you. All these weeks now, I've lived with the guilt of knowing what I needed to do." She got to her feet and faced both women. "You have no idea how it has tormented me. I don't want to lose your friendship—it means more than life to me."

Lizzy shook her head. "You aren't going to lose my friendship. Not ever."

"Nor mine," Mary assured. "Lizzy has told me how terrible things were for you. I promise I'll always be your friend."

"I've prayed so much about this. I don't know the details. I can only tell you what I overheard." Ella paused and met Mary's gaze. "Believe me, if it could have brought August justice, I would have said something immediately. But nothing I say will help you with that. My father and Jefferson Spiby own the entire county and part of the state. They have friends in powerful positions, and they will never be called to account for the things they've done."

"What have they done?" Mary asked.

"I don't even know. I overheard my father and former fiancé speaking. They said someone had seen too much. I don't recall the exact words, but the conversation ended with them resolving to take care of the matter. The next thing I knew, your brother was dead. I wasn't even sure the two events were connected. I had already planned to run away, and I knew that my chance to leave depended on being able to slip away unnoticed.

"When Father told us August was dead and the sheriff was coming, I knew I had to take advantage of that narrow bit of time. I was nearly caught coming down the back stairs of the house, but I managed to hide myself when I heard my father and Jefferson. It was then that I overheard Jefferson say that he had killed your brother."

Mary gasped and clamped her hands over her mouth. Lizzy's mouth dropped open, and her eyes grew wide. Ella felt a sense of relief that the truth was finally out there, but she had no idea what would happen now.

"I didn't see him do it, nor do I have any idea what August saw that made them think he had to die. I never dreamt my father was capable of such a thing, but I could believe it of Jefferson. I've heard horrible things about him. He even admitted to my father that this wasn't his first time to kill and it wouldn't be his last."

"We have to stop him," Mary said, lowering her hands. "He'll just keep killing people for whatever reason he deems necessary."

"I know." Ella could hear the resignation in her voice. If only they understood the hopelessness of it. "But no one will listen to me."

"You don't know that," Mary said, getting to her feet. She looked down at Lizzy. "We have to do something."

"But what?" Lizzy rose and looked from Ella to Mary. "She's right. I've met these men. They have money and power, and no one is going to speak against them."

"But Ella will. Ella can tell what she heard."

"But that's just it, it's hearsay. It's her word against theirs." Lizzy shook her head. "Ella's right, no one would dare come against them."

Ella could see in Mary's expression that she finally understood as she sank back onto the bench. "Then August's death will never be avenged. He'll never have justice."

"God will give him justice," Lizzy said, sitting beside her. She put her arm around Mary's shoulders. "God knows what happened, and He won't let evil win. We must give this over to Him and pray that He will show us what to do."

"If only we had some equally powerful men we could go to for help," Mary murmured. Her head snapped up. "What about Jason? His father is wealthy and a man of power."

"He's an Englishman. He doesn't hold any power here in America," Lizzy replied.

"But you said yourself that Jason is half American, and his mother's family is rich. He and his family must know powerful people here."

"Perhaps."

Ella could see where Mary hoped to take this. She wanted to do whatever she could to help. "If we can find someone—anyone—who will help us, I will happily testify to what I heard. I don't know if that will matter at all, but I will do what I can to help you, Mary. Please don't hate me for not speaking up sooner."

Mary's eyes met Ella's. "I don't hate you, Ella. You were afraid, and fear is something we have all experienced. I appreciate that you would tell me now, even though your fear is still very real. I knew my brother couldn't have been trampled by a horse. I know you're afraid your father and fiancé will come here and cause you harm, but I will do whatever I can to protect you from their wrath."

"We both will," Lizzy assured her.

Ella knew they were both sincere, but their words gave her very little peace.

⋇⊨ TWENTY ⊨⋇

Corabelle and Betty won't be returning to the show," Uncle Oliver announced. Some of the performers had already started arriving at the ranch as planned, while others had sent letters of regret. "I just learned that Corabelle's back injuries will keep her from performing. She twisted it pretty badly when we were on the road, and apparently while at home, she suffered a fall that caused the problem to worsen."

Lizzy looked at Ella. "She did both trick riding and Roman riding. Do you suppose you can learn some of the Roman riding act before we head off on the circuit?"

"I'm sure I can."

Uncle Oliver nodded. "I was hopeful of that." He looked at Gertie, a young woman of medium build in her early twenties. "What about you? Do you want to take on some of the Roman riding?"

The brunette shrugged. "I'm willing to give it a try, but I doubt I'll be proficient enough by the time we're on the road. I'm better with the trick riding."

"I can help," Lizzy said and turned to Jessie and Debbie, their other Roman riders. "I haven't done it in a while, but at least I've had experience. I'm sure with all of us working together, we can figure something out. If nothing else, we'll change the routine."

The ladies nodded.

Jason sat beside Lizzy and offered her a smile. "Are you certain? I remember you once saying that it is best to focus on just one area of stunt riding. If need be, I'm certain we could hire another rider."

He'd stuck to Lizzy like glue since returning from Chicago. She knew he wanted to endear himself, but being overly concerned wasn't the way to do it.

"I'll be fine. Once Ella knows the routine, they'll be back to a team of three. You said that we needed to learn each other's jobs so we could cover for one another in times of injury or absence. Ella and I have even been training with Mary, although I'm not much good at sharpshooting."

"I'm not as likely to get injured as you are," Mary threw out. "Besides, Alice is coming back. She wrote and told me, I just haven't had a chance to announce it. Since Teresa left, Alice didn't want to train with someone new, but when she found out I was rejoining the show, she decided to come back so long as her husband is rehired as crew."

Everyone looked to Jason. "Which one is he?"

"Carson Hopkins. He was my brother's best friend," Mary replied. "He wasn't sure he even wanted to return, but I encouraged him to do it in memory of August."

"Ah, yes." Jason looked to Oliver, who was nodding. Jason smiled. "He was definitely invited to return."

"Alice shoots bow from horseback. I think we can give her more time in the act," Oliver said. "Perhaps she'll have some ideas for how we might make the act even more exciting."

"I think I could add some things as well," Mary declared. "My job isn't as physically taxing as what the others girls do. If you need me to, I could do some additional tricks, even have more audience participation."

"I say, that's a capital idea," Jason piped up.

Lizzy listened as the conversation continued about how they would make the show more exciting and add some local interest as well. Jason assured them that having some contests for the locals would bring people in from far and wide.

"A sense of competition will always encourage attendance. We could have something of a challenge between the genders, perhaps?" His face lit up at this.

"I'm not sure I understand what the purpose would be," Mary commented.

Jason's expression suggested he'd just struck gold. "Imagine this. We could have an open competition at the beginning of each event—just prior to the show itself. We invite men to pay to shoot against Mary and Alice. Mary could use her rifle, and we could set up targets. Alice could have a similar contest with the bow."

Oliver nodded enthusiastically. "Yes! Yes! I can see that being very compelling. Imagine the men wanting to prove themselves against the women. Would you be willing to add that to your responsibilities, Mary?"

"Do you really suppose the men would pay to shoot against me?" Mary looked to Lizzy. "What do you think?"

"I think men tend to be ninnies any time women are involved," Lizzy said without thinking. Jason raised a brow as he glanced her way. Lizzy wasn't going to get caught in this discussion. "I have some new tricks I need to work on. I think whatever you decide will be fine. I'm sure there will be plenty of money to be made if the men think they can outshoot Mary. Goodness, if you made a kiss from her the reward, we're sure to be swimming in gold."

"There's an idea!" Uncle Oliver said, turning to Jason.

Lizzy didn't stay to hear where the rest of the conversation led. She made her way to the pens and collected Longfellow before heading to the arena. Once there, she saddled the horse and began galloping around the arena. She liked to warm him up before heading into any kind of maneuver. As they made endless circles, she thought of Wesley. He'd been so busy with the calving season that she'd seldom seen him. Mother said that Cookie was packing up food each day to send out with the men, but sometimes they didn't even make it back in before nightfall. There was so much to do, in fact, that Phillip and the older men were out helping.

Mother had also mentioned that she and Uncle Oliver wanted Wes to go on tour with the show. They felt confident that since he had experience and could be trusted, he was the perfect choice to fill August's role. Lizzy hadn't known what to think of that. The idea of Wes being with them made it much riskier for her. How could she hope to keep her feelings under control?

She signaled to Longfellow that they were going to start their routine. She brought him to a stop at the end of the arena. "Good boy," she said, stroking his neck. She slipped the reins under the bridle headpiece. "Now it's time to work."

She put him through his paces doing simple tricks—vaults, spins, and layovers. Longfellow knew what was expected and performed without flaw. When Lizzy felt they were both amply warmed up, they tried a few harder tricks. She knew better than to practice alone, but with Uncle Oliver and Jason wanting to go into details with the others, Lizzy felt the best way to spend her time was in practice. Besides, she and Longfellow rarely had trouble.

For weeks now, Lizzy had been planning out a series of tricks she could do at a full gallop, and she wanted to add one additional element that would allow her to vault from the ground into a squat on the saddle. From there she would stand up, then go head first to the left side of Longfellow, somersaulting to hit the ground with her feet and vault backward and back up. It needed to be fluid or it wouldn't look right. She hadn't quite worked out all the problems, but she was close.

She put Longfellow into a gallop and went into the pattern of vaults and spins, but when she tried the new elements, she lost her grip while vaulting backward, slammed her shoulder hard against the saddle, and lost control.

She hit the ground face first, knocking the wind from her chest. She stayed completely still, trying to force her lungs to take in air.

"Lizzy!"

She would have moaned in frustration at the sound of Wes calling her name, but she couldn't draw enough air. Of all the people to catch her in this situation, it had to be him.

He rushed to her side and rolled her over, drawing her into his arms. "Lizzy, are you all right?"

Thankfully she was starting to get control of her breathing. "I'm . . . fine."

His worried expression made her think back to what he'd told her about Clarissa.

She struggled to speak without gasping. "Really. I'm fine."

"You scared the life out me when I saw you lying here. What are you doing, practicing without someone here with you?"

He was still holding her, and Lizzy wasn't in any real hurry to get away, but his accusing tone was more than she wanted to deal with at the moment. "I had work to do." She drew a deep breath and ignored the ache in her side. "As you can see, I haven't quite perfected my new trick. Now, if you don't mind, I'd like to get up."

Wesley helped her to her feet. "You need to quit this. You're too old to do these dangerous tricks."

She put her hands on her hips. "Too old?"

"You know what I mean. The older you get, the more you risk hurting yourself in a bad way."

"Is there a good way?"

"Lizzy." His voice was full of irritation. "I don't think you should go with the show this year."

"Well, I don't think you should either."

He stared at her as if trying to figure out what to say next, but Lizzy saved him the trouble.

She reached down and picked up her hat. "I don't need you telling me what to do. If you want to be useful, then be supportive and encouraging. If you only want to find fault, you can find it with someone else."

She dusted off her backside and whistled for Longfellow. He came immediately, but Wesley took hold of his bridle. "You need to listen to reason."

"What seems to be the problem?" Lizzy's mother asked, coming to join them. Prince stuck close to her heels.

Lizzy rolled her eyes. "He's the problem. I

fell off my horse, and he acts like it's the end of the world."

"I found her on the ground, not even moving."

Lizzy stretched to her full height on tiptoes and pressed her face closer to his. "I was trying to breathe. That's why I wasn't moving."

His lips bore the tiniest hint of a smile. "Breathing wouldn't have been a problem if you hadn't been thrown to the ground."

"I wasn't thrown, I lost my grip. Now give me my horse."

"No. You need to rest and make sure you aren't hurt. Go sit down."

Lizzy heard her mother chuckle and stepped back to glare at her. "This isn't the slightest bit funny. I have a routine to perform in just a few weeks, and if I can't get the trick right, then I will have an even bigger problem." She looked at Wes and shook her finger in his face. "Stop bossing me around. You are not my father or my brother." Seeing he wouldn't yield, she let out a growl and headed for the door. "Fine. You take care of his grooming and make sure that saddle is put away properly."

She slammed the door on the way out—just for good measure.

Wes could see the amusement on Rebecca Brookstone's face. He shook his head. What could he say?

"Now that Lizzy has clearly established what you *aren't*," the older woman said, "maybe you should figure out what you *are*."

"She's impossible. I thought she was dead."

Lizzy's mother put her hand on his arm. "Wes, you can't keep her from harm. She loves what she does and daily scares the life right out of me. But I can't tell her she can't do what she loves. She'd only hate me for it. She'd hate you too."

"But she could have been killed."

"Like Clarissa."

He swallowed hard and frowned. "Yes. Like Clarissa."

"Wes, Clarissa is gone. Lizzy is her own woman, and if you want a future with her, you'll have to accept her for who she is. To do less would be to change her. Love and marriage are all about give and take. Lizzy's ready to stop riding in the show, but if you tell her she can't do it . . . she's only going to keep doing it out of defiance just to prove she can."

"I don't know how to win her heart." Longfellow was getting bored with the conversation and began to shift around. Wes gave him a pat on the neck.

Rebecca Brookstone smiled. "You've already won her heart, Wes. Now you just need to show her that you don't see her as a child or someone to boss around, but as a partner—someone to share your life with, to grow old with."

"But she won't grow old at this rate."

Rebecca grew thoughtful. "Mark didn't grow old either, but he wasn't doing anything more dangerous than sitting in a chair when he had his heart attack. None of us know when our time will come. Mark and I had some wonderful years together and a beautiful daughter. The dangers and risks were worth it. You might not have felt that way with Clarissa, but you two didn't marry for love."

He tried to hide his surprise, but Mrs. Brookstone shook her head. "You don't have to say anything about it. I know when a man and woman love each other. That's why I know you and Lizzy are in love—even if you're both too bullheaded to admit it.

"Come, Prince!" The pup snapped to attention and hugged her heel. Mrs. Brookstone took a few steps, then turned to glance over her shoulder. "If you're smart, Wes, you won't waste all your time trying to make Lizzy into someone she's not. After all, the woman she is now is the woman you fell in love with.

If you force her to change, you risk losing everything."

He watched Lizzy's mother leave by the same door Lizzy had just slammed moments ago. Was she right?

He sighed and looked Longfellow in the eye. "What am I supposed to do?"

TWENTY-ONE

Lizzy was still seething over Wesley's attitude a week later. The last of the performers had arrived only the day before. They were full of excitement about the 1901 show calendar, and Uncle Oliver and Jason had called a meeting for that afternoon. Meanwhile, Jason had done everything in his power to get Lizzy alone. He hadn't succeeded, thankfully. Lizzy had no desire to spend time in private discussions with him when she had Wes on her mind. The trouble was that Wes was always on her mind.

As everyone gathered in the large living room, Lizzy sat in the corner, wondering why Wesley's opinion mattered so much. She felt bad for the way she'd acted. He had good reason to hate trick riding, and she knew he only wanted her to be safe.

Mary plopped down beside her. "You look like you've got the weight of the world on your shoulders."

"I'm still upset over what happened last week with Wes."

"He hasn't even been around to pester you," Mary reminded her. "Your mother said the men have been so busy with calving that she's not seen much of them."

"Yes, but Wes will be back soon enough. I ran into Phillip, and he said Wes intends to take the wrangler position with the show."

"But that's a good thing. You'll have all year to work on your feelings for each other."

"Thanks everybody for being here so promptly," Uncle Oliver said as he brought the meeting to order. "We've got some exciting news. Next year's show schedule is fully set, and I'm delighted to announce we will be going abroad in the fall to England."

There were gasps, and several people had questions that spilled out all at once. Uncle Oliver held up his hands. "If you'll just quiet down, we'll give you all the details." He proceeded to explain how they would tour extensively throughout the Midwest and move toward the East Coast. They would perform almost every day but Sunday.

"The schedule will be grueling, but we will have a nice rest when we sail to London in August. We will perform in England for much of August and September, then sail home to finish out at the Pan-American Expo in Buffalo, New York."

It was exhausting just listening to the details. It was worse still when Uncle Oliver explained they would do all of this with half the crew.

"You expect us to keep a schedule like that and take on other duties?" Alice Hopkins asked.

"Not many," Uncle Oliver assured her. "We want our performers to be well rested. We realize a daily performance is going to be hard enough. We haven't worked out all of the details, and some of them won't be known until we're actually in the throe of things.

"Now, Agnes has agreed to do part of the year with us, and while she's with us, she'll continue to train her niece Brigette, who's been her assistant the last two years, to handle costumes and laundry for the troupe. Meanwhile, Brigette's good friend Sally has joined up and is training to cook and clean. By having these two on board with us, we've been able to eliminate two positions, and once Agnes retires, we'll be down another. All of this will save money in the long run." He looked to Lizzy's mother. "I presume training has been going well?"

Mother nodded. "We've only just started, but it's going well. Sally had experience in cooking for large groups, so she's quite capable." Everyone looked at the shy young woman who sat beside Agnes and her niece. "She'll be ready when it's time to go."

"Brigette too," Agnes assured everyone.

"Wonderful." Uncle Oliver flashed a big smile.

The meeting went on for over an hour before Uncle Oliver finally brought it to a close.

"I want you all to finalize the performances you plan to give so that Jason and I can review them with you one by one. We want to pack as much into the show as we can. The acts will be in twenty-minute increments as before. This year, however, two hours prior to the show, there will be a local shooting contest that each individual town will advertise. The top three winners will compete against Mary. We'll offer a prize of five dollars for the man or woman who can beat Mary."

"But it isn't likely Mary will lose." This came from Gertie.

"Exactly. No matter the outcome, Mary will pose for newspaper photographs with the three top shooters. It will all be quite celebratory, and as word gets around from town to town, more people will be driven to try their hand."

"What if I do lose?" Mary asked.

Uncle Oliver chuckled. "Given the fees we'll charge to participate in the contest, it won't be that big of a loss. If a man beats you, we'll play it up that you were distracted by his stunning good looks or something."

Lizzy put out her own thought. "What if another woman beats her?"

"Then we'll hire her on," Uncle Oliver said with a shrug, making everyone laugh. "There's more. We've also made arrangements with the towns to handle concessions. The one provision is that they must carry our banners and programs and be prepared to give back our inventory and money immediately at the close of the program. Jason will be responsible for managing this, as well as the ticket sales."

Always in the past, a couple of the older men were responsible for these things. Lizzy thought it only right that if Jason was getting rid of the men, he should be responsible for taking on their jobs.

When the meeting finally concluded, it was understood that the staff working with the horses had been cut by half and those taking care of household duties had been cut by three. Jason had also eliminated the need for two of the train cars and had re-outfitted the others. Gone was the family car, as Lizzy and Oliver both agreed they could bunk in with the others. Jason also explained how new, up-to-date arrangements for the horses allowed them to need fewer cars for the animals. She hoped—prayed—that he knew what he was doing. Transportation was hard enough on the animals.

Glad to be out of the stuffiness of the house, Lizzy started for the arena, then changed her mind. There was plenty of time, and she wanted to work with Emerson. The colt was making great strides. Phillip and Lizzy had been working with him whenever time allowed. Soon, however, she'd be gone, and the responsibility would fall solely to Phillip. She didn't want to miss an opportunity for the colt to become more familiar with her.

At one end of the barn was the extended stall where Emerson was kept during the night. Temperatures had been brutal lately, and everyone felt it wise to afford the yearling extra protection. Lizzy grabbed a lead and went to the stall gate. Emerson was used to her now and came over in search of a treat.

"Show me what you can do, and then I'll give you a reward," she told him, attaching the lead to his halter.

She opened the gate and led the colt out of the barn. He was quite good on the rope. Wes had told her they'd worked through the summer with him, and it showed.

The air was crisp, but the temperature had warmed to the mid-twenties, according to Cookie. With the sun out in full, the intensity of its heat was welcoming, and Lizzy lifted her face to let the rays wash over her. All the while, she walked with the colt beside her.

She stopped several times, teaching him to respond to her commands. When he performed correctly, she praised him. "Emerson, you are quite the little stallion. I think you'll be an amazing sire."

She continued down the main drive, stopping and doing turns with him from time to time. It was important to keep him working on these skills. While most ranchers would have put him in a field until he was three and then have someone break him in hard and fast, that wasn't Lizzy's style. She wanted to form a solid relationship with the colt. She'd trained Longfellow and Thoreau, and both now handled as if they were extensions of her own body. She didn't plan to use Emerson in the shows, but she would still like to ride him.

Lizzy had started the colt back to the barn when she saw Jason Adler making his way toward her. She sighed. "Well, we didn't need his company, did we, Emerson?"

"Goodness, Lizzy, you are hard to find at times," Jason said as he reached her side.

"I have work to do." She reached up to stroke Emerson's face. "A lot of work, actually." She started walking toward the pens. "What can I do for you?"

He chuckled. "I would be brash and say *marry me*, but I doubt that would get me any further than my previous proposal."

"No. It wouldn't get you anywhere at all." She glanced up to find him frowning. "Did you enjoy Chicago?"

"Very much. I prefer city life in the winter."

"Only the winter? I figured you were sold on the city year-round."

Jason kept pace with her, and when they reached the pen, he opened the gate for Lizzy. She led Emerson inside, then took off the lead. Reaching into her pocket, she pulled out a few slices of dried apple. The colt was to receive them, then took off to join the other horses and see who he could push around.

Lizzy laughed at his antics. "He's such a

fine animal. I'm more and more impressed with him."

Longfellow and Thoreau made their way over to her. Lizzy gave them each some apple, drawing the colt's attention.

"He's definitely pushy," she said, refusing to give him anything more.

"A fella has to be around here to get any attention," Jason replied.

She ignored the comment and attached the lead to Longfellow. "Don't worry, Thoreau, I'll send Ella to get you next." She walked Longfellow from the pen, grateful that Jason was happy to manage the gate.

"Thank you," she told him as she moved off toward the arena.

"Don't you have even a few minutes to talk with me?" Jason called after her.

He sounded so disappointed that Lizzy motioned for him to follow. "I can take a couple of minutes while I check over my saddle straps."

Jason nodded and caught up with her in two long strides. Inside the building, Lizzy tied off Longfellow, then went to the equipment stall.

"So what's on your mind?"

"You are, of course. I missed you, Lizzy. If anything, the time away only proved to me how much you've become a part of me."

She had figured he'd take this line and decided to change the subject. "I see you managed to talk Uncle Oliver into England. I'm sure that pleases you." She checked the saddle from top to bottom and back to front. She'd worked with Zeb to add a new strap for her latest trick.

"It pleases me because it will allow me to show you London and our country estate. I know you'll love it, Lizzy, and I know my parents will love you as well."

"Yes, well, I generally get along with everyone." Pleased with the saddle, Lizzy grabbed a blanket. She was about to take it and the saddle to Longfellow, but Jason was at her side, pushing her hands away. He spun her around so quickly that she nearly lost her footing.

"Please, Lizzy. Won't you at least give me a chance? I've fallen quite madly in love with you." He held fast to her arms. "You know that I want us to marry."

"But I don't." She decided against any attempt to sugarcoat her words. "I don't ever intend to marry. Not you or anyone else."

"But that's not even reasonable. You're a beautiful woman with so much to offer. Marry me, and I'll give you anything you want."

"You can't give me what I want, Jason." Her

throat went dry, and she bowed her head. She didn't even know what she wanted. "Please try to understand. I like you well enough." She forced herself to look up as he let go of her. "But I don't love you."

"You love him, don't you?"

She didn't need him to use a name to know that he meant Wesley. "Yes." She hadn't intended to admit such a thing to Jason, but now that she had, she felt the need to continue. "I never set out to, and God knows I have no intention of doing anything about it. But I do love him, and because of that, I won't give you false hope."

"You don't plan to marry him either?"

"No." She tried to keep all emotion from her voice. "As I said, I don't ever intend to marry—not that Wes has asked."

"Then he's a fool."

Lizzy smiled. "I don't think so. I think he may be the only smart one."

Jason let go a long breath. "I don't intend to stop trying to win you over and change your mind."

His statement only furthered her frustration. "What happened to us just being friends?"

"I lost my heart to you. That's what happened. I can't imagine taking any other woman for my wife."

"I am sorry, Jason. I made it clear from the

beginning that I didn't want anything more. Now, please, leave me to work."

She thought he might argue with her, but thankfully her mother appeared from the shadows of the doorway. Prince was faithfully at her heels.

"Lizzy, here you are."

Jason gave Lizzy a slight bow and exited the arena without another word. Mother came to Lizzy and glanced back over her shoulder. "I thought if I made myself known, he'd leave you be."

"Thank you. He can be a pest." Lizzy leaned down and scratched Prince behind the ear. "I am so impressed with how quickly you've brought him in line."

"He's a smart dog and learns quick."

Lizzy gave him one final pat and straightened up. "I wish everyone would learn as quickly."

"Are you speaking of yourself or Jason?" Mother asked with a smile. "I'm sorry, but I overheard a great deal of your conversation. I was in the back room taking inventory."

"I didn't realize anyone else was out here, but that's all right." Lizzy lifted the saddle in her arms. She carried it to Longfellow and placed it on the ground beside him. "I didn't say a thing to him that I wouldn't have said with you at my side."

"Why did you tell him you never intend to marry?" Mother asked.

Lizzy put the blanket atop Longfellow and smoothed it out. "Because I don't."

"That doesn't sound like you. You've always talked about wanting to marry and have a family."

"That was then." Lizzy planted the saddle atop her horse, then rocked it back and forth to make sure it was in the right place. She'd secured the cinch and flank billet before Mother put her hand on Lizzy's arm. Lizzy looked up. "What is it?"

"Why have you changed your mind about marrying? I know you still have deep feelings for Wes. I heard you tell Jason that you love him. Why don't you want to marry him?"

"First of all, Wes sees me as a child—the daughter of the man he works for . . . or worked for. Second, he doesn't return my feelings. Third . . ." She fell silent. Looking in her mother's eyes, Lizzy knew her reasoning would only cause pain. "It's not important."

"I think it is, and I want you to tell me."

"I don't want to hurt you more by remembering what you once had."

Mother's eyes narrowed slightly. "Is this about your father and I?"

"Yes. I know what it cost you to lose Father. Your love for him and his for you was such a strong and beautiful thing. Now that he's gone, you're left with all this misery and pain. I hear you cry at night, Mother. I know how much his loss has meant."

"Yes, it's been very hard," Mother admitted. "But I wouldn't trade a single day we had together to be free of this sorrow."

"You wouldn't?" Lizzy found that hard to believe.

"Do you honestly suppose I would?" Mother sounded as if Lizzy had just suggested the most ridiculous thing in the world.

"I can't imagine that a few years of happiness is worth the pain you feel now."

"That's how little you know about love." Mother put her arm around Lizzy and drew her away from Longfellow. She led them to the bench. "Sit with me a moment."

Lizzy took a seat beside her mother, and Prince settled on the ground between them. Mother clasped her hand in Lizzy's. "My darling girl, is this why you're avoiding Wes?"

"I'm not really avoiding him. He's been very busy with the calving."

Mother smiled. "I first met your father when I was just fourteen. I lost my heart to him almost immediately. I think he'd say he did the same. We were nearly inseparable from then on. We knew we'd marry and hoped we'd have a large family. Of course, the latter didn't happen. You were the only child we were able to have, but you were such a blessing. Your father often said that instead of giving us ten beautiful and intelligent children, God put the equivalent characteristics into one perfect child."

"I'm far from perfect, but I know you and Father love me dearly. I never lacked for love from either of you." Lizzy squeezed her mother's hand.

"I'm glad. I know I've never felt a lack of love from you and certainly never from your father. I don't even feel that lost to me now, which is why you must listen to me. Lizzy, avoiding love because you're afraid of losing it will leave you a very lonely and empty woman."

"But it will also keep me from knowing the pain you now know."

"Life is full of sorrows and pain. But it's also full of joy and love. Would you turn away from me because of the pain you've experienced losing your father? Would your fear of losing another parent result in you leaving me for good?"

Such a thing was unthinkable, and Lizzy was quick to say as much. "Never. That would be beyond reason."

"So too is hardening your heart against falling in love. You love Wes, and I believe the two of you belong together. Don't avoid love because you fear what might happen should he die. Don't sacrifice what is real for what may never be."

"But everyone dies." Lizzy felt her emotions welling up inside and pushed them back down. "You can't say that it may never be, because death will come."

"Yes, because it's part of life. But Lizzy, your strength is found in the Lord. I remember when you were very little and asked me what happened to us when we died. Do you remember that talk?"

"I do. I was five years old, and one of Grandmother's cats had been killed by the dog. The dog had threatened her kittens, and she died protecting them."

"Yes." Mother brushed a strand of brown hair from Lizzy's face. "I told you that when a person died they would either go home to be with God or they would be forever separated from Him."

"And I asked why." Lizzy smiled. "I used to ask why all the time."

Mother laughed. "You did indeed. But that was perhaps the most important time of all."

Lizzy remembered it well. "You told me

about Jesus dying on the cross for me to take away my sins. It made me cry because all I could think about was how that poor cat had been killed."

"I know, but it was a good way to teach you about Jesus dying for us. He saw that we were in a bad way without Him. Satan was always threatening His children, just as that dog threatened the kittens. He gave His life so that we would be able to escape Satan's torment."

"You told me that if I put my trust in Jesus and confessed my sins, I would never really die."

"And you got confused and thought I meant you'd never die at all." Mother smiled. "Death in this life isn't the end. We certainly needn't fear it if we have given our hearts to God. We will see your father again. Of this I'm certain, even though it is hard to be without him now."

"It is."

Mother got to her feet and drew Lizzy up with her. She hugged her long and hard, and when Mother pulled back, Lizzy could see the tears that streamed down her cheeks. With her guard down, Lizzy could hardly bear it.

"Lizzy, I want you to know the truth for what it is. I would bear this pain and even more. Your father's love was worth the price. Just think about that, will you?" She kissed Lizzy's cheek, then walked away. Prince cocked his head to one side as he looked at Lizzy, then took off after his mistress.

"Yes. I will." Lizzy sank back onto the bench.

The door to the arena opened, but Lizzy didn't look up. She heard Mother say something but paid no attention. No doubt Ella was coming to work on their act.

"Lizzy?"

Wesley's voice so surprised Lizzy that she jumped to her feet. He stood only a few feet away, watching her. He looked tired and worried. Had Mother said something to him?

"I'm sorry, I was lost in my thoughts." She smiled and squared her shoulders. "What can I do for you? How's the calving going?"

"Everything's going well. We're ninety percent done. I think everything will finish up by the first of the month."

"That's good." Lizzy made her way back to Longfellow to finish saddling him. She took up the breast collar and secured it in place. "I'm sure you'll be relieved to have it all done before you head out with the show. Although I still don't understand why you said yes. You hate the show."

"I do not." He moved to stand beside Longfellow. "I never hated it."

"Then why do you give me such a hard time about performing?" She straightened and raised her brow.

"Because I don't want you to get hurt. Those stunts you create are dangerous. They're getting more and more dangerous just so you can thrill an audience."

She sighed. "Stop acting like an overprotective big brother."

Wesley growled and pulled her into his arms. He kissed her with great passion, nearly bending her over backward. Lizzy gave in to the moment and let the love she felt for Wes surge. It surely couldn't hurt just this once.

When he straightened and let go of her, Lizzy could only stare at him. Her pounding heart and panting breath hardly allowed her to speak. Slowly, rational thought returned. "Why . . . why did you . . . do that?"

His eyes never left hers. "Because I want to be clear on one thing: I do not think of you as my sister."

"Then what—what do you think of me as?"

He pulled her back into his arms. "My heart."

He started to kiss her again, but a scream sounded, and Lizzy pushed back.

"That's Ella!"

Ella flew through the open door. She was nearly hysterical.

"What's wrong?" Lizzy went to the crying girl and took hold of her. "What is it?"

Ella's eyes were wide with fear. "My father . . . Jefferson . . . they're here!"

⸗ TWENTY-TWO ⸗

Lizzy was glad that Wes agreed to return to the house with her and Ella. When they arrived, they found Mother, along with Uncle Oliver and Jason, sitting in the front room.

"Ella!" Mr. Fleming jumped to his feet. "I've been half sick with worry over you." He started to come to her, but Ella backed away. He stopped and looked at her with a frown. "Whatever has come over you?"

"Stay away from me. I want nothing to do with either of you."

Jefferson joined Ella's father. "What in the world is wrong, Ella? You've had us frantic for months in search of you."

"I left because I couldn't abide being

there. I have no intention of returning home, so please go and leave me alone."

Lizzy put her arm around Ella. She could see the anger in Jefferson Spiby's expression, while Ella's father just looked confused.

"Why don't we all sit and discuss this in a civilized manner?" Mother suggested. "I'll have Irma bring us some coffee." She turned to go.

"I'd prefer something stronger," Spiby called after her.

Mother looked back and smiled. "I'm afraid we do not drink spirits in this house, Mr. Spiby. You'll have to settle for coffee, tea, or milk."

He glared at her. "Very well. I'll have coffee."

Lizzy was already ushering Ella to the far side of the room. There were two chairs by the door to the music room. If things got uncomfortable, Lizzy could take Ella out that way. Since the music room adjoined the library, which led to the hall, they could escape if need be.

Ella was trembling when Lizzy let go of her. She felt sorry for the younger woman. Ella's fear of these men was evident. Men like Mr. Fleming and Spiby counted on intimidation to get their way, and Lizzy wasn't about to stand for them trying that here. She saw

Wes take up a spot by the hallway entrance. He crossed his arms and leaned back against the doorjamb, all while watching Spiby and Fleming. Lizzy found herself wishing she'd confided in him regarding Ella. What in the world must he think?

"I'm not sure what this is all about, Ella, but your mother has been sick of heart since you ran away. She took to her bed and has hardly been up since you disappeared. I thought perhaps you had gone to your sister in Chicago, but our investigation soon proved otherwise." Mr. Fleming turned to eye Uncle Oliver. "I sent a man to ask if you were with the Brookstone group, but he was told you weren't."

"In all honesty, Uncle Oliver didn't know," Lizzy announced. "I snuck Ella onboard and hid her. He knew nothing of her being with us until days later."

"I should have known." Ella's father looked at Lizzy in disgust. "You are a most willful young woman."

"Which is better than being one who cowers and lives in fear," Lizzy countered.

Ella said nothing and kept her gaze on her folded hands.

Mr. Fleming made a dismissive noise and continued. "Ella, as I told Mr. Brookstone, we've come to take you home. I've spent a small fortune hiring a Pinkerton man to find you, and now that I have you safely in my care, we must return home. We appreciate the hospitality he and Mrs. Brookstone have given you, but you've a wedding to plan. The date has been rescheduled for April."

Ella's head snapped up. "I'm not in your care, and I won't marry Jefferson Spiby."

Jefferson gave her a hard, cold look but remained silent. Ella's father, however, wasn't about to do the same.

"You *will* marry him. We made that arrangement long ago, and you knew your obligation to him."

"I won't." Ella looked from her father to Jefferson. "I will not marry. Those were your arrangements, not mine." She focused on her father and crossed her arms. "I'm twenty-one now, and you cannot force me to marry or return home with you."

Her father seemed to have forgotten this fact. He looked momentarily confused. Lizzy wondered if it were possible he hadn't realized Ella had come of age. Surely he knew the date of his own daughter's birthday.

Mother returned with Irma close behind. The older woman carried a tray with coffee and cups. Mother had a platter of cookies. "I hope you will enjoy these," Mother said, putting the cookies on the table between Jefferson and George Fleming's chairs. "Irma just pulled them from the oven. They're oatmeal. They will hold you over until lunch. I do hope you'll join us for the meal."

Lizzy admired her mother's grace and gentility. She was no happier to see these two men in her house than Lizzy was, but Mother maintained a polite, welcoming spirit.

"As we told you, Mrs. Brookstone, we are only here to retrieve Ella, and then we must be on our way."

"I'm not going anywhere with either of you." Ella was quickly growing bolder.

"Ella, I am deeply wounded. What did I do to cause you to run away?" her father asked.

Lizzy wondered if her friend would be truthful in this gathering. No one but Lizzy and Mary knew about Ella overhearing Jefferson Spiby's confession.

Mary. Where was she? What would happen if she heard that these men had come?

A log in the hearth shifted, startling Ella. She bit her lip and looked at Lizzy, eyes wide. Lizzy patted her arm and decided to jump into the conversation.

"Ella wants to perform in our show. She's going to trick ride with me. She's very good."

Spiby chuckled. "So she ran away to join the circus. How amusing."

"Not amusing at all," Mr. Fleming declared. "I wondered at your . . . manner of dress." He paused momentarily, as if considering all that had been said. "Ella, this is ridiculous. No daughter of mine is going to be a common performer. Furthermore—"

"I'm sorry, Father, but that is exactly what I am going to do."

He looked at Ella as if she were a stranger. "This is outrageous. I demand you refuse her, Mr. Brookstone." Mr. Fleming looked at Uncle Oliver. "If not, I will discontinue doing business with you and ruin your show."

"I'm not a man to be threatened, Fleming." Uncle Oliver crossed his arms. "Especially in my own home."

"And I'm not a man to be refused," Fleming countered. "Especially where my own daughter is concerned."

Silence fell over the room, and with it, the tension increased. Lizzy didn't figure either side would resort to violence, but she knew that Mr. Fleming and Mr. Spiby hadn't anticipated anyone taking a stand against them.

Then, as she had feared, Mary appeared in the doorway. Lizzy had no idea how she'd found out about the men's arrival, but she could very nearly read Mary's thoughts. She kept her expression void of emotion, but her eyes seemed to burn. When her gaze met Lizzy's, it was clear that she wanted nothing more than to use the guns strapped at her side.

"Ah, Mary," Mother said, smiling. "Mary is our sharpshooter."

The men barely nodded in acknowledgment before returning their attention to Ella. Lizzy wondered if her friend would be able to hold her temper. Mary knew these men were responsible for the death of her brother. If they had killed Lizzy's father, she knew she wouldn't find it easy to do and say nothing.

Finally, after what seemed an eternity, Ella spoke. "I wonder if I might speak privately with my father."

Lizzy knew what she intended to do. It was Ella's one chance to be rid of her father and Mr. Spiby. No doubt Ella figured that if she threatened to tell what she knew, then perhaps they would be willing to leave her alone. That was how Lizzy would have played it.

"I would be happy to speak with you, Ella." Her father's expression looked hopeful.

"Come with me to the dining room. It won't take us but a moment."

Ella left the gathering without so much as a backward glance. She was terrified of her father and Jefferson but knew she would have to face at least one of them. Her father seemed the lesser of two evils. Jefferson was a killer, after all. She could only hope and pray that wasn't also true of her father.

Once in the dining room, Ella pulled the pocket doors closed and went to the far side of the room. Her father followed.

"Why are you doing this, Ella? You know your responsibilities."

She put the table between herself and Father. Her voice was barely a whisper. "I know what you and Jefferson did." She decided the direct approach was best. "I know Jefferson killed August Reichert."

Her father paled. "You know no such thing."

"I overheard you two discussing it." She gripped the back of the chair. "I know that August saw something you didn't want him to see. I know that you felt he had to be dealt with, and I heard Jefferson confess to murdering him. I also heard Jefferson say that he has killed before. I'm prepared to go to the authorities."

Her father considered this for a moment. Then, as Ella had feared, he shrugged off the entire matter. "You know as well as I do that no one is going to come against me or Jefferson. No one is going to believe you—an ungrateful child, a frightened bride-to-be. You have no proof."

"You don't know that."

"I do." Her father's confidence had returned. "No one back home is going to lift a finger against either one of us, so you'd do well to get your things and come back with us now. I'm willing to overlook all of this, and once you're married, I'm sure Jefferson will as well."

"Jefferson has never overlooked nor forgiven any infringement against him, Father. You know that as well as I do. Would you truly turn me over to that man, knowing what he is capable of doing?"

"Rumors—all rumors. He would never hurt you. He loves you and will give you everything your heart desires." Her father pulled out a handkerchief and dabbed his forehead. "Now, get your things."

Ella eyed him suspiciously. "Why are you so determined for me to marry him? You know he is evil, even if you won't admit it to me. Do you really want to give your child to a murderer?"

"Jefferson will never harm you, Ella. We have an agreement between us."

"What agreement?"

Father pocketed his handkerchief. "It's none of your concern. It's enough for you to know that a contract was arranged, and your marriage to Jefferson is part of it."

"It's your contract, not mine. I will not marry him."

"If you can get him to release you from it, then I'll have no more to say on it. However, I'm fairly confident Jefferson will never let you go. He loves you, Ella."

"Jefferson Spiby doesn't know how to love." Ella skirted the table. Once she reached the doors, she pushed them back and turned to her father. "It's best we join the others so I can make it clear once and for all where I stand."

"Be careful what you say, Ella. Words once spoken can never be taken back."

Ella marched across the hall and entered the living room. She pointed a finger at Jefferson, who had jumped to his feet. "I am not marrying you. I know exactly what you are and"—she paused, glancing at Mary—"what you've done." She returned her gaze to Jefferson, and from the look in his eyes, Ella knew he understood. "I will never marry you." The other men had also risen, and she looked at them. "I do not wish to cause you any problem with the show, so if you prefer that I leave, I will. However, I would very much like to continue with you."

"I'm happy to have you stay on, Ella." Oliver Brookstone looked at Jefferson and then her father. "I won't turn you out. They may threaten as they wish."

"You'll be sorry you took a stand against us," Ella's father said, moving to Jefferson's side. "I am no longer asking, Ella. I'm prepared to take you by force if necessary."

"I think it might be best if you two returned to town," Mrs. Brookstone interjected. "There's a lovely hotel there, and I believe you will be quite comfortable. That will give everyone some time to think. You could return tomorrow and join us for lunch—if you're prepared to act in a civilized manner."

Father began sputtering. "After I offered you the hospitality of my home, you would send me to a hotel in that poor excuse for a town?"

Mrs. Brookstone nodded. "I'm sorry, Mr. Fleming, but our house is full to overflowing. Not only that, but our party posed no threat to you or your family when we stayed with you. You're threatening to remove one of my guests by force."

Ella watched as her father assessed the situation. She prayed he wouldn't resort to violence. It had never occurred to her until that moment that Jefferson probably carried a gun. Would he dare to threaten this family? She was about to yield to her father's demands when he spoke up.

"Very well. We will retire to a hotel for the evening and return again tomorrow at noon." He fixed Ella with a hard look. "You will return with us. No matter what you think you can do or say—I will not allow you to remain behind." He looked at Jefferson. "Let's go."

Jefferson looked as if he might refuse, but then to Ella's surprise, he nodded and threw Mrs. Brookstone a broad grin. "I look forward to joining you for dinner tomorrow."

She gave a gracious smile. "I hope we all enjoy a more amiable time."

Lizzy all but held her breath until the two men exited the house. She wondered if her mother might later send a note taking back the invitation to lunch. She never wanted to see those men again. They were clearly evil.

"Oliver! Are you all right?"

Her mother's urgent voice seized Lizzy's attention. Her uncle had paled and sunk onto a chair, clutching his chest. Lizzy froze. It was just like Father.

Wes and Mother were at his side. Mary

quickly joined them and began loosening her uncle's tie. "What is it, Oliver?" Mother asked.

"I think that was a bit more than I was up to," he replied. "I suppose I'm not entirely recovered from my trip."

Lizzy was taken back in time to when her father had his heart attack. He had been sitting and talking, doing nothing strenuous, when he'd grabbed his chest. She would never forget the look of fear in his eyes. It was the same look as in Uncle Oliver's.

"Wes, can you get him upstairs to bed?" Mother asked.

"Sure thing."

"I can walk." Uncle Oliver got to his feet, but his legs gave out, and Wes lifted him in his arms.

"It's all right, Oliver. I'll carry you. That way if it's something more, you won't be exerting yourself."

"Mary, tell Irma I need her. Lizzy, go find Phillip. Have him go to town and get the doctor. Tell him to say nothing to Mr. Fleming, however. I don't want them knowing how their visit affected Oliver."

Mary hurried off, but Lizzy stood frozen in place. She could barely breathe.

"Lizzy!" Mother's raised voice broke through her daze. "Go send Phillip for the doctor!"

Lizzy nodded as she forced her feet to move. Half stumbling forward, she fought to get ahold of her emotions. She searched the pens and then the barns for Wes's younger brother and finally found him working with one of the saddles in the tack room. She felt close to hysterics.

"Phillip! You need—you have to go right now. We need a doctor."

He stepped toward her. "What's happened?"

"Uncle Oliver." She found it difficult to make sense of what she wanted to say. "Oh, Phillip, go to Miles City and get the doctor. My uncle may be dying."

Phillip started for the pen to get his horse, but Lizzy stopped him.

"Wait!"

He turned, and Lizzy rushed to his side.

"Mr. Fleming and Mr. Spiby were just here. They upset Uncle Oliver, and Mother said to say nothing to them if you should cross paths. She doesn't want them to know their effect on my uncle. Just get the doctor without making a scene and say nothing to them."

"Sure thing, Miss Lizzy."

After he'd gone, Lizzy felt her chest tighten as her thoughts ran wild. What would happen to them if Uncle Oliver died? It would mean the end of the show and perhaps even the ranch. What would she and Mother do then?

Tear came to her eyes as she fell to her knees. *God, why is this happening? Isn't it enough that we lost Father? Must we lose Uncle Oliver too? Must we lose everything?*

She wasn't able to hold back the rush of anguish. How could God take all the best they had and leave them with nothing? Father had been everything to her and Mother. She could still see him lying on his deathbed. His face was pasty, almost colorless. She remembered lifting his hand to her cheek. The tips of his fingers were bluish gray, as were his lips. He was dying. She knew that but couldn't bring herself to accept it.

There on the barn floor, Lizzy buried her face in her hands and wept. Nothing would ever be the same without him. It hurt so much to know he was gone and she was all alone.

You aren't alone, Lizzy.

The words echoed in her heart, and she knew the truth of them. She had Mother and Uncle Oliver, but they would die too. They would die and leave her with no one. Then there was Wes. She had loved him for so long and wanted nothing but his love in return. But now that he offered it—now that happiness was within her grasp—Lizzy was terrified. He would die too.

Mother had said, *"I would bear this pain and even more. Your father's love was worth the price."*

Lizzy thought of the love she'd shared with her father. He had comforted her when she was afraid, encouraged her when she was sure she couldn't go on. Father had taught her so much about life and love. Wasn't this pain worth the love they'd shared? Lizzy wasn't sure she could answer that question. It hurt so much to be without him.

She felt strong arms wrap around her and pull her close. She knew without even looking that it was Wes. The thought of his death, of having to say good-bye to him, only made her cry all the more.

"It's all right, Lizzy."

Why couldn't he understand? It wasn't going to be all right. It was all wrong. Life was just one painful experience after another, and she wanted no more of it. How could she bear even one more loss?

"Go," she sobbed. "Just go."

Wes tightened his hold. "Sweetheart, you cry all you want. I'm not going anywhere. I'm never going to leave you."

His words were whispers of comfort, but they were also lies. Lizzy pulled away, but

Wes refused to let her go. She was blinded by her tears, but she could see the love in his expression.

"Yes, you will," she said, struggling to break free. "Everybody leaves. Everybody dies. You'll die too, and I can't bear the thought. I'd rather be dead myself than lose anybody else . . . especially you."

⊰⊱ TWENTY-THREE ⊰⊱

Mary did what she could to help Mrs. Brookstone, but all the while she wanted nothing more than to ride after Fleming and Spiby and shoot them both. She burned in anger. It wasn't right that they should go about their business while her brother lay cold in the ground.

"Stop fussing," Oliver Brookstone demanded of his sister-in-law. "I'm just fine."

"You haven't been 'just fine' since Mark died," Mrs. Brookstone said in blunt honesty. "You have carried the burden of grief and responsibility like the weight of the world, and now it's catching up with you."

Oliver's face reddened as he struggled to

sit up in the bed. "Nonsense. Just let me get my breath, and I'll be fit as a fiddle."

Mrs. Brookstone glanced at Mary. "Take off his boots."

"You don't need to do that," he protested.

Mary didn't listen to him. She removed his boots and set them by the bed. She had no idea what was wrong with Mr. Brookstone. Lizzy said he had started drinking again during the show tour and that he had once been quite the drinker. It was clear that he wasn't under the influence of spirits at the moment, but that might have been the problem. Mary had heard that folks who drank a lot got liver-sick when they went without a drink for a while. Grandma said it had something to do with the liver expecting a certain amount of alcohol—needing it, so to speak. Mary thought about suggesting a drink but decided against it. The Brookstones weren't ones to keep liquor in the house or even on the property, and if Oliver Brookstone was hiding some, he wasn't going to say.

"Mary, please ask Irma to come back up here. Then you go about your business. I know you have to practice for the show."

"I'm happy to stay if you need me." She glanced at Oliver Brookstone and smiled. "I'm rather fond of Mr. Brookstone and would do anything to assure his quick recovery."

"Nonsense. I'm fine. I just let Fleming get me worked up. I can't abide a man who thinks he can push around little gals like Ella and not have to answer for it. I don't care if he is her father. Given what Ella has told us and what we saw with our own eyes . . ." He fell silent, leaned back against the pillow, and let out a breath. "I can't abide cruelty."

Mary nodded, knowing their cruelty had also gotten her brother killed.

Mrs. Brookstone patted his arm. "You're clearly exhausted. I knew you shouldn't have taken that trip. We're both getting too old for this kind of life." She glanced at Mary. "Go ahead, dear. I'll be just fine."

Mary left and found Irma ironing in the kitchen. "Mrs. Brookstone asked that you come help her again."

"Happy to." Irma put the iron back on the stove. "Did she ask me to bring anything?"

"No. Just to come."

Irma nodded. "Well, I'll take a little coffee and some cookies just in case. Could be Oliver just needs something to eat."

Mary grabbed her coat and headed outside. For a moment she stared down the long drive from the ranch. It would take hours for Ella's father and Jefferson Spiby to drive back to Miles City. She could get her horse and cut across the land. She had taken several rides with Lizzy and on her own. Mary figured she knew the lay of the land well enough to ambush the men responsible for her brother's death. The temptation to confront them and learn why they had killed her brother was strong.

The air had warmed the night before, and most of the snow had melted. Despite the cold temperatures, Mary knew it would be difficult to slog her way across some of the open range. She knew too that killing two men in cold blood wasn't the right thing to do. She wasn't even sure she could pull the trigger with a man in her sights, even if that man was her brother's killer. No, as much as she wanted them to pay for what they had done, she knew it was better to go about it legally.

Mary stuffed her hands in her coat pockets and turned toward the arena. She and Alice were supposed to be practicing their horseback shooting act. She glanced at the cloudy skies overhead. "I promise, August, I will get justice for you."

Ella was in the arena when Mary came through the door. She was sitting alone, and there was no sign of Alice.

"Are you all right?" Mary asked.

"No. I doubt I'll ever be all right again. I can't abide that my father and Jefferson Spiby will get away with murder."

"You don't know that," Mary said, sitting beside Ella.

"But I do. I told my father that I know what happened."

Mary took Ella's hands and turned her. "What did he say?" She studied Ella's face for any clue.

"He said what I knew he'd say. No one will believe me, and he has friends enough to make sure nothing ever happens to cause him problems."

"And Mr. Spiby?"

Ella shook her head. "Something intricately connects the two of them. So much that my father would force me to marry a man known for his cruelty and abuse. Not only that, but Father knows him to be capable of murder, yet he would give his daughter away to such a man."

"I am sorry, Ella." Mary sighed. "I considered riding after them."

"To kill them?"

Mary was surprised by Ella's matter-of-fact manner. "Yes." She barely whispered the word. She wasn't proud of her desire to see them dead. After all, bad or good, they were human beings, and life was sacred. If she killed them, she'd be no better than they were.

"I'm sorry. I'm so sorry I brought anyone else into this."

Mary put her arm around Ella's shoulder. "You didn't. They did this. They brought it on themselves when they decided to kill my brother. Whether you had come here or not, I would have eventually ended up there to question them about what happened. I might have ended up dead as well."

"I just don't know what to do. My father has threatened to ruin the show if I stay, yet I cannot return. I won't give myself to Jefferson. I would rather die." Tears slipped down Ella's cheeks. "Maybe that's the answer."

"No!" Mary hugged her close. "No more death. I want justice for my brother, but not at the price of your life."

Ella pulled away and looked at Mary. Her face was contorted in grief. "Then what are we going to do?"

Mary shook her head as she got to her feet. "I don't know. I suppose we must pray even more about it than we have. God won't be mocked, Ella. He knows the truth of what happened, even if no one else does. Surely He will show us what must be done."

"I won't leave you, Lizzy." Wes wanted nothing more than to bring her peace of mind and heart. "I promise."

"You can't." She jumped up from the barn floor. "You can't make promises like that. One day we will all die. You. Me. You can't promise to never leave."

"All right." He stood, at a loss as to what he could say. Only one thing came to mind. "But you know that death isn't the end of things."

Lizzy began to pace. "I know that. I know Father is with Jesus, just as the thief on the cross is. But it doesn't help. If Uncle Oliver dies, Mother and I will be alone to face overwhelming circumstances. If Mother dies . . ."

"You won't be alone." Wes took hold of her. "So long as I have breath in my body, you will neither one be alone. And even if I die, you'll still have God. Have you forgotten that, Lizzy?"

He walked her over to a bale of hay and made her sit. Lizzy didn't protest, much to his relief.

"Look, I have a few things I need to say to you. First, I have to beg your forgiveness for how I've acted the last couple of years. I was wrong to put a wall between us. I was wrong to blame you for what happened to Clarissa." He pushed back his dark hair. "I felt guilty when Clarissa accused me of being in love with you. Not at first, because I didn't see it that way. I cared about you very much, but I cared about your entire family. I came to this ranch when I was just eighteen. I'd left my mother and father and brother, hoping to make my own way. I wanted to prove myself. Your family was more than gracious and took me in like a son."

"Father always said you *were* a son to him," Lizzy murmured.

"I know. He told me that as well. I loved him, Lizzy. He was like a second father to me, especially after mine died. I'll never forget how he helped me get past my grief. He told me just what I've been saying to you."

She looked up. "He did?"

Wesley nodded. "He said that death, while hard on the ones left behind, was nothing but joy for the man or woman who loved God. He told me we should learn to put aside our grief and rejoice for the one who'd gone home."

"I know." Lizzy sighed. "But it hurts so much. It's like a burden on my shoulders pressing me down."

Wes knelt beside her. "I know. It weighs on me too. But maybe it wouldn't be quite so heavy if we bore it together."

She touched his cheek, much to his surprise.

"I never thought about how much Father's death would hurt you. It was selfish of me only to think of my pain. I'm sorry."

He pressed his hand over hers. "I know you are, just as I'm sorry for how much you're hurting. Just don't let that pain cause you to wall yourself away from everyone. I can tell you from experience, it doesn't take away the pain."

He stood and drew Lizzy up with him, then looked for several long moments into her brown eyes. Why had it been so hard to see how much she meant to him—how much he loved her? "Lizzy, I—"

"Hello? Lizzy? Are you out here?"

Wes let go of her at the sound of Ella calling Lizzy's name.

"I'm here." Lizzy held Wesley's gaze a moment longer. "Thank you for talking with me. For your kindness."

She squared her shoulders and headed to the front of the barn. Wes could hear her speaking with Ella, but not enough to know what was being said. He wanted to run after Lizzy and declare his love—force her to admit hers for him. But for all his desire, Wes felt there was a better time and place. Right now, she needed to come to terms with her fears, and he felt that such a declaration would only interfere with God's plan.

Not only that, but he still had unfinished business.

Later that afternoon, after hearing that Oliver was suffering nothing more than exhaustion, Wes rode out to the little family cemetery. The Brookstone cemetery sat atop a rolling rise that overlooked the river. Wes had helped Mark and Oliver Brookstone bury their parents here. Together they had put a fence around an area twenty feet by twenty feet, and prayed they wouldn't have to bury anyone else there for a long, long time.

He remembered how Mrs. Brookstone had fought against all the elements Montana had to offer to grow a small collection of pines to stand vigil over the graves. He'd helped her water the trees and protect them from animals and the wind. There was little Wes had ever seen Rebecca Brookstone attempt without success, and this was no exception. The small seedlings she had planted the summer after losing her father-in-law were now sturdy, mature trees. They bore up under the drought and snows much as the family had over the years.

Wes dismounted his horse and made his way to Clarissa's grave at the far side of the fenced area. Due to the shelter of the trees, there was still some snow here and there, and her headstone was covered. With his gloved hand, he wiped the snow aside and read the inscription.

Clarissa DeShazer
1872–1898
Beloved Wife and Daughter

He stood back and took off his hat. "But you were neither, and for that I am sorry."

He stared at the stone for a long time. He knew Clarissa wasn't there—just her earthly body—but still he felt the need to speak to her, and this seemed like the only reasonable place.

"We never lied to each other about why we married," he began. "We both knew it was wasn't a love match, although I cared about you and I think you cared about me." He looked out across the cemetery to the river. "I thought I could keep you safe—protect you. I thought I could save you from the world and all those folks who would hurt you, and instead I ended up hurting you myself.

"It helps to know that you understood it was never intentional, Rissa, but it's burdened me nevertheless. I never meant to wrong you. I honestly never thought of Lizzy as a potential wife—at least not then. I cared about her and wanted to keep her safe, and I know I talked a lot about her and what she was doing. I didn't figure I was committing adultery, but maybe after a fashion, that's what it was. Either way, I let her come between us. I cared a great deal about her—loved her—but not the way you thought I did. But now I do."

He turned the black Stetson in his hands and shrugged. "I guess I wanted to tell you that I'm sorry. I'm sorry I didn't put everything in God's hands rather than do what I thought best. I learned a painful lesson about trying to take God's place. I'm sorry too that I could never give you the love you deserved. I know, though, that you finally have it. I know, given you put your trust in God before you died, that you finally know the only love that truly lasts forever. Just the same, I hope you forgive me."

Wes felt a peace settle over him. He could finally lay Clarissa to rest.

Gazing at the heavens, he continued. "Lord, I ask You to forgive me too. I was such a fool. Young and ignorant. I tried to take Your place. I thought that I could make things right and fix the problems Clarissa had. I thought I could do that with Phillip too. I've made a poor savior, Lord.

"From now on, I just want to put everything in Your hands. I'm asking You to make me a better man. Help me hear Your voice and heed Your directions rather than take my own counsel."

He thought of what had transpired earlier in the day with Lizzy. "Help her, Lord. She's hurting, and I know I can't make that better. I want to. I truly do, but I know she needs to come to You with it and not me. I love her, Lord. I don't know why it took me so long to see it or to understand that she's the only woman I want to spend my life with, but now that You've helped me realize it, I'm praying You'll help me be the man Lizzy needs. I'm praying You'll make me a man after Your own heart so that I always put You first and seek Your direction for my life."

Wes glanced one last time at the headstone. He'd done what he'd come to do and felt assurance deep in his soul that he could put the past behind him now and focus on the future. Whatever that future might hold.

TWENTY-FOUR

A strong wind had blown most of the night, and that, coupled with the memory of all Wes and her mother had said, kept Lizzy from sleeping. At one point she sat up in bed and drew her knees to her chest. At times like these, she knew there was nothing to do but pray.

"Lord, I'm so afraid." She hugged her arms around her legs. "Wes cares for me just as I've so often prayed he would. I love him, but I can't bear the thought of him dying. I know death isn't the end. I know Father is there with You now, so why can't I let go of this pain—this fear?"

Rocking in bed, Lizzy tried to remember all the Bible verses she'd ever memorized, but nothing came to mind. It was as if in putting up her wall of protection, she'd pushed out the Holy Spirit along with everything else. For a moment, she panicked. Had God left her alone because of her hard heart?

She fumbled for the matches on her nightstand. Finally she found them and lit the lamp. The glow did little to comfort her. She pulled open the nightstand drawer and retrieved her Bible. Just having it in hand helped soothe her spirit. It was only then that she realized she hadn't read it in a long time. A very long time. In fact, she hadn't read it since her father died.

"Oh, God, I'm so sorry." Tears trickled down her cheeks. "I didn't know. I didn't see. I was so lost in my pain that I pushed You away with everyone else." She began to sob and cradled the Bible against her chest.

After a few minutes, there was a light tapping at her door. When the door opened, Lizzy saw her mother's worried face.

"Lizzy, are you all right?"

"No. No, I'm not." Lizzy cried all the harder.

Mother sat beside her. She pulled Lizzy close as she had done when Lizzy was a child. "There, there, my darling. Tell me what's wrong."

"I'm what's wrong." Lizzy buried her face against her mother's neck.

"What are you talking about?"

Lizzy's voice was ragged. "I pushed God away. I didn't want any more pain, so I was determined not to love. I didn't realize that's what I was doing, but it was."

Mother nodded. "I know."

"Can He forgive me? Will He come back?"

"Oh, Lizzy." She brushed back Lizzy's dampened hair. "He never left you. He's just been waiting for you."

"Are you sure?"

"Of course. God promised He would never leave us nor forsake us. Even when we walk away, God is still there. But if you don't believe me—talk to Him. I promise He's listening. He's right here with us now."

Lizzy knew that her mother spoke the truth. She could feel it in her heart. For the first time in a long time, she could feel God's presence.

"Forgive me," she whispered, bowing her head. "Forgive me for pushing You away."

The peace that had been missing for so many months washed over her in warm waves. Lizzy felt herself relax in her mother's arms. For a long while she stayed in that loving hold, knowing that nothing in the world could hurt her.

After a time, Mother lifted Lizzy's face. She looked quite serious.

"What is it?" Lizzy asked.

"I hope you realize that your comfort just now is from the Lord, not me."

It was as if she'd read Lizzy's mind. "But it's your arms around me."

"And His around us both. Lizzy, I love you so dearly. You are my child—my only child. I could not have been happier with a dozen children. But I'm only human, and one day I will go home to be with God. I don't want to worry that you'll fall apart and leave your faith behind."

"I can't imagine life without you." Lizzy shook her head. "I couldn't imagine it without Father either." She thought of all her mother had said and began to see the truth. "I suppose God gives us people at different times to teach us and help us."

"To love us too," Mother added. "It's not good to be alone—at least not for long. God knows exactly the right person to send along on our journey. Whether it's parents when we are young or friends . . . or a mate. But it's God Himself who is our mainstay, our comfort, our hope. People do what they can, but they will leave or die . . . just as I will one day. It doesn't mean we can't cherish them while they're here, but we mustn't depend on them for our hope. That comes from God alone."

It seemed so simple, yet it had taken Lizzy such a long time to see the truth. "I understand, Mother. I do. I see it now. I put my trust in my earthly father rather than my heavenly Father."

"People make poor saviors." Mother smiled. "I had to learn the truth of that myself. I think God has been working to teach us both the same truth. He is enough, Lizzy. No matter who else walks in or out of our lives. God will fill the empty places in our hearts, but we must allow Him access. He never forces us to receive Him."

When Lizzy woke hours later, she found her Bible still cradled in her arms. Mother had gone, but the covers were neatly tucked around Lizzy, reminding her of when she was a child. She waited for the pang of loneliness and sadness to come, and when it didn't, she smiled. God had filled the empty place left by her father's death. God had taken His rightful place in her heart.

A million thoughts went through her mind as she made her way downstairs for breakfast. She felt freer than she had in months, but there were still a lot of problems. What would happen with Ella's father and former fiancé? What kind of trouble could Fleming and Spiby cause for the Brookstone show? And then there was Wes. What in the world was she supposed to do about him?

"Are you just now going down?" Ella asked.

Lizzy turned to see Ella following her down the stairs. She had dark circles under her eyes. "Yes. And you?"

"I couldn't sleep at all for fear of what Father and Jefferson have planned. I just wanted to pull up the covers and hide in my bed." Ella reached Lizzy's side. "What am I going to do? Do you suppose they'll come back today like they said?"

"All we can do is take it moment by moment. I honestly believe, however, that God has already taken care of all this. He will show us what to do and say. I feel sure of it."

Ella paused on the step. "You sound different today. Did something happen?"

Lizzy nodded. "I realized how foolish I was acting. I was trying to hold God and everyone else away from me so that I could avoid getting hurt. Mother helped me see that and some other things. I can tell you more after breakfast, but I honestly feel as though I've come back to life."

They reached the bottom step and heard voices in the dining room. Ella grabbed Lizzy's arm. "They're back. They're here."

"Your father and Mr. Spiby?" Lizzy asked in a whisper.

Ella's expression answered for her. She looked terrified. Lizzy held her back from going into the dining room. She waited to hear what her mother would say.

"Gentlemen, you are very welcome to sit and partake of breakfast with the rest of us. My brother-in-law, however, will not be joining us. He's been under the weather since traveling to Chicago, and I made him promise he'd remain in bed today."

"That's not a problem, Mrs. Brookstone." Lizzy knew that voice but couldn't quite place it. It wasn't either Mr. Fleming or Mr. Spiby. "We wouldn't want to inconvenience you."

"I assure you, Sheriff, there's plenty for everyone," Mother replied. "Please have a seat. We all eat together. I can make introductions to the show's performers in a moment when Lizzy and Ella join us."

Ella grew paler. "They brought the sheriff here?"

Lizzy leaned close. "Apparently, but that's a good thing. With the sheriff here, they won't cause any trouble."

Ella's expression was still panicked. She shook her head and backed away. "I don't want to face them."

"I know, but I hardly see how we can avoid it. Come on." Lizzy took Ella's hand and led her into the dining room.

"Ah, there they are," Mother said, smiling. To Lizzy's surprise, she wasn't wearing her black mourning clothes. Instead she wore a simple brown skirt and white blouse. Apparently God had worked in her heart as well.

"Sorry we're late, Mother," Lizzy said. She released Ella and went to her mother's side. "You look lovely this morning." She kissed Mother's cheek, then glanced at the three men who stood at the end of the table. "Good morning, Sheriff. Mr. Fleming. Mr. Spiby."

The men gave her a nod of greeting, but none spoke. Ella avoided them altogether and took the chair between Mary and Alice. The other performers lined the far side of the table, looking as uncomfortable as Lizzy felt.

Lizzy helped her mother into a chair. "I'm hungry enough to eat a bear." She claimed her seat as Wes walked into the room.

He glanced at the trio of men standing at the end of the table. "Morning, Sheriff. Gentlemen." He looked at Lizzy and her mother. "Sorry I'm late."

"You're fine, Wes. Lizzy and Ella just got here themselves," Mother declared. She looked again at the trio. "Gentlemen, I must ask you to either join us for breakfast or wait in the front room until we've concluded here."

The sheriff smiled. "I'm no fool. I know better than to pass up a good meal." He took a seat beside Wesley.

Fleming and Spiby exchanged glances, then took the empty chairs at the end of the table.

Mother gave a nod. "Wes, would you offer thanks?"

Everyone bowed their heads. Lizzy wondered if Ella's father and fiancé would have the decency to at least pretend to pray. She couldn't resist raising her head just enough to spy on them. Spiby sat rigidly, observing the occupants of the table while Wes said grace. Lizzy's gaze met his. Spiby smirked like he'd caught her stealing eggs from the henhouse.

There was something so dark, so evil in his nature, that Lizzy could feel it. His expression left her cold.

"Amen," most everyone murmured.

Lizzy turned to her mother. She kept her voice low. "I see we have uninvited guests." There was enough noise going on with the passing of food that she felt certain no one could overhear her.

"Yes, they showed up just as we were coming to the table. I think they're figuring to use the law to get their way." Mother handed her a platter of biscuits. "Although with Ella being of age, I'm not sure what they hope to do."

"You won't turn her out, will you?"

Mother shook her head. "Of course not. She can stay, whether she works in the show or remains here with me."

Lizzy kissed her mother again, then took two biscuits and passed the platter to her right. "Thank you. And thank you for last night. I am truly renewed."

"As am I," Mother said, nodding. "I think your father is probably smiling in heaven to see us moving forward and putting our sadness behind us."

The conversation around the table mostly lent itself to the upcoming tour. Jason Adler didn't show up until they were nearly done.

He explained that he'd had breakfast with Uncle Oliver in his room.

"I need to go over some of the show's details with the crew as soon as they conclude their meal. I'll wait in the living room." He left as quickly as he'd appeared.

"What's that all about?" Lizzy asked her mother.

"I believe Jason and Oliver made some changes to the way the acts will be presented. At least, that's what they were discussing this morning when I took your uncle a tray."

Little by little, the ladies excused themselves to seek out Jason. When only Lizzy, Mother, Wes, and Ella remained, Ella's father pushed back from the table.

"I don't wish to seem ungrateful for the lovely meal, but I would like to be on my way back to town."

"Of course," Mother replied. "Feel free to go whenever you choose."

Ella's father frowned. "That isn't the point. I've come for my daughter, as you well know."

"Yes, I do realize your purpose here," Mother said. "However, I also know that the young lady has reached her majority. If she chooses to remain here with us, I am perfectly content with that decision." She looked at Ella and smiled.

"She will return home with us," Mr. Fleming insisted. "I brought the sheriff so there wouldn't be any trouble."

Mother looked at the sheriff. "You know us well enough to know there won't be trouble. I'm sorry you came all this way. Mr. Fleming and Mr. Spiby were here yesterday, as they might have mentioned. Their daughter told them then that she intended to remain here to perform with the show."

The sheriff looked at Mr. Fleming. "You led me to believe your daughter wasn't of age."

"She's not qualified to make decisions, whether she's of age or not. She is rather simple-minded, and I am trying to protect her."

"From what?" Lizzy couldn't help interjecting.

Mother put her hand on Lizzy's arm. "It's best that you let them work this out. Why don't you and Wes meet with the others? I'll stay here with Ella."

Lizzy didn't want to go, and she was certain Ella didn't want her to leave. Still, she didn't want to dishonor her mother by arguing. She put her napkin on the table. "Very well."

The minute she stepped outside the dining room, however, Lizzy stopped. Wes nearly ran into her.

"What are you doing?" he asked.

She put her finger to her lips and pulled him away from the door. To her surprise, however, Wes all but dragged her into the living room, where Jason was talking about how Mary and Alice's act would play out.

"I think the timing will be better in the long run," Jason declared. He smiled at Wes and Lizzy as they entered the room. "Ah, Mr. DeShazer. I was hoping you might speak to the group about how you and your men will handle the animals and equipment."

Lizzy moved to where Mary sat by the music room door. She waited until Wes had begun talking to nudge Mary. When several of the girls started asking questions of Wes and Jason, Lizzy pulled Mary into the adjoining room.

"I want to hear what Ella's father and the others are saying. I figure you want to know as well."

Mary nodded.

Lizzy led her through the music room into the library. From there, they slipped out of the library via the hall door and made their way to the kitchen's rear entrance. Lizzy spied Irma and put a finger to her lips as she and Mary snuck over to the dining room door. It was open only a fraction, but it was enough to hear what they were saying.

"I'm sorry you made the trip all the way out here, Sheriff. I can vouch for Miss Fleming's sound mind. She is not at all feeble nor incapable of reason. I believe her father has only suggested this because he plans for Ella to be married to his business partner."

"Is that true, Fleming? Is this the only reason you came here?"

"She's my daughter, and I demand she return with us."

"She's twenty-one," the sheriff replied. "Mrs. Brookstone, I'm sorry for inconveniencing your day."

"It wasn't an inconvenience at all. It was good to see you again."

Lizzy and Mary exchanged a glance. Would that put an end to it?

"I wonder if I might speak privately for a moment with my fiancée?" Jefferson Spiby asked. "Perhaps we could take a walk?"

"I have no desire to speak with you, Jefferson." Ella's voice sounded stronger than earlier. Perhaps she felt confident, given Mother's support.

Lizzy opened the door just a little wider to hear better. She knew from where everyone had been sitting earlier that the only person who might notice her was Ella.

"I'm not asking for much, my dear. I'd simply like to speak to you. If you are still determined to remain here after that, I won't protest."

Ella glanced up and caught sight of Lizzy. She bit her lip as she seemed to contemplate something. Lizzy wondered what she was thinking.

"Very well," Ella finally said. "I will take a short walk with you, but keep in mind that it is rather cold outside." She looked again at Lizzy, then got to her feet. The sound of other chairs moving left no doubt that the men were getting to their feet. "If it's too cold," Ella said, meeting Lizzy's gaze, "I can show you where I train."

Lizzy pulled back. "Get our coats. We're going to follow her. I don't want Ella to be alone with that madman for even a moment."

Mary nodded and quickly left the kitchen. Irma looked at Lizzy with concern. "What are you planning now?"

"It's nothing to worry about. If anyone comes looking for us, however, I'd appreciate you not mentioning that we were here."

"I won't lie, Lizzy."

"Nor would I ask you to." Mary returned with their work coats, and Lizzy quickly slipped into hers. "Just don't volunteer anything."

Irma smiled. "I suppose I can do that much."

Lizzy and Mary slipped out the back door.

"It is rather cold out, my dear. Is there someplace we might speak privately without subjecting ourselves to this bitter chill?" Jefferson asked Ella.

She nodded. She'd seen Lizzy watching her from the kitchen door and prayed that her friend was even now continuing her vigil. "As I mentioned, we can step into the arena where I train."

"Honestly, my darling, I don't know why you would do such a thing. It's hardly the calling of a proper young woman."

"Perhaps I'm not proper."

Ella opened the arena door rather than allow Jefferson to do so. She stepped inside, grateful that large windows on either end allowed for decent light. Some of the girls had been training earlier and had lit the large lanterns that further brightened the arena. Ella walked out to the center, knowing that if Lizzy had made it to the equipment room to hide, she'd be able to see what was going on.

"Say what you wish to say, Jefferson, and let's be done with it."

He looked at her thoughtfully. "You've certainly grown bold."

She shrugged. "Let's just say I've learned my value."

"You hardly dress as if you know it. Look at you."

Ella glanced down at her outfit. Today she'd donned a dark navy split skirt that had been banded at the knee like her other performance skirts. On top she wore a loose yellow calico blouse, and over this a canvas coat Lizzy had found for her. Her boots and gloves completed the outfit.

"I see nothing wrong with the way I'm dressed." She looked back up.

Jefferson scowled. "It's most inappropriate for a young lady. Especially one who is to be my wife."

"Jefferson, I'm going to be training with Lizzy in a few minutes, so it's quite appropriate that I dress in this manner. If I were attending a formal ball, then it might be different. Furthermore, I am not going to marry you."

He stepped toward her, and Ella backed up a few steps and put out her hands. "Stay right there. I won't be manhandled by you."

"You're wrong there, Ella. On both accounts. You will marry me, and I will handle you as I please."

She shook her head. "I have only to scream, and half the hands on this ranch will come to my rescue. Heed my warning, Jefferson."

He stopped advancing and cocked his head. "You need to learn your place. Your father has let you have your way long enough. Call for your ranch hands if you must, but I will not allow them to come between me and the arrangement I have with your father."

"Your arrangement with Father is just that. Your arrangement. Not mine." Ella could see she was only making Jefferson angrier, but she didn't care. Movement behind him gave her confidence that she wasn't alone. She saw Lizzy and Mary only momentarily, but it was enough to bolster her courage.

Unfortunately, after taking her eyes off Jefferson, she didn't realize he had closed the space between them. He grabbed her throat and held her fast.

"Go ahead and scream for your friends. By the time they get here, I will have snapped this scrawny neck of yours."

"I see. Well, you did say that killing August Reichert wouldn't be your last time."

Jefferson's eyes turned dark and his expression cold. "So you know what I'm capable of."

"Yes, but not why. You killed the Brookstone wrangler because he'd seen too much. But what exactly did he see? Did he witness you kill someone else? Goodness, how many people have you killed?"

"That's none of your concern. What's important is that I will add you to the number if you continue this nonsense."

Ella looked into his eyes, unafraid. "Then kill me. I would rather be dead than married to you."

❖⇜ TWENTY-FIVE ⇝❖

Lizzy felt an icy chill run up her spine at Ella's declaration. It had been ominous enough to hear Jefferson Spiby admit to killing August and others, but to see him threatening Ella with death was too much. Mary moved beside her, as silent as the grave. Lizzy turned to see what she was doing and nearly gasped at the sight of her friend taking aim with her pistol.

She reached out to Mary and shook her head, but Mary merely moved Lizzy's hand away. The look in her eyes was determined. She intended to kill Spiby.

Lizzy put her lips against Mary's ear. "You can't do this. We've heard him admit

what he did. Now we can bear witness to
the sheriff."

Mary shook her head. "He deserves to
die." Her words were barely audible, but Jefferson Spiby's rang through the arena. Both
Lizzy and Mary returned their attention to
the scene in the arena.

"I won't kill you . . . just yet. But if you
don't do as I command, you'll wish you were
dead." Ella said nothing, and he continued.
"We will marry this afternoon in Miles City
before boarding the train. That way you will
never get the chance to do anything like this
again."

Ella tried to pull away from his hold, but
it only angered him more. "You think your
friends here can keep you from danger, but I
promise I'll make them suffer. I'll make each
of them suffer for your defiance."

"They've . . . done . . . nothing wrong."
Ella was barely able to speak.

"I don't care." He lowered his voice, making it hard for Lizzy to hear what he was saying. "I will hurt them. I will kill them."

Ella tried again to break free, but Jefferson
held her fast.

"I thought you'd rather be dead," he said.

Ella gasped for air and tried to pull Jefferson's hands away from her neck. Lizzy looked
at Mary. If she was going to kill him, why

didn't she? At least now she had a good reason. If she didn't shoot him, he would kill Ella.

Mary stared straight ahead. Lizzy thought she looked frozen. "Mary?" she whispered. "Mary?"

Lizzy looked again toward Ella fighting for her life. She got to her feet. "Stop!" she yelled.

Jefferson didn't even seem to hear her.

Lizzy looked down at Mary. "Do something."

Mary pulled the trigger. The sound echoed in the arena, and Jefferson let out a roar. He held his arm as he scanned the room to see who was responsible. Rage marred his face.

Ella stumbled away from him. She coughed and sputtered, but at least she was alive.

"Don't move, or I'll shoot you again," Mary declared from her perch.

"You'll pay for this." Jefferson growled in pain. "You will pay for this."

The arena doors flew open, and Wesley and the sheriff rushed in. They stopped at the sight of Jefferson holding his arm, writhing in pain.

"What's going on here? We heard a shot," the sheriff said, looking around the arena.

Lizzy stepped out of the shadows. "He tried to kill Ella. He admitted to killing August Reichert."

Wesley closed the distance between them with incredible speed and took hold of Lizzy. "Are you all right?"

She saw the worry in his expression. "I'm just fine."

"Sheriff, I demand you take that woman into your custody. She tried to kill me," Jefferson declared as the sheriff approached.

This brought Mary out of hiding. She walked toward Jefferson with her pistol still at the ready. "She didn't shoot you. I did. I could have killed you. God knows I wanted to, given you admitted to murdering my brother."

Jefferson looked at the sheriff. "She's mad. I admitted no such thing."

Lizzy stepped away from Wes. "He did so. He threatened to kill my family and friends here if Ella didn't do exactly as he wanted." She looked at Jefferson, who seemed almost confused. "We can both bear witness to what he said, Sheriff."

Ella joined them, still rubbing her neck. "He tried to strangle me."

Jefferson seemed to gather his wits. "They're making this up. They're trying to keep Ella from returning with us." He pulled back his hand to reveal the blood on his arm. "I'm the injured one."

The sheriff looked at Ella and then back

to Jefferson. "It looks like we'd better get you some help. I suggest we go back to the house."

He took hold of Jefferson but looked at Mary. "You can put that away. He's going nowhere for the moment."

Mary lowered her gun. "All right, but I'll be right behind you." She looked at Ella. "I won't let him hurt you again."

The two girls followed the sheriff and Spiby from the arena, leaving Lizzy and Wes alone. Wes watched her with grave concern.

"I'm fine, Wes. Stop looking at me like I'm going to die."

"I thought maybe you had."

She pulled his face down to hers and kissed him on the lips. He didn't have time to react before she stepped away with a grin. "See? I couldn't be better. Come on, we need to follow them. I heard and saw it all, including Jefferson Spiby confessing to killing August."

Wes followed her back to the house, but she knew he had to be confused about everything that had just happened. Especially the kiss. She felt bad that she hadn't explained anything to him.

There was utter chaos in the living room when Lizzy and Wes entered the house. The sheriff was trying to calm everyone down.

Thankfully, the other performers and Jason had gone.

"Take a seat, folks. We may be here awhile," the sheriff said, pushing Spiby onto a wooden chair.

Everyone with the exception of Ella's father sat. Mr. Fleming, however, was indignant and paced back and forth. "What in the world is going on? Who shot this man?"

"I did," Mary admitted. "Because he was about to kill your daughter."

"Bah! I don't believe it. Jefferson would never harm a hair on her head." He looked at Ella. "Tell the truth."

"He tried to strangle me," Ella said, her voice hoarse.

"I did no such thing." Jefferson vehemently denied the accusation while writhing in pain. "You and your friends lured me to that place in order to kill me."

The sheriff looked at Mary. "Why were you there?"

"To protect Ella."

"That's right, Sheriff," Lizzy interjected. "I was listening when you were all talking in the dining room. I knew Ella was terrified of Mr. Spiby and her father and wanted to keep an eye on her."

"This is madness," Ella's father declared. "She isn't terrified of me or of Jefferson. She's merely been listening to the bad counsel of this woman and her family."

"That's uncalled for, Fleming," Wes said. He put his hands on Lizzy's shoulders. "This family has done nothing wrong. They're good, godly folks who took in your daughter when she ran away."

"I suggest that Elizabeth Brookstone encouraged her to run away."

"I did," Lizzy admitted. "Not only that, but I would again."

"See there!" Fleming yelled, pointing his finger. "She admits it."

Mother came into the room with Irma on her heels. Irma held a tray of bandages and other medicinal articles. Mother went to Jefferson and helped him out of his coat. She then ripped open the already torn sleeve to get a better look.

Everyone stopped talking for a moment, almost mesmerized by her ministering. When the wound was clean, Mother smiled. "It's nothing more than a graze. Hardly even that. We'll bandage it up, and you'll be fine. Probably won't even notice it in a day or two."

"I'll notice it plenty, and it'll be a wonder if I don't get blood poisoning. I need a drink," Jefferson grumbled.

"I can't accommodate you there, Mr. Spiby.

I have no alcohol on the property. We don't allow it."

Jefferson swore at her, much to everyone's dismay. Mother said nothing, however, and instead reached for a bottle and poured a generous amount onto the wound.

Jefferson came up out of his seat, cursing all the more. "Are you trying to kill me?"

Mother pushed him back into his chair. Wes left Lizzy's side and stood behind Jefferson. He put his hands on the angry man's shoulders. "I'll help you stay still," Wes said sarcastically.

"This is my own special concoction, Mr. Spiby," Mother said. "It will help ensure you don't get blood poisoning."

This seemed to calm everyone down again, and the sheriff looked to Ella. "You say this man and your father were responsible for killing a man in Kentucky. Did you see them kill him?"

"No. I heard them talking about it as if they'd done nothing more than kill a rabbit."

The sheriff looked at Ella's father. "What about it, Mr. Fleming? What happened to the Brookstone wrangler?"

"He was trampled by a horse. Nothing more. The county sheriff was there, as well as the local doctor. If he was murdered, the authorities would never have said it was an accident."

"Yes, they would have," Ella countered. "Because you own them. They're all so obligated to you and afraid of you that they wouldn't dare have said otherwise."

This seemed to silence the older man. He finally took a seat, shaking his head. "I have given you everything, and this is how you repay me."

Jefferson balled his right fist and pounded it on his knee. "I'm telling you, it's this place and these people. They're all a bunch of hooligans."

The sheriff shook his head. "Mister, I've known these folks for most of my life. I can't say the same about you or your friend." He looked at George Fleming. "As far as I can see, you have no rights where this young lady is concerned."

"Well, I have rights," Jefferson declared. "I have the right to file charges against that woman." He pointed at Mary.

Ella stepped forward. "You do that, and I'll press charges against you for this." She opened the neck of her blouse to reveal the bruises that were already starting to show.

Jefferson clenched his jaw. The sheriff looked at him, as did everyone else in the room. "Very well," he muttered. "Let the devil have them both."

"He can't, Mr. Spiby," Mother said as she finished with his arm. "The Lord already has them, and the Good Book says He won't let them be plucked from His hand. Seems to me you might want to seek Him out as well. Maybe then you wouldn't be so inclined to anger."

Jefferson pushed away from Wes and got to his feet. He grabbed his coat. "I've had enough of this place, George. Let's go."

The sheriff put out his hand. "Not so fast. There's still this matter of murder back in Kentucky. I think you and Mr. Fleming better accompany me back to Miles City. I need to hear from the officials in Kentucky as to whether you're wanted."

"This is madness!" George Fleming got to his feet. "Pure madness. We are highly regarded in our state. You have no right to hold this man."

Lizzy went to Ella. She clasped the girl's hand and gave it a squeeze. With any luck at all, they'd soon be rid of these men and get justice for Mary's brother.

"I am willing to testify to what I've heard Mr. Spiby say," Ella said, causing everyone to turn to her. "And Father, if you have any decency left in you, you'll bear witness as well."

Her father shook his head. "You don't know what you're saying. You stupid little fool. You'll be sorry for this."

Lizzy pulled Ella close. "You're hardly in a position to threaten her."

"I'll never forgive you if you go through with this nonsense, Ella." Her father's eyes narrowed. "You'll never be welcomed back. You'll be forever estranged from your family."

Mother stepped forward. "She'll always have a home with us. I'm happy to have her here with me or with the show. Whatever she chooses."

"You're all fools," Fleming sneered. "You'll be sorry for this." He looked around the room. "I'll destroy you and your show!"

"Mr. Fleming, you do what you feel you must, but I will tell you this much. We have long lived under the protection of God Almighty. Your threats are no concern to me." Mother looked at the sheriff. "Now, I will take you up on the offer to escort them away from here." Her gaze went from the sheriff to Spiby and then settled on Fleming. "Gentlemen— and I use that term with great hesitation— you are no longer welcome on Brookstone property."

<hr/>

After the sheriff left with Fleming and Spiby, Wes wanted nothing more than to be alone with Lizzy. She'd kissed him, and in that moment, he'd known something had changed. But there'd been Spiby's injury and Ella's accusations to deal with. Then, just as he thought they'd have a moment to themselves, his brother had shown up, announcing problems that needed his attention. What in the world were they all going to do if he went on the road with the show?

By the time he was free to seek Lizzy, she was busy training in the arena. He thought of what Rebecca Brookstone had said about not trying to change her daughter. Wes had prayed a great deal about this matter and knew she was right. Lizzy was nearly ready to give up the show on her own. What Wes needed to do was give her a reason to leave trick riding. He smiled to himself. She had kissed him, so she must love him. He just had to persuade her that she loved him more than performing.

In the arena, all the trick riders were gathered to go through their acts from beginning to end. Lizzy was critiquing and instructing from the sidelines as Ella, Debbie, and Jessie went through their Roman riding and acrobatics.

"That's good. Really good," Lizzy called to them. "You've got that looking smoother than ever."

Wes watched as Jessie stood atop a team of horses. She held them in a steady line while Debbie and Ella did a variety of maneuvers.

It was funny how he didn't feel at all nervous watching them, yet their tricks were just as dangerous.

The ladies finished their act and came to where Lizzy stood. "I think you've got a winner. The more motion, the more the audience will perceive danger and thrills." Lizzy grinned. "It's all about making the ladies faint and the men cheer for more."

"It does look good," Wes offered.

Lizzy turned and met his gaze. "I didn't know you were here."

"I came to see you."

"I'm glad you did." She looked back at the trio of riders. "Go on with your practice. I'm going to speak with Wesley." She pulled on her coat and motioned him toward the door. "Shall we?"

He followed her outside. The skies were filling with clouds. Cookie had told him that morning to expect snow because his lumbago was acting up. In Montana, it could snow most any time of year, but you could be guaranteed of its arrival if Cookie said as much.

They walked a ways down the long drive before Wes worked up the nerve to stop Lizzy. He turned her and looked into her eyes for a long moment.

"I love you." There. He'd said the words, and now the chips could fall where they would.

She grinned. "I've waited nearly a lifetime to hear you say that."

"You're only twenty-eight, so it hasn't been that long."

Lizzy laughed. "You were just telling me the other day how twenty-eight was ancient."

"I said no such thing." He could see the change in her. "You're different. Something's happened to you."

She nodded. "Yes. It has. You might say I had a 'come to Jesus' moment." She shrugged. "I've been wrapped up in fear ever since Father died. I couldn't bear the thought of losing one more person, so I tried to close myself off to everyone . . . including God, although I didn't realize it at the time."

"What happened to change that?"

"Everything. You. Mother. I suppose even Ella and her troubles all moved me to see that I couldn't stop loving people just because of my fears. Then last night I was truly at a crossroads. I couldn't bear it anymore. I realized I hadn't even picked up my Bible in months . . . not since my father's death."

Wesley nodded. "I know how that can be. With me it was shame and guilt that made me want to hide from God. Just like Adam in the Garden of Eden."

"We've both come through a great deal, and I'm ashamed to say that I didn't perform very well."

He chuckled. "If we're being rated on performance, then we're both in trouble."

"Thankfully, God doesn't do business that way."

He shoved his cold hands in his pockets. "So what happens now?" She still hadn't declared her love for him, and Wes felt a little concerned. In her new understanding of heart, was there room for him?

She stepped closer. "It's cold out here. You do realize there are much warmer places to be."

He drew out his hands and wrapped his arms around her. "Like here in my arms?"

Lizzy nodded. "For one. Wes, when you are near, I feel whole. Complete. The way Father made my mother feel. When he died, I was heartbroken, but it was nothing compared to what my mother was going through. I didn't want to love you if it meant hurting so badly. Then Mother talked to me. She said she wouldn't trade what she had with my father for anything. She said the pain was unimportant compared to the love they'd shared, and I started to see that she was right. I want your love, no matter the pain."

"No doubt there will be some." He reached

down to cup her chin. "But I know that with God, there is nothing we can't face."

"I agree." She gazed into his eyes. "I love you, Wesley. I've loved you since I was ten years old, and it amazes me how that love has changed and grown and become what it is today."

"And what's that?" he asked, almost afraid to know the answer.

"Ours." Her voice was filled with tenderness. "It's not just mine or yours. It's ours."

"I like the sound of that," he said, lowering his mouth to hers. "I like it lot."

Tracie Peterson is the award-winning author of over one hundred novels, both historical and contemporary. Her avid research resonates in her stories, as seen in her bestselling HEIRS OF MONTANA and ALASKAN QUEST series. Tracie and her family make their home in Montana. Visit Tracie's website at www.traciepeterson.com.

Sign Up for Tracie's Newsletter!

Keep up to date with Tracie's news on book releases and events by signing up for her email list at traciepeterson.com.

Also from Tracie Peterson!

In the early 1900s, Camri Coulter's search for her missing brother, Caleb, leads her deep into the political corruption of San Francisco—and into the acquaintance of Irishman Patrick Murdock, whom her brother helped clear of murder charges. As the two try to find Caleb, the stakes rise and threats loom. Will Patrick be able to protect Camri from danger?

In Places Hidden, GOLDEN GATE SECRETS #1